The [...] gnal Log spoke [...] human. It was a thin, high, alien squeaking—and yet, somehow, not alien enough. The consonants were ill-defined, and there was only one vowel sound.

"*Eeveengeer* tee *Deestreeyeer. Eeveengeer* tee *Deestreeyer*. Heeve tee. Heeve tee eer we eepeen feer!*"

The voice that answered was not a very convincing imitation of that strange accent. . . .

"A woman," whispered Sonya. "Human. . ."

Playing for time, thought Grimes. *They did their best. . .*

"Dee!" screamed the inhuman voice. "Heemeen sceem, dee!"

. . . "'Die,'" repeated the Commodore slowly. "'Human scum, die!'" He said, "Whoever those people are, they wouldn't be at all nice to know."

"That's what I'm afraid of," Sonya told him. "That we might get to know them. Whoever they are—and wherever, and whenever. . . ."

**But get to know them they would—
and under the worst
possible circumstances, as**

Contraband
from Otherspace

JOHN GRIMES RIMWORLD
DOUBLE-ADVENTURES

THE ROAD TO THE RIM
   & THE HARD WAY UP
THE INHERITORS &
   THE GATEWAY TO NEVER
THE DARK DIMENSIONS & THE RIM GODS
INTO THE ALTERNATE UNIVERSE &
CONTRABAND FROM OTHERSPACE

watch for more John Grimes Adventures
by A. Bertram Chandler
coming soon
from ACE Books

SF

Into the Alternate Universe

A. Bertram Chandler

SF
ace books
A Division of Charter Communications Inc.
A GROSSET & DUNLAP COMPANY
360 Park Avenue South
New York, New York 10010

An ACE Book

Cover art by Rowena Morrill

Second Ace printing: November 1972
Third Ace printing: March 1979

For my nose-to-grindstone keeper

I

THE INEVITABLE freezing wind whistled thinly across the Port Forlon landing field, bringing with it eddies of gritty dust and flurries of dirty snow. From his office, on the top floor of the Port Administration Building, Commodore Grimes stared out at what, over the long years, he had come to regard as his private kingdom. On a day such as this there was not much to see. Save for *Faraway Quest,* the Rim Worlds Government survey ship, the spaceport was deserted, a state of affairs that occurred but rarely. Soon it would resume its usual activity, with units of the Rim Runners' fleet dropping down through the overcast, from Faraway, Ultimo and Thule, from the planets of the Eastern Circuit, from the anti-matter systems to the Galactic West. But now there was only the old *Quest* in port, although a scurry of activity around her battered hull did a little to detract from the desolation of the scene.

Grimes stepped back from the window to the pedestal on which the big binoculars swiveled on their universal mount. He swung the instrument until *Faraway Quest* was centered in the field of view.

He noted with satisfaction that the bitter weather had done little to slow down the work of refitting. The flare of welding torches around the sharp stem told him that the new Mass Proximity Indicator was being installed. The ship's original instrument had been loaned to Captain Calver for use in his *Outsider;* and the *Outsider,* her Mannschenn Drive unit having been rebuilt rather than merely modified, was now falling across the incredibly wide and deep gulf of light years between the island universes.

And I, thought Grimes sullenly, *am stuck here. How long ago was my last expedition, when I took out the old* Quest *and surveyed the inhabited planets of what is now the Eastern Circuit, and the anti-matter worlds to the Galactic West? But they say that I'm too valuable in an administrative capacity for any further gallivanting, and so younger men, like Calver and Listowel, have all the fun, while I just keep the seat of my office chair warm. . . .*

"Commodore Grimes!"

Grimes started as the sharp female voice broke into his thoughts, then stepped back from the instrument, turning to face his secretary. "Yes, Miss Willoughby?"

"Port Control called through to say that they've just given landing clearance to *Star Roamer.*"

"*Star Roamer?*" repeated the Commodore slowly. "Oh, yes. Survey Service."

"Interstellar Federation Survey Service," she corrected him.

He smiled briefly, the flash of white teeth momentarily taking all the harshness from his seamed, pitted face. "That's the only Survey Service that piles on any gees." He sighed. "Oh, well, I suppose I'd better wash behind the ears and put on a clean shirt. . . ."

"But your shirts are *always* clean, Commodore Grimes," the girl told him.

He thought, *I wish you wouldn't take things so literally,* and said, "Merely a figure of speech, my dear."

"E.T.A. fifteen minutes from now," she went on.

"And that's the Survey Service for you," he said. "Come in at damn nearly escape velocity, and fire the braking jets with one-and-a-half seconds to spare. But it's the Federation's tax payers that foot the fuel bills, so why should we worry?"

"You were in the Survey Service yourself, weren't you?" she asked.

"Many, many years ago. But I regard myself as a Rimworlder, even though I wasn't born out here." He smiled again as he said, "After all, home is where the heart is ..." And silently he asked himself, *But where is the heart?*

He wished that it was night and that the sky was clear so that he could see the stars, even if they were only the faint, far luminosities of the Galactic Rim.

Star Roamer came in with the usual Survey Service *éclat*, her exhaust flare a dazzling star in the gray sky long before the bellowing thunder of her descent reverberated among the spaceport buildings, among cranes and gantries and conveyer belts. Then the long tongue of incandescence licked the sparse drifts and frozen puddles into an explosion of dirty steam that billowed up to conceal her shining hull, that was swept from the needle of bright metal by the impatient wind, fogging the wide window of Grimes' office with a fine drizzle of condensation.

She sat there on the scarred concrete—only a little ship, and yet with a certain air of arrogance. Already the beetle-like vehicles of the port officials were scurrying out to her. Grimes thought sourly, *I wish that they'd give our own ships the same prompt attention.* Remembering his own Survey Service days he felt a certain nostalgia. *Damn it all,* he thought, *I piled on more gees as a snotty-nosed Ensign than as Astronautical Superintendent of a shipping line and Commodore of the Rim Worlds Naval Reserve. . . .*

He stood by the window, from which the mist had now cleared, and watched the activty around *Star Roamer.* The ground vehicles were withdrawing from her sleek hull, and at the very point of her needle-sharp prow, the red light, almost painfully bright against the all-surrounding grayness, was blinking. He heard Miss Willoughby say, "She's blasting off again." He muttered in reply, "So I see." Then, in a louder voice, "That was a brief call. It must have been on some matter of Survey Service business. In that case, I should have been included in the boarding party. As soon as she's up and away, my dear, send word to the Port Captain that I wish to see him. *At once.*"

There was a flicker of blue incandescence under *Star Roamer's* stern and then, as though fired from some invisible cannon, she was gone, and the sudden vacuum of her own creation was filled with peal after crashing peal of deafening thunder. Grimes was aware that the speaker of the intercom was squawking, but could not make out the words.

His secretary did. Shouting to be heard over the dying reverberations she cried, "Commander Verrill to see you, sir!"

"I should have washed behind the ears," replied Grimes. "But it's too late now."

II

She hasn't changed much, thought Grimes, as she strode into his office. She was wearing civilian clothes—a swirling, high-collared cloak in dark blue, tapered black slacks, a white jersey of a material so lustrous that it seemed almost luminous. *And that outfit,* went on the Commodore to himself, *would make a nasty hole in a years salary. Rob Roy tweed and Altairian crystal silk . . . The Survey Service looks after its own.* Even so, he looked at her with appreciation. She was a beautiful woman, and on her an old flour sack would have looked almost as glamorous as the luxurious materials that adorned her fine body. In her pale blonde hair the slowly melting snow crystals sparkled like diamonds.

"Welcome aboard, Commander," said Grimes.

"Glad to be aboard, Commodore," she replied softly.

She allowed him to take the cloak from her, accepted the chair that Miss Willoughby ushered her towards. She sat down gracefully, watching Grimes as he carefully hung up her outer garment.

"Coffee, Commander Verrill? Or something stronger?"

"Something stronger." A smile flickered over her full lips. "As long as it's not your local rot-gut, that is."

"It's not. I have my sources of supply. Nova Caledon Scotch-on-the-rocks?"

"That will do nicely. But please omit the rocks." She shivered a little theatrically, "What a vile climate you have here, Commodore."

"It's the only one we have. Say when."

"Right up, please. I need some central heating."

And so you do, thought Grimes, studying her face. *So you do. And it's more than our weather that's to blame. You did what had to be done insofar as that mess involving you and Jane and Derk Calver was concerned, but to every action there's an equal and opposite reaction—especially once the glow of conscious nobility has worn off.*

She said, "Down the hatch."

"Down the hatch," he replied. "A refill?"

"Thank you."

He took his time about pouring the drinks, asking as he busied himself with glasses and ice cubes and bottle, "You must be here on important business, Commander. A courier ship all to yourself."

"Very important," she replied, looking rather pointedly towards Miss Willoughby, who was busying herself with the papers on her desk in a somewhat ostentatious manner.

"H'm. Yes. Oh, Miss Willoughby. I'd like you to run along to the Stores Superintendent, if you wouldn't mind, to straighten up the mess about *Rim Falcon's* requisition sheets."

"But I still have to run through *Rim Kestrel's* repair list, sir."

"*Rim Kestrel's* not due in for a week yet, Miss Willoughby."

"Very well, sir."

The girl straightened the litter on her desk, got up and walked slowly and with dignity from the office.

Sonya Verrill chuckled. "Such sticky-beaking would never be tolerated in the Service, Commodore."

"But you don't have to put up with civilian secretarial staff, Commander. Come to that, I well recall that when I was in the Service myself an occasional gift of some out-world luxury to a certain Lieutenant Masson—she was old Admiral Hall's secretary— could result in the premature release of all sorts of interesting information regarding promotions, transfers and the like."

"Things are different now, Commodore."

"Like hell they are. Anyhow, Sonya, you can talk freely now. This office is regularly debugged."

"Debugged, John?"

"Yes. Every now and again high-ups in the various Ministries decide that they aren't told enough of Rim Runners' affairs—of course, the *Aeriel* business made me very unpopular, and if Ralph Listowel hadn't got results, serendipitous ones at that, I'd have been out on my arse. And then *your* people manage to plant an occasional bug themselves."

"Come off it, John."

"Still playing the little, wooly, lamb, Sonya?"

She grinned. "It's part of my job. Perhaps the most important part."

"And what's the job this time?"

"There won't be any job unless our Ambassador to the Rim Confederation manages to talk your President into supplying help. But I think that he will. Relations have been fairly friendly since your autonomy was recognized."

"If you want a ship," said Grimes, "the charter rates will be favorable to ourselves. But surely the Federation has tonnage to spare. There are all the Commission's vessels as well as your own Survey Service wagons."

"Yes, we've plenty of ships," she admitted. "And plenty of personnel. But it's know-how that we're after. You hardly need to be told that your people have converted this sector of Space into your own backyard, and put up a big sign, *No Trespassing*. Even so, we hear things. Such as Rim Ghosts, and the winds of it that blew your pet *Aeriel* through about half a dozen alternative time tracks. And there was that business of the wet paint on Kinsolving's Planet years ago—but that, of course, was before you became autonomous, so *we* had the job of handling it...."

"And the Outsider's ship..." supplied Grimes.

"No. Not in the same class, John. She'd drifted in, or been placed there, by visitors from another Galaxy. And, in any case, we're already in on that." She held out her glass for a refill.

"You're welcome, Sonya, but..."

"Don't worry John. Olga Popovsky, the Beautiful Spy with hollow legs—that's me."

"You know your own capacity."

"Of course. Thank you. Now, as I was saying, our top brass is interested in all the odd things that seem to happen only in this sector of Space, and the Rhine Institute boys are interested too. It was decided that there was only one Intelligence Officer in the Service with anything approaching an intimate knowledge of the Rim. I needn't tell you who that is. It was decided, too, that I'd work better if allowed to beg, borrow or steal Rim Worlds' personnel. Oh, the Service can afford to pay Award rates, and above. Frankly, when I was offered the job I almost turned it down. I know the Rim—but my memories of this sector of Space aren't all too happy..." She leaned forward in her chair, put her slim hand on Grimes' knee. "But..."

"But what, Sonya?"

"All this business of Rim Ghosts, all these theories about the curtains between the alternative universes wearing thin here, on the very edge of the expanding Galaxy... You know something of my history, John. You know that there have only been two men, real men, in my life. Bill Maudsley, who found the Outsiders' quarantine station, and who paid for the discovery with his life. And Derek Calver, whose first loyalties were, after all, to Jane... Damn it all, John, I'm no chicken. I'm rather tired of playing the part of a lone wolf—or a lone bitch, if you like. I want me a man—but the right man—and I want to settle down. I shall be due a very handsome gratuity from the Service when I retire, and there are still sparsely settled systems in this Galaxy where a little, one-ship company could provide its owners and operators with a very comfortable living...."

"So?"

"So it's bloody obvious. I've been put in charge of this wild goose chase—and with any luck at all I shall catch me my own wild gander. Surely there must be some alternative Universe in which I shall find either Bill or Derek, with no strings attached."

"And what if you find them both at once?" asked Grimes.

"As long as it's in a culture that approves of polyandry," she grinned. Then she was serious again. "You can see, John, that this—this research may well fantastically advance the frontiers of human knowledge."

"And it may well," he told her, "bring you to the haven where you would be." He raised his glass to her. "And for that reason, Sonya, I shall do everything within my power to help you."

III

AFTER SONYA had left he pottered around his office for a while, doing jobs that could have been done faster and better by Miss Willoughby. When his secretary returned from her visit to the Stores Superintendent and, with a display of efficiency, tried to take the work from his hands, he dismissed her for the day. Finally, realizing that he was accomplishing nothing of any value, he put the papers back in their files and, having drawn himself a cup of coffee from the automatic dispenser, sat down to smoke his battered pipe.

He felt sorry for Sonya Verrill. He knew much of her past history—more, in fact, than she had told him. He was sorry for her, and yet he envied her. She had been given fresh hope, a new goal towards which to strive. Whether or not she met with success was not of real importance. If she failed, there would be other goals, and still others. As an officer of the Survey Service Intelligence Branch she was given opportunities for travel denied even to the majority of professional spacemen and women. Grimes smiled at the corniness of the thought and muttered, "Someday her prince will come . . ."

Yes, he envied her. She, even within the framework of regulations that governed her Service,

12

had far more freedom of movement than he had. He strongly suspected that she was in a position to be able to select her own assignments. *And I,* he thought, *am marooned for the rest of my natural— or, if I so desire, unnatural—life on this dead-end world at the bitter end of sweet damn' all . . .*

Come off it, Grimes, he told himself. *Come off it, Grimes, Commodore Grimes, Rim Worlds Naval Reserve. Don't be so bloody sorry for yourself. You've climbed to the top of your own private tree.*

Even so . . .

He finished his coffee, poured himself another cup. He thought, *I should have offered to put her up during her stay on Lorn.* And then he was glad that he had not made the offer. She was used to luxury— luxury on a government expense account, but luxury nonetheless—and surely would have been appalled by his messy widower's establishment. His children were grown up, and had their own homes and, in any case, incurable planetlubbers that they were, would have little in common with one who, after all, was a professional adventuress.

So . . .

So I can enjoy adventures—although not in the same sense—vicariously, he thought. *I'll do what I can for Sonya, and hope to receive in return a first-hand account of all that happens to her. She said that she would want a ship—well, she shall have* Faraway Quest. *It's time that the poor old girl was taken for another gallop. And she'll be wanting a crew. I'll put out the call for volunteers before I get definite word that the expedition has been approved —just quietly, there's no need to get the politicians' backs up. Rimworlders, she specified. Rimworlders born and bred. I can see why. People raised on the Rim are far more likely to have counterparts in the alternative Universes than those of us who have, like myself, drifted out here, driven out here by the winds of chance. I shouldn't have much trouble in raising a team of officers, but a Master will be the problem. Practically all our Captains are refugees from the big, Earth-based companies, or from the Survey Service.*

But there was no urgency, he told himself.

He drew yet another cup of coffee and, carrying it, walked to the wide window. Night had fallen and the sky had cleared and, work having ceased for the day, there was no dazzle of lights from the spaceport to rob the vision of keenness.

Overhead in the blackness was one bright star, the Faraway sun, and beyond it lay the faint, far nebulosities. Low in the east the Lens was rising, the upper limb only visible, a parabola of misty light. Grimes looked away from it to the zenith, to the dark immensities through which Calver in his *Outsider* was falling, perhaps never to return. And soon Sonya Verrill would be falling—but would she? could she?—through and across even stranger, even more fantastic gulfs, of Time as well as of Space.

Grimes shivered. Suddenly he felt old and alone, although he loathed himself for his self pity.

He left his office, fell down the dropshaft (what irony!) to the ground floor, got out his monocar from the executives' garage and drove home.

Home was a large house on the outskirts of Port Forlon. Home was a villa, and well kept—the maintenance service to which Grimes subscribed was highly efficient—but sadly lacking in the touches of individuality, or imagination, that only a woman can supply.

The commodore drove his car into his garage and, after having shut off the engine, entered the house proper directly from the outbuilding. He did not, as he usually did, linger for a few minutes in the conservatory that housed his collection of exotic plants from a century of worlds. He went straight to his lounge, where he helped himself to a strong whisky from the bar. Then he sat down before his telephone console and, with his free hand, punched the number for library service.

The screen lit up, and in it appeared the head and shoulders of a girl who contrived to look both efficient and beautiful. Grimes smiled, as he always did, at the old-fashioned horn-rimmed spactacles that, some genius had decided, made the humanoid robot look like a real human librarian. A melodious contralto asked, "May I be of service, sir?"

"You may, my dear," answered Grimes. (A little subtle—or not so subtle—flattery worked wonders with often tempermental robots.) "I'd like whatever available data you have on Rim Ghosts."

"Visual sir, or *viva voce?*"

"*Viva voce*, please." (Even this tin blonde, with her phony feminity, was better than no woman at all in the house.)

"Condensed or detailed, sir?"

"Condensed, please. I can always ask you to elaborate as and if necessary."

"Very good, sir. The phenomenon of the Rim Ghosts occurs, as the name implies, only on the Rim. Sightings are not confined to single individuals, so therefore cannot be assumed to be subjective in nature. A pattern has been established regarding these sightings. One member of a party of people will see himself, and be seen by his companions, in surroundings and company differing, sometimes only subtly, from those of actuality. Cases have been known in which an entire group of people has seen its Rim Ghost counterpart.

"For a while it was thought that the apparitions were prophetic in character, and the orthodox explanation was that of precognition. With the collection of a substantial body of data, however, it became obvious that prophetic visions comprised only about 30% of the total. Another 30% seemed to be recapitulations of past events, 20% had a definite here-and-now flavor, while the remaining 20% depicted situations that, in our society, can never arise.

"It was in the year 313 A.G. that Dr. Foulsham, of the Terran Rhine Institute, advanced his Alternative Universe Theory. This, of course, was no more than the reformulation of the idea played around with for centuries by speculative thinkers and writers, that of an infinitude of almost parallel Time Tracks, the so-called Worlds of If. According to Dr. Foulsham, on Earth and on the worlds that have been colonized for many generations, the barriers between the individual tracks are . . ." The robot paused.

"Go on, my dear," encouraged Grimes. "This is only a condensation. You needn't bother trying to break down fancy scientific terminology."

"Thank you, sir. The barriers, as I was trying to say in suitable language, are both high and thick, so that a break-through is almost impossible. But on the very rim of the expanding Galaxy these barriers are ... tenuous, so that very often a fortuitous break-through does occur.

"An example of such a breakthrough, but visual only, was that achieved by Captain Derek Calver and his shipmates when he was serving as Chief Officer of the freighter *Lorn Lady*. The ship was pro-ceeding through deep space, under Mannschenn Drive, when another vessel was sighted close alongside. In the control room of the other space-craft Calver saw himself—but he was wearing Master's uniform—and most of the others who were with him in *Lorn Lady's* control compartment. He was able, too, to make out the name of the strange ship. It was the *Outsider*. Some months later, having become the recipient of a handsome salvage award, Calver and his shipmates were able to buy a second-hand ship and to operate as a small tramp shipping company. They christened her the *Outsider*. This, then, was obviously one of the precognitive appari-tions, and can be explained by the assumption that the Alternative Universe in which Calver's career runs almost parallel to his career in *this* Universe possesses a slightly different time scale.

"Physical breakthrough was inadvertently achieved by Captain Ralph Listowel in his ex-perimental light jammer *Aeriel*. Various members of his crew unwisely attempted to 'break the light bar-rier' and, when the ship was proceeding at a veloc-ity only fractionally less than that of light, dis-charged a jury rigged rocket hoping thereby to out-run the photon gale. They did not, of course, and *Aeriel's* crew became Rim Ghosts themselves, ex-periencing life in a succession of utterly strange cul-tures before, more by luck than judgment, returning to their own. The unexpected result of this ill-advised experiment was the developing of a method whereby atomic signs may be reversed, thereby making possible intercourse between our planets and the anti-matter worlds.

"There is no doubt that the Rim Ghost phenomenon is one deserving of thorough investigation, but with the breakaway of the Rim Worlds from the Federation it has not been possible to maintain full contact with either the Survey Service or the Rhine Institute, which bodies, working in conjunction, would be eminently capable of carrying out the necessary research . . ."

"You're out of date, duckie," chuckled Grimes.

"I beg your pardon, sir?"

"You're out of date. But don't let it worry you; it's not your fault. It's we poor, inefficient humans who're to blame, for failing to feed new data into your memory tanks."

"And may I ask, sir, the nature of the new data?"

"Just stick around," said Grimes, "and some day, soon, I may be able to pass it on to you."

If Sonya comes back to tell me, he thought, and his odd mood of elevation evaporated.

IV

A WEEK PASSED, and for Commodore Grimes it was an exceptionally busy one. *Rim Mammoth*—ex-*Beta Geminorum*—had berthed, and that ship, as usual, was justifying her reputation as the white elephant of Rim Runners' fleet. A large consignment of fish had spoiled on the passage from Mellise to Lorn. The Chief Reaction Drive Engineer had been beaten up in the course of a drunken brawl with the Purser. The Second, Third and Fourth Officers had stormed into the Astronautical Superintendent's presence to aver that they would sooner shovel sludge in the State Sewage Farm than lift as much as another centimeter from a planetary surface under the command of the *Mammoth's* Master and Chief Officer.

Even so, Grimes found time to initiate his preliminary inquiries. To begin with, he had his secretary draw up a questionnaire, this asking for all relevant data on the sighting of Rim Ghosts. It seemed to him that Sonya Verrill would require for her crew personnel who were in the habit of sighting such apparitions. Then, having come to the reluctant conclusion that a lightjammer would be the most suitable research ship, he studied the schedules of such vessels as were in operation, trying to work out which one could be withdrawn from service with the minimal dislocation of the newly developed trade with the anti-matter systems.

Rather to his annoyance, Miss Willoughby issued copies of the questionnaire to the crew of the only ship at the time in port—*Rim Mammoth*. The officers of that vessel were all in his black books, and it had been his intention to split them up, to transfer them to smaller and less well-appointed units of the fleet. Nonetheless, he studied the forms with interest when they were returned. He was not surprised by what he discovered. The Master and the Chief Officer, both of whom had come out to the Rim from the Interplanetary Transport Commission's ships, had no sightings to report—Captain Jenkins, in fact, had scrawled across the paper, *Superstitious Rubbish!* The Second, Third and Fourth Officers, together with the Psionic Radio Officer, were all third generation Rim Worlders, and all of them had been witnesses, on more than one occasion, to the odd phenomena.

Grimes ceased to be annoyed with Miss Willoughby. It looked as though the manning problem was already solved, insofar as executive officers were concerned. The Second, Third and Fourth Mates of *Rim Mammoth* were all due for promotion, and Captain Jenkins' adverse report on their conduct and capabilities could well result in the transfer of their names to the bottom of the list. So there was scope for a little gentle blackmail. Volunteers wanted for a Rim Ghost hunt! You, and you, and you!

But there was a snag. None of them had any sail training. How soon would Sonya Verrill want her ship? Would there be time to put the officers con-

cerned through a hasty course in the handling of
lightjammers? No doubt he would be able to find a
team of suitably qualified men in the existing lightjammer fleet, but all of them were too useful where
they were.

It was while he was mulling this problem over in
his mind that Commander Verrill was announced.
She came into his office carrying a long envelope.
She held it out to him, grinning. "Sealed orders,
Commodore."

Grimes accepted the package, studying it cautiously. It bore the crest of the Rim Confederation.

"Aren't you going to open it?"

"What's the rush?" he grunted.

But he picked up the paper knife from his desk—
it had been the deadly horn of a Mellisan sea uni-
corn—and slit the envelope, pulling out the contents.

He skipped the needlessly complicated legal lan-
guage while, at the same time, getting the gist of it.
As a result of talks between the President of the Rim
Worlds Confederation and the Ambassador of the
Intersteller Federation, it had been decided that the
Confederation was to afford to the Federation's
Suvey Service all possible assistance—at a price. One
Commodore Grimes was empowered to negotiate
directly with one Commander Verrill regarding the
time charter of a suitable vessel and the em-
ployment of all necessary personnel. . . .

Grimes read on—and then he came to the para-
graph that caused him to raise his eyebrows in surprise.

Commodore Grimes was granted indefinite leave
of absence from his post of Astronautical Superintendent of Rim Runners, and was to arrange to

hand over to Captain Farley as soon as possible. Commodore Grimes was to sail as Master of the vessel chartered by the Survey Service, and at all times was to further and protect the interests of the Rim Confederation. . . .

Grimes grunted, looked up at the woman from under his heavy eyebrows. "Is this your doing, Sonya?"

"Partly. But in large measure it's due to the reluctance of your government to entrust one of its precious ships to an outsider."

"But why me?"

She grinned again. "I said that if I were obliged to ship a Rim Confederation sailing master, I insisted on exercising some little control over the appointment. Then we all agreed that there was only one Master of sufficiently proven reliability to meet the requirements of all concerned . . ." She looked a little worried. "Aren't you glad, John?"

"It's rather short notice," he replied tersely and then, as he watched her expression, he smiled. "Frankly, Sonya, before you blew in aboard *Star Roamer* I'd decided that I was sick and tired of being a desk-borne Commodore. This crazy expedition of yours will be better than a holiday."

She snapped, "It's not crazy."

His eyebrows went up. "No? An interstellar ghost hunt?"

"Come off it, John. You know as well as I that the Rim Ghosts are objective phenomena. It's a case of paranormal physics rather than paranormal psychology. It's high time that somebody ran an investigation—and if you people are too tired to dedigitate, then somebody else will."

Grimes chuckled. "All right, all right. I've never seen a Rim Ghost myself, but the evidence is too—massive?—to laugh away. So, while Miss Willoughby starts getting my papers into something like order for Captain Farley—he's on leave at present, so we won't have long to wait for him—we'll talk over the terms of the charter party.

"To begin with, I assume that you'll be wanting one of the lightjammers. *Cutty Sark* will be available very shortly."

She told him, "No. I don't want a lightjammer."

"I would have thought that one would have been ideal for this . . . research."

"Yes. I know all about Captain Ralph Listowel and what happened to him and his crew on the maiden voyage of *Aeriel*. But there's one big snag. When *Aeriel's* people switched Time Tracks, they also, to a large extent, switched personalities. When *I* visit the Universe next door I want to do it as me, not as a smudged carbon copy."

"Then what sort of ship do you want?"

She looked out of the window. "I was hoping that your *Faraway Quest* would be available."

"As a matter of fact, she is."

"And she has more gear than most of your merchant shipping. A Mass Proximity Indicator, for example . . ."

"Yes."

"Carlotti Communication and Direction Finding Equipment?"

"Yes."

Then, "I know this is asking rather much—but could a sizeable hunk of that anti-matter iron be installed?"

He grinned at her. "Your intelligence service isn't quite as good as you'd have us believe, Sonya. The *Quest* has no anti-matter incorporated in her structure yet—as you know, it's not allowed within a hundred miles of any populated area. But there's a suitably sized sphere of the stuff hanging in orbit, and there it stays until *Faraway Quest* goes upstairs to collect it. You know the drill, of course—the anti-matter, then an insulation of neutronium, than a steel shell with powerful permanent magnets built into it to keep the anti-matter from making contact with normal matter. A neutrino bombardment and, presto!—anti-gravity. As a matter of fact the reason for the *Quest's* refitting was so that she could be used for research into the problems arising from incorporating anti-gravity into a ship with normal interstellar drive."

"Good. Your technicians had better see to the installing of the anti-matter, and then ours—there's a bunch of them due in from Elsinore in *Rim Bison*—will be making a few modifications to the Carlotti gear. Meanwhile, have you considered manning?"

"I have. But, before we go any further, just what modifications do you have in mind? I may as well make it clear now that the Carlotti gear will have to be restored to an as-was condition before the ship comes off hire."

"Don't worry, it will be. Or brand new equipment will be installed." She paused and glanced meaningfully at the coffee dispenser. Grimes drew her a cup, then one for himself. "Well, John, I suppose you're all agog to learn what's going to happen to your beloved *Faraway Quest*, to say nothing of you and me and the mugs who sail with us. Get this straight, I'm no boffin. I can handle a ship and navigate well enough to justify my Executive Branch commission, but that's all.

"Anyhow, this is the way of it, errors and omissions expected. As soon as the necessary modifications have been made to the ship, we blast off, and then cruise along the lanes on which Rim Ghost sightings have been most frequent. It will help, of course, if all members of the crew are people who've made a habit of seeing Rim Ghosts . . ."

"That's been attended to," said Grimes.

"Good. So we cruise along quietly and peacefully —but keeping our eyes peeled. And as soon as Ghost is sighted—Action Stations!"

"You aren't going to open fire on it?" demanded Grimes.

"Of course not. But there will be things to be done, and done in a ruddy blush. The officer of the watch will push a button that will convert the ship into an enormously powerful electro-magnet, and the same switch will actuate the alarm bells. Automatically the projector of the modified Carlotti beacon will swing to bring the Ghost into its field. The boffins tell me that what *should* happen is that a bridge, a temporary bridge, will be thrown across the gulf between the Parallel Universes."

"I see. And as *Faraway Quest* is an enormously powerful magnet, the other ship, the Ghost, will be drawn into our Universe."

"No," she said impatiently. "Have you forgotten the anti-matter, the anti-gravity? The *Quest* will have one helluva magnetic field, but no mass to speak of. She'll be the one that gets pulled across the gap, or through the curtain, or however else you care to put it."

"And how do we get back?" asked Grimes.

"I'm not very clear on that point myself," she admitted.

The Commodore laughed. "So when I man the *Quest* it will have to be with people with no ties." He said softly, "I have none."

"And neither have I, John," she told him. "Not any longer."

V

Captain Farley was somewhat disgruntled at being
called back from leave, but was mollified slightly
when Grimes told him that he would be amply
compensated. As soon as was decently possible the
Commodore left Farley to cope with whatever problems relative to the efficient running of Rim Runners
arose—after all, it was Miss Willoughby who really
ran the show—and threw himself into the organiz-
ing of Sonya Verrill's expedition. What irked him
was the amount of time wasted on legal matters.
There was the charter, of course, and then there was
the reluctance of Lloyd's surveyors to pass as space-
worthy a ship in which Mannschenn Drive and anti-
matter were combined, not to say one in which the
Carlotti gear had been modified almost out of recog-
nition. Finally Sonya Verrill was obliged to play hell
with a Survey Service big stick, and the gentlemen
from Lloyds withdrew, grumbling.

Manning, too, was a problem. The Second, Third
and Fourth Mates of *Rim Mastodon* agreed, quite
willingly, to sign on *Faraway Quest's* articles as
Chief, Second and Third. The Psionic Radio Officer
was happy to come along with them. After a little
prodding at the ministerial level the Catering and
Engineering Superintendents supplied personnel for

their departments. And then the Institute of Spacial
Engineers stepped in, demanding for its members
the payment of Danger Money, this to be 150% of the
salaries laid down by the Award. Grimes was
tempted to let them have it—after all, it was the
Federation's taxpayers who would be footing the
bill—and then, on second thoughts, laid his ears
back and refused to play. He got over the hurdle
rather neatly, persuading the Minister of Shipping
and the Minister for the Navy to have *Faraway
Quest* commissioned as an auxiliary cruiser and all
her officers—who were, of course, reservists, called
up for special duties. Like Lloyds, the Institute retired grumbling.

As a matter of fact, Grimes was rather grateful to
them for having forced his hand. Had the *Quest*
blasted off as a specialized merchant vessel only,
with her crew on Articles, his own status would
have been merely that of a shipmaster, and Sonya
Verrill, representing the Survey Service, would have
piled on far too many gees. Now he was a Commodore on active service, and, as such, well and tru-
ly outranked any mere Commander, no matter
what pretty badge she wore on her cap. It was, he
knew well, no more than a matter of male pride, but
the way that things finally were he felt much hap-
pier.

So, after the many frustrating delays, *Faraway
Quest* finally lifted from her berth at the Lorn spaceport. Grimes was rusty, and knew it, and allowed
young Swinton—lately Second Officer of *Rim Mammoth*, now Lieutenant Commander Swinton, First
Lieutenant of R.W.S. *Faraway Quest*—to take the
ship upstairs. Grimes watched critically from one of

the spare acceleration chairs, Sonya Verrill watched
critically from the other. Swinton—slight, fair-haired,
looking like a schoolboy in a grown-up's cut-down
uniform—managed well in spite of his audience.
The old *Quest* climbed slowly at first, then with
rapidly increasing acceleration, whistling through
the overcast into the clear air beyond, the fast thinning air, into the vacuum of Space.

Blast-off time had been calculated with considerable exactitude—"If it had been more exact,"
commented Grimes, "we'd have rammed our hunk
of anti-matter and promptly become the wrong sort
of ghosts . . ."—and so there was the minimum
jockeying required to match orbits with the
innocent-looking sphere of shining steel. The *Quest*
had brought a crew of fitters up with her men with
experience of handling similar spheres. Working
with an economy of motion that was beautiful to
watch they gentled the thing in through the special
hatch that had been made for it, bolted it into its
seating. Then it was the turn of the physicists, who
set up their apparatus and bathed the anti-iron in a
flood of neutrinos. While this operation was in
progress, two tanker rockets stood by, pumping tons
of water into the extra tanks that had been built into
the *Quest's* structure. This, Grimes explained to his
officers, was to prevent her from attaining negative
mass and flying out of her orbit, repelled rather than
attracted by Lorn and the Lorn sun, blown out of
station before the landing of the assorted technicians
and the loading of final essential items of stores and
equipment.

At last all the preliminaries were completed.
Faraway Quest was fully manned, fully equipped,

and all the dockyard employees had made their transfer to the ferry rocket. This time Grimes assumed the pilot's chair. Through the viewports he could see the globe that was Lorn, the globe whose clouds, even from this altitude, looked dirty. Looking away from it, he told himself that he did not care if he never saw it again. Ahead, but to starboard, a lonely, unblinking beacon in the blackness, was the yellow spark that was the Mellise sun. The commodore's stubby fingers played lightly over his control panel. From the bowels of the ship came the humming of gyroscopes, and as the ship turned on her short axis the centrifugal force gave a brief illusion of off-center gravity.

The Lorn sun was ahead now.

"Sound and alarm, Commander Swinton," snapped Grimes.

The First Lieutenant pressed a stud, and throughout the ship there was the coded shrilling of bells, a succession of Morse R's short-long-short, short-long-short. *R is for rocket,* thought Grimes. *Better than all this civilian yapping into microphones.*

Abruptly the shrilling ceased.

With deliberate theatricality Grimes brought his fist down on the firing button. The giant hand of acceleration pushed the officers down into the padding of their chairs. The Commodore watched the sweep-second hand of the clock set in the center of the panel. He lifted his hand again—but this time it was with an appreciable effort—again brought it down. Simultaneously, from his own control position, Swinton gave the order, "Start Mannschenn Drive."

The roar of the rockets cut off abruptly, but before there was silence the keening song of the Drive pervaded the ship, the high-pitched complaint of the ever-spinning, ever-precessing gyroscopes. To the starboard hand, the great, misty lens of the Galaxy warped and twisted, was deformed into a vari-colored convolution at which it was not good to look. Ahead, the Mellise sun had taken the likelihood of a dimly luminous spiral.

Grimes felt rather pleased with himself. He had a crew of reservists, was a reservist himself, and yet the operation had been carried out with naval snap and efficiency. He turned to look at Sonya Verrill, curious as to what he would read in her expression.

She smiled slightly and said, "May I suggest, sir, that we splice the mainbrace?" She added, with more than a hint of cattiness, "After all, it's the Federation's taxpayers who're footing the bill."

VI

THE SHIP having been steadied on to her trajectory, Grimes gave the order that Sonya Verrill had suggested. All hands, with the exception of the watchkeeping officers, gathered in *Faraway Quest's* commodious wardroom, strapping themselves into their chairs, accepting drinking bulbs from the tray that Karen Schmidt, the Catering Officer, handed around.

When everybody had been supplied with a drink the Commodore surveyed his assembled officers. He wanted to propose a toast, but had never possessed a happy knack with words. The only phrases that came to his mind were too stodgy, too platitudinous. At last he cleared his throat and said gruffly, "Well, gentlemen—and ladies, of course—you may consider that the expedition is under way, and the mainbrace is in the process of being spliced. Perhaps one of you would care to say something."

Young Swinton sat erect in his chair—in Free Fall, of course, toasts were drunk sitting—and raised his liquor bulb. He declaimed, trying to keep the amusement from his voice, "To the wild ghost chase!"

There was a ripple of laughter through the big compartment—a subdued merriment in which, Grimes noted, Sonya Verrill did not join. He felt a

32

strong sympathy for her. As far as she was concerned this was no matter for jest, this pushing out
into the unknown, perhaps the unknowable. It was,
for her, the fruition of months of scheming, persuading, wire-pulling. And yet, Grimes was obliged
to admit, the play on words was a neat one. "Very
well," he responded, "to the wild ghost chase it is."

He sipped from his bulb, watched the others
doing likewise. He reflected that insofar as Rim
Worlds personnel was concerned it would have
been hard to have manned the ship with a better
crew—for this particular enterprise. All of them,
during their service in the Rim Runners' fleet, had
acquired reputations—not bad, exactly, but not
good. Each of them had exhibited, from time to
time, a certain ... scattiness? Yes, scattiness. Each of
them had never been really at home in a service
that, in the final analysis, existed only to make the
maximum profit with the minimum expense. But
now—the Federation's taxpayers had deep pockets—
expense was no object. There would be no tedious
inquiries into the alleged squandering of reaction
mass and consumable stores in general.

Insofar as the Survey Service personnel—the
Carlotti Communications System specialists—were
concerned, Grimes was not so happy. They were an
unknown quantity. But he relied on Sonya Verrill to
be able to handle them—after all, they were her
direct subordinates.

He signaled to Karen Schmidt to serve out another
round of drinks, then unstrapped himself and got
carefully to his feet, held to the deck by the magnetized soles of his shoes. He said, "There's no need to
hurry yourselves, but I wish to see all departmental

heads in my day room in fifteen minutes."

He walked to the axial shaft, let himself into the tubular alleyway and, ignoring the spiral staircase, pulled himself rapidly forward along the guideline. A vibration of the taut wire told him that he was being followed. He turned to see who it was, and was not surprised to see that it was Sonya Verrill.

She sat facing him across his big desk.

She said, "This is no laughing matter, John. This isn't just one big joke."

"The wild ghost chase, you mean? I thought that it was rather clever. Oh, I know that you've your own axe to grind, Sonya—but you have to admit that most of us, and that includes me, are along just for the hell of it. Your people, I suppose, are here because they have to be."

"No. They're volunteers."

"Then don't take things so bloody seriously, woman. We shall all of us do our best—my crew as well as yours. But I don't think that anybody, apart from myself, has any clue as to your private motives."

She smiled unhappily. "You're right, of course, John. But . . ."

There was a sharp rap at the door. "Come in!" called Grimes.

They came in—Swinton, and the burly, redhaired Calhoun, Chief Mannschenn Drive Engineer, and scrawny, balding McHenry, Chief Reaction Drive Engineer. They were followed by the gangling, dreamy Mayhew, Psionic Radio Officer, by little, fat Petersham, the Purser, and by the yellow-haired, stocky Karen Schmidt. Then came Todhunter, the dapper little Surgeon, accompanied by Renfrew, the

Survey Service Lieutenant in charge of the modified
Carlotti gear.

They disposed themselves on chairs and settees,
adjusted their seat straps with practiced hands.

"You may smoke," said Grimes, filling and lighting his own battered pipe. He waited until the others' pipes and cigars and cigarettes were under way,
then said quietly, "None of you need to be told that
this is not a commercial voyage." He grinned. "It is
almost like a return to the bad old days of piracy.
We're like the legendary Black Bart, Scourge of the
Spaceways, just cruising along waiting for some fat
prize to wander within range of our guns. Not that
Black Bart ever went ghost hunting. . . ."

"He would have done, sir," put in Swinton, "if
there'd been money in it."

"There's money in anything if you can figure the
angle," contributed McHenry.

This was too much for Sonya Verrill. "I'd have
you gentlemen know," she said coldly, "that the
question of money doesn't enter into it. This expedition is classed as pure scientific research."

"Is it, Commander Verrill?" Grimes' heavy eyebrows lifted sardonically. "I don't think that we
should have had the backing either of your Government or of ours unless some farsighted politicians
had glimpsed the possibility of future profits. After
all, trade between the Alternative Universes could
well be advantageous to all concerned."

"If there *are* Alternative Universes," put in
Calhoun.

"What do you mean, Commander? I specified
that the personnel of this ship was to be made up of
those who have actually sighted Rim Ghosts."

"That is so, sir. But we should bear in mind the possibility—or the probability—that the Rim Ghosts *are* ghosts—ghosts, that is, in the old-fashioned sense of the word."

"We shall bear it in mind, Commander," snapped Grimes. "And if it is so, then we shall, at least have made a small contribution to the sum total of human knowledge." He drew deeply from his pipe, exhaled a cloud of blue smoke that drifted lazily towards the nearest exhaust vent. "Meanwhile, gentlemen, we shall proceed, as I have already said, as though we were a pirate ship out of the bad old days. All of you will impress upon your juniors the necessity for absolute alertness at all times. For example, Commander Swinton, the practice of passing a boring watch by playing three-dimensional noughts and crosses in the plotting tank will cease forthwith." Swinton blushed. This had been the habit of his that had aroused the ire of the Master and the Chief Officer of *Rim Mastodon*. "And, Commander Calhoun, we shall both of us be most unhappy if the log desk in the Mannschenn Drive Room is found to be well stocked with light reading matter and girlie magazines." It was Calhoun's turn to look embarrassed. "Oh, Commander McHenry, the Reaction Drive was in first class condition when we blasted off from Port Forlorn. A few hours' work should suffice to restore it to that condition. I shall not expect to find the Reaction Drive Engine Room littered with bits and pieces that will eventually be reassembled five seconds before planetfall." The Surgeon, the Purser and the Catering Officer looked at each other apprehensively, but the Commodore pounced next on the Psionic Radio Officer. "Mr.

Mayhew, I know that it is the standard practice for you people to gossip with your opposite number all over the Galaxy, but on this voyage, unless I order otherwise, a strict listening watch only is to be kept. Is that understood?"

"You're the boss," replied Mayhew dreamily and then, realizing what he had said, "Yes, sir. Of course, sir. Very good, sir."

Grimes let his glance wander over Todhunter, Petershamm and Schmidt, sighed regretfully. He said, "I think that is all. Have you anything to add, Commander Verrill?"

"You seem to have cleared up all the salient points insofar as your own officers are concerned," said the girl. "And I am sure that Mr. Renfrew is capable of carrying out the orders that he has already been given."

"Which are, Commander?"

"As you already know, sir, to maintain his equipment in a state of constant, manned readiness, and to endeavour to lock on to a Rim Ghost as soon as one is sighted."

"Good. In that case we all seem to know what's expected. We stand on, and stand on, until . . ."

"I still think, sir," said Calhoun, "that we should be carrying a Chaplain—one qualified to carry out exorcism."

"To exorcise the Rim Ghosts," Sonya Verrill told him, "is the very last thing that we want to do."

VII

THEY STOOD on ...

And on.

Second by second, minute by minute, hour by hour the time was ticked away by the ship's master chronometer; watch succeeded watch, day succeeded day. There was normal Deep Space routine to keep the hands occupied, there were the frequent drills—at first carried out at set times and then, as every officer learned what was expected of him, at random intervals—to break the monotony. But nothing was sighted, nothing was seen outside the viewports but the distorted lens of the Galaxy, the faint, far, convoluted nebulosities that were the sparse Rim stars.

Grimes discussed matters with Sonya Verrill.

He said, "I've been through all the records, and I still can't discover a pattern."

"But there is a pattern," she told him. "On every occasion at least one member of the group to sight a Rim Ghost has seen his own alternative self."

"Yes, yes. I know that. But what physical conditions must be established before a sighting? What initial velocity, for example? What temporal precession rate? As far as I can gather, such things have had no bearing on the sightings whatsoever."

"Then they haven't."

"But there must be some specific combination of circumstances, Sonya."

"Yes. But it could well be something outside the ship from which the ghost is sighted, some conditions peculiar to the region of Space that she is traversing."

"Yes, yes. But what?"

"That, John, is one of the things we're supposed to find out."

Grimes said, "You know, Sonya, I think that perhaps we are on the wrong track. We're trying to do the job with technicians and machinery . . ."

"So?"

"How shall I put it? This way, perhaps. It could be that the best machine to employ would be the human mind. Or brain."

"What do you mean?"

"That Calhoun may have something after all. It will not surprise you to learn that I have, on microfilm, a complete dossier on every Rim Worlds' officer in this ship. I've been through these dossiers, hoping to establish some sort of pattern. As you know, every Rim Worlder in this ship has at least one Rim Ghost sighting to his name. Now, our Mr. Calhoun, or Commander Calhoun if you like—you recall his remarks at our first conference, just after we'd lined up for the Mellise sun?"

"I do. He was saying that the Rim Ghosts might be *real*—or should one say *unreal?*—ghosts."

"Yes. Anyhow, Calhoun was born on the Rim. On Ultimo, to be exact. But his parents were migrants. From Dunglass."

"Yes. . . ."

"You know Dunglass?"

"I was there once. An odd world. Ruled by a theocracy ... Or is 'theocracy' the right word? But the United Reformed Spiritualist Church runs the show, after a fashion."

"Probably as well as any other government on any other world. Anyhow, the U.R.S.C., as no doubt you know, has its share of heretics. Calhoun's parents were such. Apparently the house in which they lived was haunted, and they employed a bootleg exorcist to lay the ghost. This was frowned upon by the authorities, so much so that the Calhouns decided to emigrate. Now, one can be a heretic without being either an atheist or an agnostic. The Calhouns still *believe*, although reserving the right to believe in their own way. Their only son was brought up in their religion."

"And so what?"

"So—ignoring telepathy, telekinesis, teleportation and the like—what proportion of psychic phenomena is due to the activities of the dear departed, and what proportion is due to a ... leakage —from one Universe through to another?"

"H'm. I must confess that this was a line of approach that never occurred to me. I don't pretend to be an expert on so-called psychic matters, but if we did hold a seance, shouldn't we require a medium?"

"We have one—Mr. Mayhew."

"Yes. But as you know, all these Rhine Institute graduates insist that there's nothing supernatural about their psionic talents. Furthermore, one can be telepathic without being clairvoyant."

"Can one, Sonya? I'm not so sure. There are quite a few recorded cases of clairvoyance, and many of them can be explained by telepathy. Even the pre-monitory ones can be accounted for by assuming the reception of a telepathic broadcast from a Universe with a slightly different Time Scale. There is no need to assume that the Rim Ghosts are a supernatural phenomenon. If we do pay lip service to one of the supernatural religions it will only be to create the right conditions for our own experiments."

She said, "You rank me, John, and you're in command of this ship and this expedition. But I still don't like it."

"You think that we're selling out, as it were, to the supernaturalists?"

"Frankly, yes."

"I don't see it that way. What is natural, and what is supernatural? Can you draw a dividing line? *I* can't."

"All right." She unstrapped herself and got to her feet, the slight effort pushing her up and clear from the chair. She hung there, motionless, until the feeble gravitational field of her shoe soles pulled her back to the deck. Then, contact having been made with solidity, she flung her hands out in an appealing gesture. "Do what you can, John, any way you like. But do it. You've guessed how hard it was for me to persuade our top brass to pour time and money into what your Commander Swinton called a wild ghost chase. Unless we get results, there'll never be another one. And you know that I want results. And you know the sort of results I want." Her hands fell to her sides. "Only—only I've stood on my own flat feet for so long that it rather hurts to have to call in outside assistance."

"It won't be outside assistance, Sonya. We shall be

working with and through our own people, aboard
our own ship. All that we shall be trying to do will
be the creation of conditions favorable to a leakage
from one Universe to another."

"As you say. As you say." She laughed briefly. "After all, men and women have been in the habit of
selling their souls to the Devil from the very beginnings of human history. Or mythology." She paused.
"No, history is the better word."

He said, exasperated, "But we won't be selling
our souls to the Devil. If it makes Calhoun any hap-
pier to think that he's gained a few converts to the
odd faith of his parents, what does it matter?" He
reached out for his telephone, pressed a numbered
stud. "Mr. Mayhew? Commodore here. Can you
spare me a moment?" He pressed another stud.
"Commander Calhoun? Commodore here. Would
you mind stepping up to my quarters?"

Sonya Verrill pulled herself back into her chair,
buckled herself in and she and Grimes sat back to
wait.

Mayhew was first to arrive in Grimes' day cabin.
He was untidy as always, his uniform shirt sloppily
buttoned, one shoulderboard hanging adrift, his
wispy gray hair rumpled, his eyes vague and unfocused. He stifled a yawn. "Yes, sir?"

"Take a seat, please, Mr. Mayhew." There was a
sharp rap at the door. "Come in!"

Calhoun entered, somewhat ostentatiously wip-
ing his hands on a piece of waste. He, too, was told
to be seated.

"Commander Calhoun," said Grimes, "I believe
that you were brought up in the beliefs of the United

Reformed Spiritualist Church?"

"No, sir." The engineer's reply was a stressed negative. "No, sir. I was brought up in the beliefs of the United Primitive Spiritualist Church." He seemed to realize that his answer had caused a certain confusion in Grimes' mind, so went on, "You will know something of Dunglass, sir. You will know that there were people, my parents among them, who advocated a return to the old beliefs, the old, the only true faith. The right to exorcise, for example . . ."

"Yes, Commander. I understand. But you believe in the existence of the Rim Ghosts?"

"Of course, sir—although it has yet to be determined if they are good or evil manifestations. If they are evil, then exorcism should be practiced."

"Yes, of course. As you are well aware, most of us in this ship do not hold the same views as yourself regarding the phenomena of the Rim Ghosts. But you will agree that it is desirable that contact be made with one or more of the apparitions—after all, this is the purpose of this expedition. And if such contact is made . . ." Grimes paused. "If such contact is made, it might well be to the advantage of your church."

"That is so, sir."

"Perhaps you might help us to make such a contact."

"How, sir? I do not think that tampering with the Drive controls will achieve any useful result."

"That was not in my mind. But it had occurred to me, Commander, that there are certain rites practiced by your Church . . ."

"A seance, you mean, Commodore? But I have no

mediumistic talents. If such had been the case I
should not be here now; I should have entered our
priesthood."

"But you know the drill?"

"Yes, sir. I am conversant with the rites and cere-
monies. But without a medium they are valueless."

"Here is our medium," said Grimes, nodding towards the almost asleep Mayhew.

The Psionic Radio Officer jerked awake. "Come
off it!" he ejaculated. "I'm a technician, not a cheap
fortune teller!" Then, "I beg your pardon, sir. What
I meant to say is that the Rhine Institute has always
been opposed to superstition."

"Religion is not superstition, you half-witted
teacup reader!" shouted Calhoun.

"Gentlemen, gentlemen . . ." soothed Grimes.
"Need I remind you that we are under Naval dis-
cipline, and that I could order you, Commander
Calhoun, to organize a seance, and you Mr.
Mayhew, to officiate as medium?"

"Even in the Navy, *sir,*" said Calhoun, his freckles
standing out sharply against the suddenly white
skin of his face, "there are lawful and unlawful com-
mands."

"And," Grimes told him coldly, "bearing in mind
the peculiar purpose of this expedition, such a command made by myself would be construed as lawful by the Board of Admiralty. But many centuries
ago, back in the days when navies were made up of
wooden ships sailing Earth's seas, there used to be a
saying: 'One volunteer is worth ten pressed men.'
Surely, Commander, you will not hesitate to volunteer to play your part in an experiment that, when
made public, could well result in a flood of converts
to your faith?"

"If you put it that way, sir, But ..."

"And surely, Mr. Mayhew, you will not hesitate to play your part? After all, it could well lead to a Fellowship of your Institute. ..."

"But, sir, the superstition ..."

"If you dare to use that word again, Mayhew ..." threatened Calhoun.

"Commander! Please remember where you are. And Mr. Mayhew, I am asking you to respect Commander Calhoun's beliefs. If that is ineffective I shall order you to do so—with the usual penalties if the order is willfully disobeyed."

The pair of them lapsed into a sulky silence.

Grimes went on, "I shall leave matters in your hands, Commander. You are the only person in the ship qualified to carry out the necessary organization. And you, Mr. Mayhew, will co-operate fully with Commander Calhoun." He smiled briefly. "And now, gentlemen, perhaps a little refreshment before you engage yourself upon what are, after all, somewhat unusual duties. ..."

When they were gone, mellowed by the alcohol, almost friendly towards each other, Sonya Verrill said, "The big stick and the carrot ... I hope the combination gets results."

"I hope it gets the results we want," replied Grimes. "We don't want to raise any ghosts of the wrong sort."

"No," whispered Sonya, her face suddenly pale and strained. *"No."*

VIII

THE PREPARATIONS for the seance took much longer than Grimes had anticipated. But it was obvious that Calhoun, religiously as well as professionally, was a perfectionist. The most time-consuming operation was the construction of a harmonium, during which the wardroom piano was cannibalized for its keyboard, this being cut down from seven and a half octaves to five. The engineer's workshop was able to turn out the necessary bellows and treadles, and the brass vibrators or "reeds." The ivory from the surplus keys was utilized in the manufacture of the various stops. Grimes, watching with interest the fabrication of the archaic instrument, listening wincingly to the caterwauling notes of its initial tests—"We must get the *wheezing* quality . . ." insisted Calhoun—was inclined to deplore the sacrifice of what had been a well-cared-for and versatile music maker, the life and soul of many a good party during previous expeditions in *Faraway Quest*. But the seance had been his idea initially, so he felt that he had no right to criticize.

Then the wardroom was stripped of its fittings. The comfortable, well padded chairs were removed and replaced by hard metal benches. The paneling was covered by dingy gray drapes—bedsheets that had been passed through a dye concocted from peculiar ingredients by Dr. Todhunter and Karen Schmidt. Dimmers were fitted to the light switches, and some of the flourescent tubes were removed and replaced by bulbs giving a peculiarly dingy red illumination. And there were other accessories to be made: A tin speaking trumpet, and a tambourine, both of which were decorated with lines and blobs of luminous paint.

At last everything was ready.

Grimes sent for his First Lieutenant. "Commander Swinton," he said, "we shall hold our seance at 2100 hours this evening, ship's time. Please see to it that all departments are notified."

"Ay, ay, sir."

"And wipe that silly grin off your face!"

"Sorry, sir. But you must admit that after that toast, when we spliced the mainbrace, this is turning out to be a wilder ghost chase than any of us anticipated."

"From Commander Calhoun's viewpoint it's somewhat less wild than it was, Swinton. As far as he's concerned we're dropping all the scientific flummery and returning to the primitive methods, the tried and trusted methods, of his religion. And all the evidence indicates that these methods do work after a fashion. They create the right atmosphere. They raise—*something*. From inside, a release of the wild talents possessed by those present at the seance? From Outside? From the next Time Track but three? I don't know, Swinton. I don't know—yet."

"It will be an interesting experiment."

"Yes. And I'm pleased that Mr. Mayhew has been persuaded to look at it in that light."

"I suppose that he *has* got mediumistic talents, sir?"

"He must have, Swinton. What is a medium but a telepath?"

"Could be, sir. Could be. But..."

"Don't say that Commander Calhoun has converted *you?*"

"He's tried hard enough, sir. Oh, I'm willing to believe that his Church, in either the Primitive or the Reformed versions, has produced some interesting phenomena, but I've yet to be convinced that they're supernatural, any more than the Rim Ghosts are. I can't understand why the Rhine Institute hasn't done more to investigate Spiritualism."

"Because, my boy, it hasn't been allowed to. It's *scientific*. Every time that one of its investigators sniffs around a Spiritualist Church he's given either the cold shoulder or the bum's rush. You know the line of talk—'There are some things that we aren't *meant* to know. Faith is all-important; knowledge is a device of the Devil.' And so on. And so on."

"Then I'm surprised that Calhoun was among the volunteers for this expedition."

"You shouldn't be. Commander Calhoun has an axe to grind. He hopes that something will be discovered that will be useful to his Reformed Church. Exorcism by remote control, for example..."

"But that would be dragging in Science."

"As a servant, not as a competitor."

"I think I see..." The young man still looked dubious, however. "Will that be all, sir?"

"Yes, thank you, Commander Swinton.. Oh, just one more thing. As soon as this ... experiment is over, please get the wardroom looking like a wardroom, and not like a down-at-the-heels meeting house."

"That, sir, will be a pleasure."

Grimes dined in his own quarters that night—the wardroom, as it was at this time, was far too comfortless. Sonya Verrill kept him company. They enjoyed their meal together. Although it was simple it was well cooked and nicely served, and the wines from the Commodore's private stock were an excellent accompaniment to the food. While they were eating they chatted about minor matters and listened to the background music softly tinkling from Grimes' playmaster.

And then, after Grimes had produced two bulbs of vintage port and a box of fine cigars imported from Caribbea, they talked more seriously.

She said, "I hate to admit it, John, but I'm rather frightened."

"You, of all people? Why, Sonya?"

"As long as this expedition was being run on scientific lines it was ... How shall I put it? It was, in spite of my own private reasons for being here, *fun*. Something in it, as you said, of the old days of piracy —but only playing at pirates. A Carlotti beacon instead of a real gun or laser projector, and a sort of atmosphere about it all of, "Bang! You're dead!" But now ... As I told you, I've been on Dunglass. It's a dreary world, with cities that are no more than straggling towns, streets and streets of mean little houses and Meeting Halls that are just sheds designed, one would think, with a deliberate avoidance of pleasing proportion. And the feeling all the time that one is being watched, disapprovingly, by the ghosts of all the countless millions who have gone before.

"I went to one or two of their services. Partly out of curiosity, and partly because it was my job, as an Intelligence Officer. Cold, cold halls—with a chill that didn't seem to be natural—and dreary hymn singing by drab people, and dim lights, and a voice that seemed to come from nowhere giving advice about the most trivial matters—and some that weren't so trivial. . . .

"Yes, I remember it well. There was this voice—a man's voice, deep, although the medium was a skinny little woman. The man sitting next to me whispered that it was Red Eagle, a Spirit Guide. He went on to say that this Red Eagle was, or had been, a Red Indian, an American Indian. I wondered what Red Eagle was doing so many light years away from home, but it occurred to me that Time and Space, as we know them, probably mean nothing to spirits, so kept quiet. The voice said, "There is a stranger here tonight, a woman from beyond the sky.' Well, most of those present must have known who I was. The voice went on, 'I have a message for the stranger. I see a ship. I see a ship falling through the emptiness, far and far away . . .' Once again, so what? I was a spacewoman and it was no secret. 'Far away, far away, where the stars are few and dim, far and few . . . And I see the name of the ship, in gold letters on her prow . . . I can read the name . . . *Outsider* . . .' And that meant nothing to me—*then*. 'I see the Captain, brave in his black and gold. You know him. You will know him again . . .' And then there was a description of the Captain's appearance, and I knew that it was Derek Calver. As you are aware, I first met Derek when he was Second Mate of the old *Lorn Lady*. 'There is another man. He is one of the officers, although he, too, has been a Captain. He is afraid, and he is disgraced, and he is locked in his cabin . . .' And once again there was the description—even to the laser burn on the left buttock and the funny little mole just above the navel. It was Bill all right. Bill Maudsley. 'He is sick, and he is afraid, and you are not with him, and he knows that he has lost you forever. There is a bottle, and he drinks from it, and the spilled fluid drifts around the air of the cabin in a mist, in a spray. He looks at the empty bottle and curses, then smashes it on the wall. The broken, splintered neck is still in his hand, and he brings the sharp, jagged end of it across his throat . . .'

"I just sat there, in a sick, numb silence. I wanted to ask questions, but I couldn't in front of all those strangers. But there was nothing more. Nothing at all. Red Eagle had said his piece as far as I was concerned, and passed on all sorts of trivial messages to other members of the congregation. Bill Brown's grandmother was concerned because he wasn't wearing his long underwear, and Jimmy Smith's Aunt Susan wanted to tell him that trade would pick up next year, and so on, and so on.

"After the . . . meeting? Service? After the service I stayed on to have a talk with the minister. He was very sympathetic, and arranged for me to have a private sitting with the medium. It wasn't very satisfactory. Red Eagle seemed to be somewhat peeved at being called away from whatever it was that he was doing, and just told me that I should search

long and far, and that I should and should not find
that for which I was searching.

"And what can be made of that?

"Shall I succeed in my search by becoming a
ghost myself, before my time? I hope not. I'm too
fond of life, John—life on this gross physical plane. I
like good food and wine and tobacco and books and
music and clothes and ... and all the other things
that make life, in spite of everything, so well worth
living. There's far too much vagueness about what
comes after. Oh, there are the stock protestations—'It
is very beautiful here, and everybody is happy ...'—
but ... It could be faulty transmission and reception,
but I always get the impression that the After Life is
lacking in character, and color and, but of course,
the good, lusty pleasures of the flesh ...

"Even so, I was shaken. Badly shaken."

"It could be explained by telepathy, Sonya."

"No, John, it couldn't be. I was not thinking about
Bill Maudsley at the time—not until that message
came through, and even then I was thinking only
about Derek Calver. I didn't know that Bill had
shipped as his Mate. And as for ... And as for the
shocking manner of his death, that I did *not* know
about. I did not know about it officially for a matter
of months, which was the time it took for the news
to drift in from the Rim. But I checked up. I ran all
available data through one of our Master Computers, and got one of our Specialist Navigators to
run his own check, and there were no two ways
about the answer. Bill must have taken his own life
at the very time that I was sitting in that dreary
Meeting Hall in Dovlesville, on Dunglass...."

"It might be as well if you didn't attend the seance, Sonya," Grimes told her.

"And leave the show to you lousy secessionists?" she flared, with a flash of her old spirit. "No sir!"

IX

WHEN GRIMES and Sonya Verrill went down to the wardroom they found that all was in readiness for the seance. The uncomfortable benches—it was fortunate, thought the Commodore, that the ship was falling free so that the only contact between buttocks and an unyielding surface was that produced by the gentle restriction of the seatbelts—had been arranged in rows, facing a platform on which were a table, three chairs and the harmonium. Calhoun, contriving to look like a nonconformist minister in spite of his uniform, occupied one of the chairs at the table. Mayhew, his usual dreaminess replaced by an air of acute embarrassment, sat in the other. Karen Schmidt was seated at the musical instrument.

As soon as the Commodore and Sonya had taken a bench in the front row the engineer, unbuckling his seat belt, got carefully to his feet. His voice, as he made the initial announcement, was more of a street corner bray than a pulpit bleat. "Brethren," he said, "we are here as humble seekers, gathered in all humility, to beg that our loved ones on the Other Side will shed light on our darkness. We pray to Them for help—but we must, also, be prepared to help Them. We must cast out doubt, and replace it by childlike faith. We must *believe*." He went on in a more normal voice, "This, I assure you, is essential. We must put ourselves in a receptive mood, throwing our minds and our hearts open to the benevolent powers on the other side of the veil..." Then, the engineer briefly ascendant over the lay preacher, "We must strive to create the right conditions insofar as we are able..."

Meanwhile, one of his juniors was making his way along the tiers of benches distributing mimeographed sheets. Grimes looked at his curiously. It was, he saw, a hymnal.

"Brethren!" cried Calhoun, "we will join in singing the first hymn."

Karen Schmidt was having trouble with the harmonium—the operation of treadles in the absence of a gravitational field requires a certain degree of concentration. At last, however, she got the thing going and suddenly and shockingly the introductory chords blared out.

Then they were all singing to the wheezing, gasping accompaniment:

"Lead, Kindly Light, amid the encircling gloom,
"Lead Thou me on ..."

The hymn over, Calhoun prayed. Although himself an agnostic, Grimes was impressed by the sincerity of the man. He began to wish that he could believe in something.

There was another hymn, and then the lights were dimmed until only the dull-glowing red globes remained. The lines and blobs of luminous paint picking out the simple apparatus—the speaking trumpet and the tambourine—on the table gleamed eerily. Suddenly it was very quiet in the wardroom; the muted noises of machinery, the sobbing of pumps and whizzing of fans, the thin, high keening of the Mannschenn Drive, accentuated the silence rather than diminished it. It was very quiet—and very cold.

Physical or psychological? Grimes asked himself as he shivered.

His eyes were becoming accustomed to the almost-darkness. He could see the dark forms of Calhoun and Mayhew, sitting motionless at the table, and Karen Schmidt hunched over the harmonium. He turned his head to look at Sonya. Her face was so pale as to seem almost luminous. He put out his hand to grasp hers, gave it a reassuring squeeze. She returned the pressure, and seemed reluctant to relinquish the physical contact.

Mayhew cleared his throat. He said matter-of-factly, "There's something coming through. . . ."

"Yes?" whispered Calhoun. *"Yes?"*

Mayhew chuckled. "It's only a routine message, I'm afraid. *Flora Macdonald . . .*"

"But you must have heard of her," insisted Calhoun in a low voice. "She lived in the eighteenth century, on Earth. She was a Jacobite heroine. . . ."

Mayhew chuckled again. "Not this *Flora Macdonald.* She's a Waverley Royal Mail cargo liner,

and she's off Nova Caledon . . . All the same, this is
remarkable range I'm getting, with no amplifier. It
must be that the brains of all you people, in these
somewhat peculiar circumstances, are supplying
the necessary boost. . . ."

"Mr. Mayhew, you are ruining the atmosphere!"

"Commander Calhoun, I consented to take part in
this experiment on the understanding that it was to
be treated as an experiment."

Something tinkled sharply.

At the table, forgetting this disagreement, Calhoun
and Mayhew were staring at the tambourine.
Grimes stared too, saw that something had broken
its magnetic contact with the steel surface, that it
had lifted and was drifting, swaying gently, carried
by the air currents of the ventilation system.

*But the exhaust ducts were in the bulkhead be-
hind the platform, and the thing, bobbing and jingl-
ing, was making its slow, unsteady way towards
the intake ports, on the other side of the wardroom.*

Grimes was annoyed. This was no time for prac-
tical jokes. Telekinesis was an uncommon talent, for
some reason not usually found among spacemen,
but not so uncommon as all that. There was, the
Commodore knew, one telekineticist in *Faraway
Quest's* crew—and he would be on the carpet very
shortly.

But . . .

But he was the Third Mate, and he was on watch
and, in any case, all the tests that he had undergone
had proven his incapability of any but the most trivial telekinetic feats.

So this, after all, was no more than some freak of
air circulation.

The harmonium wheezed discordantly.

Calhoun was on his feet, furious. "Can't you people take things seriously? This is a religious service! Miss Schmidt, stop that vile noise at once! Stop it, I say! Lights, somebody! Lights!"

The incandescent tubes flared into harsh brilliance. The tambourine steadied and hung motionless, and then behaved in the normal manner of a small object floating loose in Free Fall, drifting very slowly with the air current towards the exhaust ducts. But at the harmonium Karen Schmidt still twitched and shuddered, her feet erratically pumping, her hands falling at random on the keyboard. Her eyes were glazed and her face vacant; her mouth was open and little globules of saliva, expelled by her stertorous breathing, hung about her jerking head in a glistening cloud.

Grimes unsnapped his seat belt and got to his feet. "Dr. Todhunter! See to Miss Schmidt, will you?"

But all Calhoun's anger had evaporated.

"No!" he shouted. "No! Be seated, everybody!"

"Like that woman," Sonya Verrill was whispering tensely.

"Let me pass!" It was Todhunter, trying to make his way through the packed rows of benches. "Let me pass."

And then Karen Schmidt spoke.

But it was not with her own voice. It was with the voice of a man—deep, resonant. At first the words seemed to be an unknown language—a strange but hauntingly familiar tongue. And then, with a subtle shift of stress and tempo, they were understandable.

"Falling ... falling ...

"Through the night and through the nothingness

you seek and you fall . . .

"But I am the onlooker; I care not if you seek and find, if you seek and fail.

"I am the onlooker."

Calhoun was taking charge. "Who are you?"

"I am the onlooker."

"Have you a message?"

"I have no message." There was laughter that seemed to come from nowhere and everywhere. "Why should I have a message?"

"But tell us. Shall we succeed?"

"Why should I tell you? Why should you succeed? What is success, and what is failure?"

"But there must be a message!" The initial awe in Calhoun's voice was being replaced by exasperation. Grimes was reminded of those primitive peoples, sincere believers, who maltreat the images of their gods should those deities fail to deliver the goods.

Again the uncanny laughter. "Little man, what message do you want? Would you know the day and hour and manner of your death? Would you live the rest of your life in fear and trembling, striving to evade the unavoidable?" The hands of the medium swept over the keyboard, and the instrument responded—not discordantly, not wheezingly, but with the tones of a great organ. And the music was the opening bars of the "Dead March" in *Saul*. "Is this the message you crave?"

Sonya Verrill, standing stiff and straight, cried, "Is this all you have for us? Is that the limit of your powers—to tell us all what we know already, that some day we must die?"

For the last time there was the sound of laughter,

and the voice said quietly, "Here is your message."

And then came the shrilling of the alarm bells, the repetition of the Morse symbol A, short long, short long, short long . . .

Action Stations.

X

SHE HUNG there on *Faraway Quest's* port beam, matching velocity and temporal precession rate, a big ship, conventional enough in design, nothing at all strange about her, except that both radar and mass proximity indicator screens remained obstinately blank. Already the oddly twisted directional antenna of the *Quest's* Carlotti apparatus was trained upon her, like the barrel of some fantastic gun, already the whine of the emergency generators, feeding power into the huge solenoid that was the ship, was audible over and above the still ringing alarm bells, the sounds of orderly confusion.

"Nothing showing on the screens, sir," the Third Officer was reporting. "And the transceiver is dead."

Swinton was already at the huge mounted binoculars. He muttered, "I think I can read her name ... *Rim Ranger* ..."

"And that," said Grimes, "is what I had in mind for the next addition to our fleet.... Interesting..."

"Call her on the lamp, sir?"

"No. If all goes well we shall soon be able to communicate through the usual channels. Ready, Mr. Renfrew?"

"Ready and standing by, sir," answered the Survey Service lieutenant.

"Good." And then Grimes found that he was groping for words in which to frame his order. He had almost said, "Fire!" but that was hardly applicable.

"Make contact!" snapped Sonya Verrill.

Renfrew, strapped into his seat at the controls of his apparatus, did look like a gunner, carefully laying and training his weapon, bringing the target into the spiderweb sights. One of his juniors was snapping meter readings: "Red twenty five, red fifty, red seventy five, eighty five ... Red ninety, ninety-five ... six ... seven ... eight ... nine..."

There was a long pause and the men around the modified Carlotti gear were muttering among themselves. Swinton, who was still watching the other ship, announced, "She's flashing. Morse, it looks like..."

"Stand by!" shouted Renfrew. "Now!"

The Carlotti gear whined intolerably, whined and crackled, and the men serving it sneezed as arc-engendered ozone stung their nostrils. There was tension, almost unbearable strain, a psychological rending—and Grimes realized that he was seeing double, that every person, every piece of apparatus in the control room was visually duplicated. But it was more than a mere visual duplication—that was the frightening part. One image of Swinton was still hunched over the eyepieces of the binoculars, the other had turned to stare at Renfrew and his crew. One image of Renfrew still had both hands at the console of his apparatus, the other had one hand raised to stifle a sneeze. And there was a growing confusion of sound as well as of sight. It was—the old, old saying flashed unbidden into Grimes' mind —an Irish parliament, with everybody talking and nobody listening.

And it was like being stretched on a rack, stretched impossibly and painfully—until something snapped.

The other ship, *Rim Ranger*, was there still, looming large in the viewports, close, too close. A voice— it could have been Swinton's—was yelping from the transceiver, "What ship?" Then, "What the hell are you playing at, you fools?"

Grimes realized that he was in the Captain's chair, although he had no recollection of having seated himself. His own control console was before him. There was only one way to avoid collision, and that was by the use of rocket power. (And he had given strict orders that the Reaction Drive was to be kept in a state of readiness at all times.) There was a microsecond of hesitation as his hand swept down to the firing key—the jettison of mass while the Mannschenn Drive was in operation could have unpredictable consequences. But it was the only way to avoid collision. Even with the solenoid cut off there was enough residual magnetism to intensify the normal interaction due to the gravitational fields of the two vessels.

But he was gentle, careful.

From aft there was only the gentlest cough, and

acceleration was no more than a nudge, although heavy enough to knock unsecured personnel off balance and tumble them to the deck.

And outside the viewports there was nothing—no strange ship, no convoluted, distorted Galactic lens, no dim and distant luminosities.

This was the Ultimate Night.

XI

SOME HOURS later they came to the unavoidable conclusion that they were alone in absolute nothingness. Their signaling equipment—both physical and parapsychological—was useless, as were their navigational instruments. There was nobody to talk to, nothing to take a fix on. Presumably they were still falling free (through *what?*)—still, thanks to the temporal precession fields of the Drive, proceeding at an effective velocity in excess of that of light. But here—whatever *here* was—there was no light. There was no departure point, no destination.

After conferring with his senior officers Grimes ordered the Mannschenn Drive shut down. They had nowhere to go, and there was no point in wasting power or in subjecting the complexity of ever-precessing gyroscopes to unnecessary wear and tear. And then he passed word for a general meeting in the wardroom.

That compartment was, of course, still wearing its drab camouflage as a meeting house. The tin speaking trumpet adhered to the surface of the table still; the tambourine clung to the bulkhead hard by one of the exhaust ducts. But this time it was Grimes who took the main platform seat, with Sonya Verrill at his side. Pale and shaken, still dazed after her involuntary mediumism, Karen Schmidt seated herself again at the harmonium. Grimes looked at her curiously, then shrugged. She might as well sit there as anywhere else.

He called the meeting to order. He said, "Gentlemen, you may carry on smoking, but I wish to point out that it may be some little time before we are able to lay in fresh supplies." He was grimly amused as he noticed Todhunter, who was in the act of selecting a fresh cigarette from his platinum case, snap it hastily shut and return it to his pocket. He went on, "Gentlemen, I accept the responsibility for what has happened. I know that the reduction of the ship's mass while the Mannschenn Drive is in operation may, and almost certainly will, have unpredictable consequences. I was obliged to throw away reaction mass. And now we don't know where—or *when*—we are."

Sonya Verrill interrupted him sharply. "Don't be silly, John. If you hadn't used the rockets there'd be no doubt as to our condition, or the condition of the people in the other ship. A collission, and none of us wearing suits . . ."

"She's right," somebody murmured, and somebody else muttered something about proposing a vote of confidence.

But this, thought Grimes, was no time to allow democracy to raise its head. He had nothing against democracy—as long as it stayed on a planetary surface. But in Deep Space there must be a dictatorship —a dictatorship hedged around with qualifications and safeguards, but a dictatorship nonetheless. Too, he was not sure that he liked Sonya Verrill's use of his given name in public. He said coldly, "I ap-

preciate your trust in me, but I do not think that any
useful purpose would be served by putting the matter to the vote. As commanding officer I am fully
responsible for this expedition." He allowed himself
a brief smile. "But I am not omniscient. I assure you
that I shall welcome any and all explanations of our
present predicament, and any proposals as to ways
and means of extricating ourselves from this . . ." he
finished lamely, "mess."

Swinton, seated in the front row with the other
departmental heads, started to laugh. It was not hysterical laughter. Grimes glared at the young officer
from under his heavy brows, said icily, "Please
share the joke, Commander Swinton."

"I'm sorry, sir, but it *is* rather funny. When we
had the seance Miss Schmidt, at the console of that
most peculiar poor man's organ, played on the
white keys, and on the black keys. But *you*, at *your*
console, played in the cracks."

"What do you mean, Commander Swinton?"

"That we're in one of the cracks. We jumped
tracks, but when we tried to jump back we didn't
make it. We fell into the crack."

"Very neat, Swinton," admitted Grimes. "A very
neat analogy. We've fallen into the gulf between Universes. But how are we to climb out?"

"Perhaps Commander Calhoun could help. . . ."
suggested Renfrew. "When we held the seance we
got in touch with . . . something."

Karen Schmidt cried, "No! No! You've not had
something utterly alien taking charge of your mind
and your body. I have, and I'll not go through it
again!"

Surprisingly Calhoun also showed a lack of enthusiasm. He said carefully, "That ... entity was not at all helpful. If we had succeeded in making contact with one of the regular Guides, all would have been well. But we didn't. And I fear that should we succeed in getting in touch with that same entity we shall merely expose ourselves in further derision."

"Well?" asked Grimes, breaking the silence that followed Calhoun's little speech.

Once again the Survey Service lieutenant spoke up. "I see it this way, sir. The Mannschenn Drive got us into this mess, perhaps it can get us out of it. Although the fact that my own apparatus was functioning at the time has some bearing on it. But, putting it crudely, it boils down to the fact that the mass of the ship was suddenly reduced while two Time-twisting machines—the Mannschenn Drive and the Carlotti Beacon—were in operation. As you know, experiments have been made with both of them from the Time Travel angle; no doubt you have heard of Fergus and the crazy apparatus he set up on Wenceslaus, the moon of Carinthia.... Well, I shall want the services of the Mannschenn Drive engineers and of everybody in the ship with any mathematical training. I think I know what we can do to get out of this hole, but it would be as well to work out the theory, as far as is possible, first."

"And what do you have in mind, Mr. Renfrew?" asked Grimes.

"Just this, sir. A duplication as far as possible of the conditions obtaining when, as your Commander Swinton puts it, we fell into the crack, *but with those conditions reversed in one respect.*"

"Which is?"

"The running of the Mannschenn Drive in reverse."

"It can't be done," stated Calhoun flatly.

"It can be done, Commander, although considerable modification will be necessary."

"We can give it a go," said Swinton.

"Yes," agreed Grimes. "We can give it a go. But it is essential that nothing be done in practice until the theory has been thoroughly explored. I have no need to tell you that a reversal of temporal precession might well age us all many years in a few seconds. Or there is another possibility. We may be flung into the far future—a future that could be extremely unhospitable. A future in which the last of the suns of this Galaxy are dying, in which the worlds are dead. Or a future in which one of the non-humanoid races has gained supremacy—the Shaara, for example, or the Darshans. Oh, we maintain diplomatic relations with them, but they don't like us any more than we like them."

"Mr. Renfrew," said Sonya Verrill, "holds a Master's degree in Multi-Dimensional Physics."

"And I, Commander Verrill, hold a Master Astronaut's certificate. I've seen some of the things that happen when a Mannschenn Drive unit gets out of control, and I've had firsthand accounts of similar accidents, and I've a healthy respect for the brute."

"But it is essential that no time be wasted," said Renfrew.

"Why, Lieutenant? What Time is there in this ... Limbo? Oh, there's biological time, but as far as air, water and food are concerned the ship is a closed economy. I regret that the bio-chemists failed to plant a cigarette tree in our 'farm,' but we still have the facilities for brewing and distilling."

"Then, Commodore, at least I have your permission to make a start on the math?"

"Of course."

Renfrew spoke half to himself. "To begin with, all three executive officers are qualified navigators. There is no reason why, with two of them working in their watches below, the third one should not do his share of the calculations."

"There is a very good reason why not," remarked Swinton.

"Indeed, Commander? I was forgetting that in spite of your status as a Reserve Officer you are really a civilian. Would that be breaking your Award, or something equally absurd?"

Swinton flushed, but replied quietly. "As long as we are serving in what, legally speaking, is a Rim Worlds warship, governed by the Articles of War, we are not civilians. My point is this—that it is essential that a good lookout be kept at all times, by all means. The officer of the watch must be fully alert, not tangled up in miles of taped calculations spewing from the control room computer."

"But we're in absolute nothingness," growled Renfew.

"Yes, but . . ."

"But we're in a crack," finished Grimes for him, feeling a childish happiness at having beaten his First Lieutenant to the draw. "And all sorts of odd things have the habit of falling into cracks!"

XII

Faraway Quest fell through the nothingness, drifting from nowhere to nowhere, a tiny bubble of light and heat and life lost in an infinite negation. Her electronic radio apparatus was useless. And Mayhew, the Psionic Radio Operator, crouched long hours in his cabin, staring into vacancy and listening, listening. He resorted to drugs to step up the sensitivity of both himself and the dog's brain that was his organic amplifier, but never the faintest whisper from Outside disturbed the telepath's mind.

And the work went on, the laborious calculations that, even with the ship's computers fully employed, took days, longer in the programing than in the actual reckoning. There were so many variables, too many variables. There were so many unknown quantities. There were too many occasions when the words *Data Insufficient* were typed on the long

71

tapes issuing from the slots of the instruments.

And Grimes, albeit with reluctance, held himself aloof from the activity. He said to Sonya, "Why keep a dog and bark yourself?" But he knew that he, at least, should be free to make decisions, to take action at a second's notice if needs be. He was grateful that the woman was able to keep him company. She, like himself, could not afford to be tied down. She was in command of the Survey Service personnel and directly subordinate to the Commodore insofar as the overall command of the expedition was concerned. And there were administrative worries too. Tempers were beginning to fray. The latent hostility between members of different services, and between members of different departments, was beginning to manifest itself. And as Grimes knew full well, unless something happened soon there would be other worries.

They were castaways, just as surely as though they had been the crew and passengers of a ship wrecked on some hitherto undiscovered planet. There were thirty of them: eight Survey Service officers, twenty two Rim Worlds Naval Reservists. Of the thirty, eight were women. As long as this had been no more than a voyage—not a routine voyage, to be sure. but a voyage nonetheless—sex had not been a problem. As long as all hands were fully occupied with mathematical work and, eventually, the modifications of the Mannschenn Drive, sex would not be a problem. But if every attempt to escape from the crack in Time failed, and if the ship were to drift eternally, a tiny, fertile oasis in a vast desert of nothingness, then something would have to be done about it. Spacemen are not monks, neither are spacewomen nuns.

"We may have to face the problem, Sonya," said Grimes worriedly as the two of them, cautiously sipping bulbs of Dr. Todhunter's first experimental batch of beer, talked things over.

She said, "I've already been facing it, John. The disproportion of the sexes makes things awkward. Oh, I know that in one or two cases it doesn't matter —my own Sub-Lieutenant Patsy Kent, for example. But even if she doesn't draw the line at polyandry, there's no guarantee that her boyfriends will take kindly to it."

He said, "We may be crossing our bridges before we come to them, if we ever do come to them. But that's one of the things that a commanding officer is paid for. It looks as though we may have to devise some workable system of polyandry...."

"Include me out," she said sharply. "By some people's standards I've led a far from moral life, but I have my own standards, and they're the most important as far as I'm concerned. If the microcosmic civilization aboard this ship degenerates to a Nature red in tooth and claw sort of set-up, then I'm looking after Number One. The best bet will be to become the private, personal popsy of the Old Man of the tribe."

He looked at her carefully as she sat there in the armchair, contriving to loll even in conditions of Free Fall. She was wearing uniform shorts and her smooth, tanned legs were very long, and her carelessly buttoned shirt revealed the division between her firm breasts. He looked at her and thought, *The Old Man of the tribe ... But it's a figure of speech only. I'm not all that old.* He said drily, "I suppose that rank should have its privileges. And if I'm the Old Man of *my* tribe, then you're the Old Woman of yours."

She said, "You flatter me, sir."

He said, "In any case, all this talk is rather jumping the gun. Your Mr. Renfrew and my own bright boys may come up with the answer."

She said, "They may not—and a girl has to look after herself."

He murmured, more to himself than to her, "I wish that there were some other reason for your ... proposition."

She laughed, but tremulously, "And do you really think that there's not, John?"

"But these are exceptional circumstances," he said. "I know your reasons for embarking on this expedition. There were two men in your life, in our own Continuum, and you lost both of them. You're hoping to find what you lost."

"And perhaps I have found it. We've been cooped up in this tin coffin together long enough now. I've watched you, John, and I've seen how you've reacted to emergencies, how you've kept a tight rein on your people without playing the petty tyrant. They all respect you, John, and so does my own staff. And so do I."

He said, a little bitterly, "Respect isn't enough."

"But it helps, especially when respect is accompanied by other feelings. It would help, too, if you were to regard me, once in a while, as a woman, and not as Commander Verrill, Federation Survey Service."

He managed a grin. "This is so sudden."

She grinned back. "Isn't it?" And then she was

serious again. "All right. I don't mind admitting that the jam we're in has brought things to a head. We may never get back again—either to our own Continuum or to any of the more or less parallel ones. We may all die if one of our bright young men does something exceptionally brilliant. But let's ignore the morbid—or the more morbid—possibility. Just suppose that we do drift for a fair hunk of eternity on our little, self-sustaining desert island. As you know, some of the old gasuss-jammers have been picked up that have been adrift for centuries, with the descendants of their original crews still living aboard them. . . .

"Well, we drift. You're the boss of your tribe, I'm the boss of my smaller tribe. Our getting together would be no more than a political alliance."

He said, "How romantic."

"We're rather too old for romance, John."

"Like hell we are."

He reached out for her, and she did not try to avoid him.

He reached out for her, and as he kissed her he wondered how long it was since he had felt a woman's lips—warm, responsive—on his. *Too long,* he thought. And how long was it since he had felt the rising tide of passion and let the softly thunderous breakers (her heart and his, and the combined thudding loud in his ears) bear him where they would? How long since he had felt the skin—firm, resilient, silken-soft—of a woman, and how long since the heat of his embrace was answered with a greater heat?

Too long . . .

"Too long . . ." she was murmuring. "Too

long..." Then was silent again as his mouth covered hers.

And outside the cabin was the ship, and outside the ship was the black nothingness....

But there was warmth in the cabin, and glowing light, a light that flared to almost unendurable brilliance and then faded, but slowly, slowly, to a comforting glow that would never go out, that would flare again, and again. There was warmth in the cabin and a drowsy comfort, and a sense of security that was all wrong in these circumstances—and yet was unanswerably right.

Grimes recalled the words of the medium—or the words of the entity that had assumed control of her mind and body. *"Through the night and through the nothingness you seek and you fall..."*

And he and Sonya had sought, and they had found.

They had sought, and they had found—not that for which they were seeking—or had they? She had been seeking a lover, and he? Adventure? Knowledge?

But all that was worth knowing, ever, was in his arms. (He knew that this mood would evaporate—and knew that it would return.)

She whispered something.

"What was that, darling?"

She murmured, "Now you'll have to make an honest woman of me."

"Of course," he replied. "Provided that the Federation taxpayers kick in with a really expensive wedding present."

She cast doubts on his legitimacy and bit his ear, quite painfully, and they were engaged in a wrestling match that could only have one possible ending when the alarm bells started to ring.

This time their curses were in earnest, and Grimes, pulling on his shorts, hurried out of the cabin to the control room, leaving Sonya to follow as soon as she was dressed.

But it made no sense, he thought, no sense at all—Action Stations in this all pervading nothingness.

XIII

GRIMES, WHOSE quarters were immediately abaft the control room, was in that compartment in a matter of seconds. He found there young Larsen, the Third Mate, and with him was Sub-Lieutenant Patsy Kent, of the Survey Service. Larsen flushed as he saw the Commodore and explained hastily, "Miss Kent was using the computer, sir . . ."

"Never mind that. What is the emergency?"

The officer gestured towards the globe of darkness that was the screen of the Mass Proximity Indicator. "I . . . I don't know, sir. But there's something. Something on our line of advance."

Grimes stared into the screen.

Yes, there was something there. There was the merest spark just inside the surface of the globe, and its range . . . The Commodore flipped the switch of the range indicator, turned the knob that expanded a sphere of a faint light from the center of the screen, read the figure from the dial. He muttered, "Twelve and a half thousand miles . . ." and marveled at the sensitivity of this new, improved model. But the target could be a planetoid, or a planet, or even a dead sun. Somehow he had assumed that it was another ship, but it need not be. Twelve and a half thousand miles, and *Faraway Quest's* initial velocity before proceeding under Interstellar Drive had been seven miles a second.... (But was it still? Where was a yardstick?) Contact in thirty minutes, give or take a couple or three ... But there should be ample time to compute the velocity of approach....

The others were now in the control room: Swinton, and Jones, the Second Mate, and Renfrew. And Sonya. He could smell the faint, disturbing perfume of her and he asked himself, *What am I doing here?* He stared at the spark of light, brighter now, and closer, with a certain resentment. *Come off it, Grimes,* he thought in self-admonishment, *it's years since you were a rosy-cheeked, snotty, sulking hard because a call to duty interfered with your very first date....*

"Your orders, sir?" Swinton was asking politely, yet with a touch of urgency.

"Action Stations was sounded, and Action Stations it is. I take it that the laser projectors and the missile launchers are closed up?"

"They are, sir."

"Good. Mr. Jones, please work out velocity of approach and estimated time of contact. Mr. Renfrew, please use the Carlotti gear for the purpose for which it was originally invented and try to initiate radio communication. Mr. Larsen, get on the blower to Mr. Mayhew and shake him up. Tell him that there's something ahead—a ship? a planet?—and that I want to know if it has a crew, or a population." Then, to Swinton, "I shall be going below for a few seconds, Commander. If anything happens you will know where to find me."

He dropped down the axial shaft to his day cabin, went through to his lavatory cubicle and hastily tidied himself up. He dressed rapidly, but with care. If this were to be a first contact with some alien race he would, at least, try to look the part that he was playing, that of leader of an expedition of Earthmen into the Unknown. He snared an undergarment of filmy crystal silk that was drifting in the air currents, stowed it hastily in a convenient drawer. It was just possible that he would be entertaining guests shortly.

Then, back in the control room, he received the reports of his officers. *Faraway Quest,* they told him, was closing the target at twelve miles a second. (So *it,* whatever *it* was, was not hanging motionless in Space. Or was it?) It had now been picked up by the radar, and the indications were that it was a metallic structure, not overly large. Neither electronic nor psionic radio had been able to establish contact.

So . . .

So it was a dead ship, a vessel that years—or centuries—ago had fallen out of its own continuum, a ship whose crew had died, or whose descendants were no longer able to operate any of the machinery except what was essential for the maintenance of life? Or was it a ship in fighting trim manned by possibly hostile beings with itchy trigger fingers, maintaining a cautious silence until the *Quest* was within range of the homing missiles, the flickering laser beams?

The Commodore went to the telephone, pressed the selector stud. "Mr. Mayhew. We are closing the target. Do you hear anything?"

"No, sir."

"The target appears to be a ship. Suppose that her

Captain has ordered radio silence, what then?"

"Any unshielded mind must radiate, sir. Only trained telepaths can establish and maintain an effective shield, but even then there is leakage, a gabble of scraps of nonsense verse, meaningless mathematical formulae and the like."

"So you think that there's nothing living there, Mayhew?"

"I'd bet on it, sir."

"I hope you're right." He snapped orders to the First Lieutenant. "Commander Swinton, take the controls, please. Match velocities with the target and maintain a range of one mile."

"Ay, ay, sir." And then Swinton, seating himself in the Master Pilot's chair, was snapping his own orders, his manner assured and competent, in startling contrast to his usual callow youthfulness.

Grimes, strapped into a convenient acceleration chair, watched the young man appreciatively. He heard the whine of the stabilizing gyroscopes and felt the vibration as the ship was turned end for end —and it was odd for this maneuver to be carried out without, as a visual accompaniment, the drift of stars (even the few, faint stars of the Rim) across the viewports. And then, relatively speaking, the target was astern—astern, but still closing rapidly. *Faraway Quest's* rocket drive coughed briefly, and coughed again. The target was still closing—but slowly, slowly.

For the last time there was the subdued rumble of the rockets, the gentle pressure of deceleration, and Swinton announced, not without pride, "Target abeam, sir. Velocities matched. Range one-point-oh-five of a mile."

Grimes swiveled his chair so that he could look out of the viewports.

And outside there was nothing but blackness.

In a matter of seconds the probing beam of the searchlight found the target.

It was a ship, but no ship such as any of those in the control room had ever seen. There was a long hull that looked as though the conventional torpedo shape had been sliced in two longitudinally. At one end of it there was what looked like an assemblage of control surfaces. Grimes, out of his chair and monopolizing the huge mounted binoculars, studied it carefully. There was a rudder, and there were two screw propellers. It could be, he thought, a lightjammer, similar to the ones that he himself had designed, capable of being handled in a planetary atmosphere like an airship. But the rudder was too small, and those propellers were too heavy and had too coarse a pitch to be airscrews.

But there were the lofty masts, one forward and one aft, protruding from the flat deck.... But that would be an unusual, and not very practicable arrangement of spars to carry a lightjammer's suit of sales.... And between the masts there was a structure, white-painted, that looked more like a block of apartments, complete with balconies, than part of a ship. Roughly in the middle of this there was another mast.... No, decided Grimes, it wasn't a mast, it was too thick, too short. It, too, was white-painted, but with a black top, and carried a design in blue. Grimes studied it carefully, decided that it was supposed to be some sort of grapnel or anchor.

He relinquished the binoculars to Sonya Verrill. When she had had time to study the weird derelict he asked, "Well, Commander, what do *you* make of it?"

She replied doubtfully, "It *could* be a lightjammer, sir. But all those ports ... It'd be hard enough to make a thing like that watertight, let alone airtight. ..."

"H'm. But those ports seem to be on one half of the hull only, the half with all the odd superstructures.... Like half a ship, and half—something else ..."

"After all, sir," put in Swinton, who had been studying the thing with a smaller pair of binoculars, "there's no reason why a spaceship should be symmetrical. As long as it never has to proceed through an atmosphere it can be any shape at all that's convenient."

"True, Swinton. True. But if that thing's designed for Deep Space only, why those screw propellers? Aerodynamically speaking it's a hopeless mess, and yet it's equipped for atmospheric flight...."

"But is it?" queried Sonya Verrill. "Those absurdly heavy screws with their fantastically coarse pitch ..."

"But where's the planet?" asked Swinton.

"Come to that," countered Grimes, "where's *our* planet?" He added, "Who knows what odd combinations of circumstances threw us here, dropped us into this crack in Time? Who knows what similar combinations have occurred in the past?" And then, in a whisper, "But we're such a long way from Earth ..."

"Are we?" asked Renfrew. "Are we? What does the word 'dimension' mean in this dimensionless Limbo?"

"So I could be right," said Grimes.

"What are you driving at, John?" demanded Sonya Verrill.

"I'd rather not say, yet. It's too fantastic." He turned to his First Lieutenant. "I'll leave you to hold the fort, Swinton. I shall take away the boarding party."

XIV

THEY ASSEMBLED in the after airlock of *Faraway Quest:* Grimes, and Sonya Verrill, and Jones, and Dr. Todhunter. They waited until they were joined by Calhoun and McHenry. When the two senior engineers put in an appearance they were hung around with an assortment of tools that would have been impossible to carry in any appreciable gravitational field: hammers, and wrenches and pinch bars and burning equipment. All members of the party, of course, carried reaction pistols and, on Sonya Verrill's insistence, all were armed—Grimes with the heavy projectile pistol that he favored, the others with hand laser projectors. In addition, the Surgeon carried a small battery of cameras.

They had put on their helmets and then Grimes, plugging the lead from his suit radio microphone into the telephone socket, ordered Swinton, in the control room, to evacuate the airlock. They watched the needle of the guage drop slowly, finally coming to rest on Zero. And then the valve opened.

The strange ship hung out there in the absolute blackness, every detail picked out by the harsh glare of the searchlight. Her colors were bright, garish—the red that was almost purple, the broad band of pink paint, and then black, and then the white of the superstructure and the yellow of that odd assemblage of spars, of masts and booms.

She looked, thought Grimes, out of context.

But to any dweller in this nothingness—if there were any such dwellers—*Faraway Quest* would look out of context too.

With an odd reluctance Grimes shuffled to the sill of the airlock door, made the little jump that broke contact between his magnetic boot soles and the steel deck. His reaction pistol was ready, and with economical blasts he jetted across the mile of emptiness. And then that odd-expanse of red-purple plating was before him—and with a sudden shift of orientation he had the sensation of falling toward it head first. He used his pistol to turn himself and then to brake his speed. His landing was gentle, his boot soles making contact with the metal with no more than the slightest of jars. They made contact and they held. So, he thought, *this ship is made of iron, or steel. But if I am right, when she was built nobody had thought of using aluminum as a structural material, and plastics had not been dreamed of. . . .*

He felt the shock as Sonya Verrill landed beside him, and then Jones came in, and Todhuhter, and the two engineers. Grimes waited until Calhoun and McHenry had sorted themselves out—hampered as they were by their equipment, they had fallen clumsily—and then led the way along the surface of painted metal.

It was not easy going.

A spaceman's shuffle is a quite effective means of locomotion over a perfectly flat and smooth surface —but when the surface is made up of overlapping, riveted plates the feet must, frequently, be lifted, and there is the fear that, with magnetic contact broken, a long fall through emptiness will ensue.

But they made progress, trudging towards a near horizon that was a purple painted angle-bar, glowing dully against the blackness.

Todhunter called a halt, contorting himself so that his magnetic knee-pads touched the plating. He said, "This is odd. It looks like clumps of some sort of living organism growing on the plates. It's dead now, of course."

"What I expected," Grimes told him.

"What you expected, sir?"

"If and when we get back to Port Forlorn, Doctor, you must read a few of the books in my rather specialized library. . . . I remember that a bright young journalist from the *Lorn Argus* once did a feature article on it. She cooked up rather a neat title, *From Dug-Out Canoe to Interstellar Liner.*"

"I don't understand, sir."

"Neither do I, Doctor. But those barnacles will keep. They've been keeping for one hell of a long time."

They negotiated the angle-bar—like a ridge, it was, like the ridge of a roof with a pitch of 45 degrees—and beyond it was more of the purple-painted plating, and beyond that a stretch of pink paint, and beyond that was the dull-gleaming black. Grimes stopped at the border between the two colors, looked down at an odd, white-painted design— a circle, bisected by a line that had at one end the letter L, at the other the letter R. And from the right-hand end of this line was another line at right angles to it, and this was subdivided and lettered: TF, T, S, W, WNA. . . . .

"So this is—or was—one of *our* ships. . . ." Sonya Verill's voice was faint yet clear in his helmet phones. "Of course, those letters could be odd characters from some utterly alien alphabet, but they don't look like it to me."

"They're not," Grimes told her. "The L and the R stand for Lloyds' Register. TF is Tropical Fresh, T is Tropical, S is Summer, W is Winter, and WNA is Winter North Atlantic."

"But what does it mean? And how do you know?"

"I know because the history of shipping—all shipping—has always fascinated me. I should have recognized this ship at first glance, but I did not, because she has no right here. (But have we?) But here she is, and here we are—and we're luckier than her people because we shall be able to survive even if we can't find our way back. . . ."

And then, still in the lead, he was shuffling over the black-painted plating until he came to a section of white-painted rails. He threw his body forward, grasped the rails with his gloved hands. He remained in this position until he had once again oriented himself, until his "up" and "down" were the "up" and "down" of the long-dead people of the dead ship. He was looking into a promenade deck. There was the scrubbed planking, and ahead of him was white-painted plating, broken by teakwood doors and brass rimmed ports—and with dense, black shadows where the glare of the *Quest's* searchlights did not penetrate. With a nudge of his chin he switched on his helmet lantern; he would be needing it soon.

The wooden deck would effectively insulate his boot soles from the steel plating beneath it, so he made a scrambling leap from the rail to one of the open doorways, pulled himself into the alleyway beyond it. There were more doors—some open, some ajar and secured by stay hooks, some shut. Grimes waited until the others had joined him, then pulled himself along a sort of grab rail to the first of the partially open doors. His gloved fingers fumbled with the stay hook, finally lifted it. The door swung easily enough on its hinges, which were of polished brass.

He let himself drift into the cabin, the glare of his helmet light gleaming back at him from burnished metal, from polished wood. There was a chest of drawers, and there were two light chairs that seemed to be secured to the deck, and there were two bunks, one above the other. The upper bunk was empty.

The Commodore stared sadly at the pair of figures in the lower bunk, the man and the woman held in place by the tangle of still-white sheets. He had seen Death before, but never in so inoffensive a guise. The bodies, little more than mummies, had been drained of all moisture by their centuries-long exposure to a vacuum harder even than that of normal interstellar Space, or even that of intergalactic Space, and yet lacked the macabre qualities of the true skeleton.

Todhunter's voice was hushed. "Do you think, sir, a photograph?"

"Go ahead, Doctor. *They* won't mind."

It's a long time, he thought, *it's a long, long time since you minded anything. . . . But how did it come to you? Was it sudden? Did the cold get you first, or did you die when the air rushed out of your lungs in one explosive burst?* He turned to look at Sonya, saw that her face was pale behind the visor of her helmet. He thought, *We should be thankful. We were lucky.* He said, "We shan't learn much by looking in the other cabins."

"Then where can we learn something?" asked Calhoun in a subdued voice.

"In the control room—although they didn't call it that."

He led the way along alleyways—in some of which drifted dessicated bodies—and up companionways, careful all the time to maintain the sense of orientation adapted to the derelict. Through public rooms they passed, the glare of their helmet lanterns, broken up into all the colors of the spectrum, flung back at them from the ornate crystal chandeliers. And then, at last, they came out into the open again, on to a great expansive of planking on either side of which the useless lifeboats were ranged beneath their davits. All around them was the emptiness, and there was *Faraway Quest,* her searchlights blazing, no more than a bright and lonely star in the black sky.

From handhold to handhold they made their way, following the Commodore, until they came to more ladders, leading to a bridge that spanned the fore part of the superstructure. In the center of this bridge was a house of varnished timber with big glass windows, and in the forward compartment of this house there was the body of a man. He was standing there, held in position by the grip of his hands on a big, spoked wheel, an ornate affair of polished wood and burnished brass. He was wearing an odd, flat blue cap, and a blue, wide-collared jumper, and blue trousers that were tucked into short black boots. The skeletal face still—after how many centuries?—wore an expression of concentration as the eyes, no more than depressions in the taut skin, stared sightlessly at the compass, at the lubber's line that had not shifted a microsecond of arc from the quarter point in half a millenium. Eerily the card swung as Grimes looked at it, pulled away from its heading by the magnetic field generated by his suit transceiver.

Abaft the wheelhouse there was another compartment. In it were two men, both attired in uniforms that still, to a shipman, made sense. Grimes murmured, "Sorry, Captain," and gently lifted the body of the tall, thin man, the almost-skeleton with the neat gray beard and the four gold bands on the sleeves, away from the chart table. He looked down at the chart, at the penciled courseline, at the circled intersections of cross bearings. "Yes," he whispered. "As I thought. The South African coast . . ."

"And where is that, sir?" asked Calhoun.

"On Earth. And the time? Towards the beginning of the Twentieth Century . . ."

By his side Sonya Verrill was looking at the open pages of the Log Book. She said, "The watchkeeper recorded thunder and exceptionally vivid lightning, and also makes mention of an unusual display of phosphoresence."

"But who were they?" Todhunter was demanding. "How did they get here?"

"I can answer the first question," Grimes replied gravely. His gloved forefinger indicated the heading of the log book path. " '*Waratah*, from Durban towards Liverpool.' But she never got there.

XV

THERE WERE several big, glazed frames on the after bulkhead of the chartroom, and in one of them was a detailed plan of the ship. Grimes and his officers studied it with interest. McHenry said suddenly, "I'd like to see what their engines are like."

"I can tell you now, Commander," Grimes told him. "Steam. Reciprocating. Coal burning. As I remember the story, she put into Durban for bunkers on her way home from Australia."

"But I'd like to see them, sir." The engineer's forefinger was tracing out a route on the plan. "As long as we keep amidships and carry on down we're bound to come to the stokehold, and from there to the engineroom."

"Then carry on," said Grimes. "But I don't want you to go by yourself."

"I shall be with him," said Calhoun, and Jones said that he wanted to make a further exploration of the derelict, and Todhunter wanted to take more photographs.

Grimes and Sonya went out to the wing of the bridge, keeping a firm grasp on the teakwood rail, and watched the two engineers, the Second Mate and the Surgeon making their way along the boat deck, saw them open a door in the fiddley casing below and just forward of the funnel and vanish, one by one, into the black opening.

He heard the girl ask, "But how do you explain all this, John?"

"I can't, Sonya—although this could be the explanation of a number of mysteries. As you know, I'm something of an authority on the history of shipping. You'd think that even as far back as the Twentieth Century it would be impossible to lose, completely, anything so large as a ship. After all, in those days there was quite efficient diving gear, and sonic sounding apparatus—and, even though it was in its earliest infancy, there was radio.

"But ships did vanish—and vanish without trace.

"Take this *Waratah*, for example. She was a new ship, owned by the Blue Anchor Line, built for the cargo-passenger trade between England and Australia. On her maiden voyage she carried freight and passengers outwards, and then loaded more freight—frozen meat and general cargo—in Australia for England, also embarking passengers. She was scheduled to call at Durban on the homeward passage to replenish her coal bunkers, also to disembark and to embark passengers. One odd feature of the voyage was the number of intending travelers who experienced premonitory dreams of a warning character and, as a result of these, canceled their passages.

"Anyhow, she arrived in Durban, and bunkered, and sailed. She exchanged visual signals with another ship shortly afterwards. And that was all.

"Oh, plenty of surface ships did founder, some of them with all hands, and the loss of *Waratah* was explained away by the theory that she was extreme-

ly unstable, and rolled so badly in a heavy swell that
she capsized and went down suddenly. But this was
not in the loneliness of mid-ocean. This was in soundings, in relatively shallow water, and on a well-
frequented shipping route. But no bodies were ever
found, and not a single fragment of identifiable
wreckage...." He pointed to a lifebuoy in its rack,
the white and scarlet paint still bright, gleaming in
the beams from *Faraway Quest's* searchlights, the
black lettering, *Waratah, Liverpool,* clearly legible.
"Even if she had gone down suddenly *something*
would have broken free and floated, something with
the ship's name on it....

"She was a passenger liner, and so she became
better known than a smaller ship would have done,
and her name joined that of *Mary Celeste* on the
long list of unsolved ocean mysteries that, even to
this day, are occasionally rehashed by journalists as
fillers for Sunday supplements. As a matter of fact
that wench from the *Lorn Argus* who was writing
up my library said that she was going to do a series
called *Maritime Mysteries of Old Earth* and spent
quite a few evenings browsing among my books....

"But there was *Waratah,* and there was *Anglo-
Australian,* and there was *Cyclops.* .... And there
were the ships like *Mary Celeste,* found drifting in
perfect order without a soul on board....

"Well, I suppose we've found out *what* happened.
But how? *How?*"

Sonya said, "That analogy of playing on the black
keys, and playing on the white keys, and playing in
the cracks, was a good one. But as an Intelligence
Officer I've had to do quite a deal of research into
this sort of thing. Ocean going ships have vanished,

but so have aircraft, and so have spacecraft. And there have been many, many cases of the inexplicable disappearances of people—the crew of your *Mary Celeste,* for example, and the famous man who walked round the horses, and Ambrose Bierce, and ... and ..."

"And?"

"I suppose you're wondering why I haven't cited any modern cases. The trouble, of course, is that Space Travel has given the explainers-away far too easy a time. A ship goes missing on a voyage, say, from Port Forlorn to Nova Caledon, as the Commission's *Delta Eridani* did a couple of years back. But Space is so vast, and when you throw in the extra dimensions added by the use of any sort of Interstellar Drive, it's vaster still. When a ship is overdue, you know as well as I do that any search would be quite useless. And men and women still go missing—but if they go missing on any of the frontier planets there are so many possible causes—usually some hitherto undiscovered life form that's gobbled them up, bones, boots and all."

"Even so, records are kept."

"Of course. It takes a small city to house all the Intelligence Department's files on the subject."

They went back into the chartroom. Grimes looked at the dessicated bodies of the Captain and his watch officer, wished that the two men were able to speak, to tell him just what had happened. Perhaps, he thought, they would be able to do so. Results, of a sort, had been achieved by that first seance aboard *Faraway Quest.* He wondered, too, if Todhunter would be able to revive any of *Waratah's* people, but he doubted it. In the early days of in-

tersteller expansion a deep freeze technique had
been used, but all of those making a long, long
voyage in a state of suspended animation had undergone months of preparation before what had
been, in effect, their temporary deaths—and in many
cases, in far too many cases, the deaths had been all
too permanent. It was easy enough to say the words,
"Snap-freezing and dehydration," but the actual
technique had never been easy.

Carefully Grimes examined the Log Book. The
pages were brittle, all moisture leeched from them
by their centuries of exposure to hard vacuum. He
deciphered the crabbed handwriting in the *Remarks* column. "Mod. beam sea, v. heavy beam
swell. Vsl. rolling heavily. O'cast, with occ'l heavy
rain and violent thunderstorms. Abnormally bright
phosphoresence observed."

Thunder and lightning and abnormally bright
phosphorensence ...

So what?

He muttered, "The electrical storm may have had
something to do with it.... And possibly there was
some sort of disturbance of the Earth's magnetic
field in that locality, and something just right—or
just wrong—about the period of the roll of a steel
hull ..."

"Or possibly," she said, "there was somebody
aboard the ship who was a sort of catalyst. Remember all the dreams, all the premonitory, warning visions, that were experienced just before her
disappearance? Perhaps there are people—in fact,
our researches hint that there are, and always have
been such people—who can slip from one Time
Track to another, in many cases quite inadvertently.

As well as the records of inexplicable disappearances there are also the records of equally inexplicable appearances—men and women who have turned up from, literally, nowhere, and who have been strangers, lost and bewildered, in a strange world. . . .

"In our own case, how much was due to Mr. Renfrew's fancy apparatus and your own tinkering with anti-matter and anti-gravity, and how much was due to the mediumistic powers of your Miss Karen Schmidt?"

"Could be . . ." he admitted. "Could be . . . It's a farfetched theory, but . . ."

"Farfetched?" she scoffed. "Here we are, marooned in this absolute nothingness, and you have the nerve to accuse me of drawing a long bow!"

"Not quite nothingness," he corrected her. "The indications are that we may be in a sort of graveyard of lost ships. . . ."

"And lost people. The unfortunates who, somehow, have missed their footing from stepping to one track to the next . . . As *Waratah's* people did."

"And as we did."

"But we're lucky enough to have a self-sustaining economy."

Grimes broke off the conversation to keep Swinton, back in the control room of *Faraway Quest,* up to date with what was happening and what had been discovered, including in his report the tentative theories that had been, so far, advanced. The First Lieutenant acknowledged, then said, "I don't want to hurry you, sir. But Mr. Mayhew informs me that he's receiving very faint signals from somewhere. It could either be something or somebody extremely distant, or something quite close but transmitting feebly."

"So we aren't alone in the junkyard," said Grimes. Then, switching frequencies, he succeeded in raising the Second Mate, the doctor and the two engineers, who were still prowling in the bowels of the ship and who were most reluctant to break off their explorations. He ordered them to report to the bridge at once.

At last they appeared, babbling of pistons and furnaces and boilers and refrigerating machinery, carrying lumps of coal that they had taken from the bunkers. *Odd souvenirs*, thought Grimes—and decided that if he were able he would acquire something more useful, the books from the library, for example, or the grand piano from the First Class Lounge.... And with the thought he looked at the long dead Captain and whispered, "It's not theft. I know you wouldn't object to making a gift to a fellow shipmaster."

"What was that, sir?" asked Jones.

"Nothing," snapped Grimes. "Now let's get back to our own wagon and find out what fresh surprises they've cooked up for us."

XVI

ONCE BACK aboard his own ship, Grimes went straight from the airlock to the control room, pausing only to take off his helmet. Swinton greeted him with the words, "Mayhew is still picking it up, sir."

"Good. Can he get any kind of directional fix on it?"

"He says not. But you know what Mayhew is like, impossibly vague unless you can nail him down."

Grimes went to inspect the screens first of the radar, then of the Mass Proximity Indicator. Both instruments had been reset for extreme long range. Both showed nothing.

He went to the nearest telephone, put out his hand to take the handset from the rack, then changed his mind. He said, "I shall be with Mr. Mayhew if you want me, Commander Swinton." He made a beckoning nod to Sonya Verrill, who followed him from the control room.

He knew that it would be a waste of time tapping on the door to the Psionic Radio Officer's cabin, but did so nonetheless. He waited for a decent interval and then slid the panel to one side, letting himself and Sonya into the room. Mayhew had his back to them; he was strapped in his seat, his body hunched as though it were being dragged from an upright position by a heavy gravitational field. He was staring at the transparent cylinder, nested in its wires and pipes, in which, submerged in the bath of nutrient fluid, hung the small, gray-white mass, obscenely naked, that was the living brain of one of the most telepathic of all animals, a dog, that was the amplifier with the aid of which a skilled telepath could span the Galaxy.

They may have made a slight noise as they entered; in any case Mayhew turned slightly in his chair and looked at them with vague, unfocused eyes, muttering, "Oh. It's you." And then, in a more alert voice, "What can I do for you, sir?"

"Just carry on with what you *are* doing, Mr. Mayhew. But you can talk, I think, while keeping a listening watch."

"Of course, sir."

"This signal you've picked up, can it be vocalised?"

The telepath pondered, then said, "No, sir. It's emotion rather than words.... It's a matter of impressions rather than a definite message...."

"Such as?"

"It's hard to put into words, sir. It's dreamlike. A dim dream within a dream..."

" 'And doubtful dreams of dreams...' " quoted Grimes.

"Yes, sir. That's it."

"And who, or what, is making the transmission? Is it human? Or humanoid? Or a representative of one of the other intelligent races?"

"There's more than one, sir. Many more. But they're human."

Sonya Verrill said, "There's a chance, John, that

there may be some flicker of life, the faintest spark, still surviving in the brains of those people aboard *Waratah*. What are their dreams, Mr. Mayhew? Are they of cold, and darkness, and loneliness?"

"No, Miss Verrill. Nothing like that. They're happy dreams, in a dim sort of way. They're dreams of warmth, and light, and comfort, and . . ." he blushed ". . . love . . ."

"But it could still be *Waratah's* people."

"No. I probed her very thoroughly, very thoroughly. They're all as dead as the frozen mutton in her holds."

"How did you know that?" demanded Grimes sharply.

"It was necessary, sir, to maintain telepathic contact with the boarding party. I 'overheard' what you were telling the others about *Waratah's* last voyage."

"Sorry, Mr. Mayhew."

"And the only telepathic broadcast from the derelict was made by you and your party, sir. With these other signals I get the impression of distance—and a slow approach."

"But who the hell is approaching whom?" exploded Grimes. Then, "I was talking to myself. But we still don't know at what speed we're traveling, if we are traveling. When we matched velocities with *Waratah* did we reverse our original motion, or did we merely come to rest, or are we still proceeding the same way as we were when we fell into this bloody crack?"

"I'm not a navigator, sir," said Mayhew stiffly.

"None of us is, until there's something to navigate with. But we're interrupting you."

"Not really, sir. This is no more than one of those pleasant dreams you have sometimes between sleeping and waking...." He stiffened. "There's one coming through a little stronger than the others.... I'll try to isolate it.... Yes....

"There are blue skies, and white, fleecy clouds, and a river with green, grassy banks... Yes, and trees... And I am sitting by the river, and I can feel the warmth of the sun, and the breeze is bringing a scent that I know is that of new-mown hay..." He paused, looked at the others with a wry grin. "And I've never seen hay, let alone smelled it. But this is not *my* dream, of course. Yes. There's the smell of new-mown hay, and there's the song of birds in the trees, and my pipe is drawing well, and my rod is perfectly balanced in my hands, and I am watching the—the bait, the fly that I tied myself, drifting on the smooth surface of the stream, and I know that sooner or later a trout will rise to take it, but there is no hurry. I'm perfectly happy where I am, doing what I am, and there's no hurry...

"But there is. Behind it all, underneath it all, there *is* a sense of urgency. There's the guilty feeling, the guilty knowledge that I'm late, that I've overslept, and that something dreadful will happen if I don't wake up...."

"Odd," commented Grimes. "Do you know Earth, Mayhew?"

"No, sir."

"Do you know anything about dry flies?"

"What are they, sir?"

"You were talking about tying one just now. They're a form of bait used by fishermen who do it for sport, not commercially. The really keen anglers tie their own flies—in other words they fabricate from feathers, wire, and the odd Gods of the Galaxy alone know what else, extremely odd—but as long as the trout also think that they look edible, why worry?"

"So," said Sonya, "we have a nostalgic dry fly fisherman from Earth, who's dreaming about his favorite sport, marooned, like ourselves, in this crack in Time-Space. Or Space-Time. But, for all we know, we may be picking up this dream from Earth itself. Dimensions are meaningless here. After all, there's *Waratah . . .*"

"She's had a long time to drift," said Grimes. "But go on, Mr. Mayhew."

"He's drifted back into the happy dream," murmured Mayhew. "He's not catching anything, but that doesn't worry him."

"And can you isolate any of the others?" asked the Commodore.

"I'll try, sir. But most of them are about long, timeless days in the air and the warm sunshine . . . There is a man who is swimming, and he turns to look at the girl beside him, and her body is impossibly beautiful, pearl-like in the clear, green water. . . . And there is a woman, sitting on velvet-smooth grass while her sun-browned children play around her. . . .

"But they're getting closer, whoever they are. They're getting closer. The dreams are more distinct, more vivid. . . .

"The air is thin and cold, and the hard-packed snow is crunching under my heavy, spiked boots. It seems that I could reach out now to touch the peak with my ice-axe. . . . It's close, close, sharp and

brilliantly white against hard blue sky.... There's a
white plume steaming from it, like a flag of
surrender.... It's only snow, of course, wind-driven
snow, but it *is* a white flag. It's never been conquered—but in only a few hours I shall plant my
flag, driving the spiked ferrule deep into the ice and
rock.... They said that it couldn't be done without
oxygen and crampon-guns and all the rest of it, but
I shall do it...."

"It would be quite a relief," remarked Sonya, half
seriously, "if somebody would dream about a nice,
quiet game of chess in a stuffy room with the air
thick with tobacco smoke and liquor fumes."

Grimes laughed briefly. He said, "I have a hunch
that these are all hand-picked dreamers, hearty
open air types." The telephone buzzed sharply. He
reached out, took the instrument from its rest. "Commodore here... Yes... Yes... Secure all for acceleration and prepare to proceed on an interception
orbit."

XVII

OUTSIDE THE viewports there was nothing but blackness, and the old steamship was no more than a spark of light, a dimming ember in the screens of radar and Mass Proximity Indicator. A gleaming bead threaded on to the glowing filament that was the extrapolation of *Faraway Quest's* orbit was the new target, the ship that had drifted in from somewhere (nowhere?) on a track that would have carried her all of a thousand miles clear of the *Quest* had she not been picked up by the survey ship's instruments.

Grimes and his officers sat in their chairs, acceleration pressing their bodies into the resilient padding. Swinton, as before, had the con, and handled the ship with an ease that many a more experienced pilot would have envied. At a heavy four gravities *Faraway Quest* roared in on her interception orbit and then, with split second timing, the rockets were cut and the gyroscopes brought into play, spinning the vessel about her short axis. One last brief burst of power and she, relative momentum killed, was herself drifting, hanging in the emptiness a scant mile clear of the stranger.

The searchlights came on.

Faraway Quest's people stared through the ports

at the weird construction, only Grimes evincing no surprise. Her appearance confirmed his hunch. She was an affair of metal spheres and girders—a small one, its surface broken by ports and antennae, a large one, with what looked like conventional enough rocket lifecraft cradled about its equator, then another small one, with a nest of venturis protruding from the pole like a battery of guns. There were no fins, no atmospheric control surfaces.

Swinton broke the silence. "What the hell is that?"

"I suggest, Commander, that you take a course in the history of astronautics. That is a relic of the days of the First Expansion, when Man was pushing out toward the stars, without any sort of reliable intersteller drive to cut down the traveling time from centuries to weeks." He assumed a lecture room manner. "You will observe that the ship was not designed for blasting off from or landing on a planetary surface; she is, in fact, a true spaceship. She was constructed in orbit, and stores and personnel were ferried up to her by small tender rockets—quite possibly those same tenders that are secured about the central sphere.

"The small, leading sphere is, of course, the control room. The central sphere contains the accommodation—if you can call it such. The after sphere is the engineroom."

Swinton said thoughtfully, "And I suppose that she's manned—no, 'inhabited' would be a better word—by the descendants of her original crew and passengers. And they don't know how to use the radio. Judging by all those antennae she's not hard up for electronic gadgetry! And so they haven't heard our signals, or if they have heard them they've not been able to answer. They probably don't even know that we're around."

Grimes laughed gently. "You haven't quite got it right, Commander. She was on a long, long voyage —far longer than her designers anticipated!—but there was no breeding *en route*."

"But there's life aboard her, sir. All those queer psionic signals that Mayhew's been picking up . . ."

"Yes. There *is* life aboard her. Of a sort."

"I'm sorry, sir. I don't quite get you."

Grimes relented. "As I said, she's a relic of the First Expansion. In those days, thanks to the failure of anybody, in spite of ample forewarning, to do anything about it, the Population Explosion had come to pass, and both Earth and the habitable planets and satellites of the Solar System were over-crowded. But it was known that practically every sun had its family of planets capable of supporting our kind of life. So there was a siphoning off of surplus population—mainly of those who could not and would not adapt to life in the densely populated cities. Techniques for the suspension of animation were already in existence and so each of the big ships was able to carry an enormous number of passengers, stacked like the frozen mutton in the holds. The crew too spent most of the voyage frozen, the idea being that the spacemen would keep watches—relatively short intervals of duty sandwiched between decades of deep freeze—so that they, on arrival at their destination, would have aged only a year or so. The passengers, of course, would not have aged at all.

"Finally, with the ship in orbit about the planet of her destination, everybody would be revived and ferried down to the surface of their new home."

"I'm not sure that I'd care for that, sir."

"Neither should I. But they had no Interstellar Drive. And they didn't know, Commander, as we now know, how many of those ships were to go missing. Some of them must have fallen into suns or crashed on planetary surfaces. Others are still wandering. . . ."

"The Survey Service," put in Sonya Verrill, "has satisfactorily accounted for all but thirteen of them."

"And this one brings the number down to twelve," remarked the Commodore.

"But how did she wander *here?*" demanded Sonya.

"We can find out," Swinton told her.

"We can try to find out," she corrected him.

Grimes stared through the big binoculars at the archaic interstellar ship, carefully studied the forward sphere, the control compartment. He could make out what looked like a manually operated airlock door on its after surface. It should be easy enough, he thought, to effect an entrance.

"Surely the duty watch will have seen the glare of our lights," Swinton was saying.

"I fear that the watch will have been too long for them," said the Commodore quietly.

As before, the boarding party was composed of Grimes, Sonya Verrill, Jones, Calhoun, McHenry and Dr. Todhunter. This time, thought Grimes, there would be something for the engineers and the Surgeon to do. The big ship could be restored to running order, her thousands of people rescued from a condition that was akin to death. *And then?* wondered Grimes. *And then?* But that bridge could be crossed when it was reached, not before.

He led the way across the emptiness between the two vessels—the sleek, slim *Faraway Quest* and the clumsy assemblage of spheres and girders. He turned in his flight to watch the others—silver fireflies they were in the beam of the *Quest's* lights, the exhausts of their reaction pistols feeble sparks in the all-pervading blackness. He turned again, with seconds to spare, and came in to a clumsy landing on the still-burnished surface of the control sphere, magnetized knee and elbow pads clicking into contact with the metal. He got carefully to his feet and watched the others coming in and then, when they had all joined him, moved slowly to one of the big ports and shone the beam of his helmet lantern through the transparency.

He saw what looked like a typical enough control room of that period: acceleration chairs, radar and closed circuit TV screens, instrument consoles. But it was all dead, dead. There were no glowing pilot lights—white and red, green and amber—to present at least the illusion of life and warmth. There was a thick hoar frost that sparkled in the rays from the helmet lanterns; there was ice that gleamed in gelid reflection. The very atmosphere of the compartment had frozen.

He made his way from port to port. It was obvious that the control room was deserted—but the control room occupied only a relatively small volume of the forward globe. The rest of it would be storerooms, and hydroponic tanks, and the living quarters for the duty watch.

He said to Sonya, "We may find somebody in the accommodation. Somebody whom we can revive.

And if we don't—there are the thousands of dreamers in the main body of the ship. . . ."

He led the way around the curvature of the metal sphere, found the door that he had observed from *Faraway Quest*. He stood back while McHenry and Calhoun went to work on it. They did not have to use any of their tools; after a few turns of the recessed wheel it opened easily enough, but the inner door of the airlock was stubborn. It was only after the little party had so disposed itself in the cramped compartment that maximum leverage could be exerted that it yielded, and then barely enough for the Commodore and his companions to squeeze through one by one. It was a thick drift of snow, of congealed atmosphere, that had obstructed the inward swinging valve. The snow and the frost were everywhere, and the ice was a cloudy glaze over all projections.

They proceeded cautiously through the short alleyway, and then through a hydroponics chamber in which the ultraviolet and infra-red tubes had been cold for centuries, in which fronds and fruit and foliage still glowed with the colors of life but shattered at the merest touch. Grimes watched the explosion of glittering fragments about his inquisitive, gloved finger, and imagined that he could hear, very faintly, a crystalline tinkling. But there was no sound. The interior of the ship was frighteningly silent. There was not even the vibration of footsteps transmitted through metal plating and suit fabric; the omnipresent snow and ice muffled every contact.

They came to a circular alleyway off which numbered doors opened.

Grimes tried the first one, the one with the numeral 4. It slid aside with only a hint of protest. Beyond it was what had been a sleeping cabin. But it was not now. It was a morgue. It held two bodies. There was a big man, and he held in his right hand a knife, and the frozen film on it still glistened redly. There was a woman who was still beautiful. Todhunter's specialized knowledge was not required to determine the cause of death. There was a clean stab wound under the woman's left breast, and the man's jugular vein had been neatly slit.

They went into the next cabin. Its occupants, lying together in the wide bunk, could have been asleep—but in the clip on the bulkhead to which it had carefully returned was a drinking bulb. It was empty—but the label, upon which was a skull and crossbones in glaring scarlet, made it obvious what the contents had been.

In the third cabin there was shared death too. There was an ingenious arrangement of wires leading from a lighting fixture to the double bunk, and a step-up transformer. The end might have been sudden, but it had not been painless. The two frozen bodies, entangled in the lethal webbing, made a Laocoon-like group of statuary—but that legendary priest of Apollo had perished with his sons, not with a woman.

And in the fourth cabin there was only one body, a female one. She was sitting primly in the chair to which she was strapped, and she was clothed, attired in a black uniform that was still neat, that did not reveal the round bullet hole over the breast until a close inspection had been made.

"Cabin Number One..." said Calhoun slowly.

"Could she have been the Captain?"

"No," said Grimes. "This, like the others, is a cabin for two people. And there's no sign of a weapon...." Gently he brushed a coating of frost from the woman's sleeve. "Gold braid on a white velvet backing... She will have been the Purser."

They found the Captain in a large compartment that lay inboard from the alleyway. He, too, was formally clothed in gold-buttoned, gold-braided black. He was huddled over a desk. The automatic pistol was still in his hand, the muzzle of the weapon still in his mouth. Frost coated the exit wound at the back of his head, robbing it of its gruesomeness. Before him was a typewriter and beside the machine was a small stack of paper, held to the surface of the desk by a metal clip.

Grimes read aloud the heading of the first page:

"TO WHOM IT MAY CONCERN ...

"IF AND WHEN ...

"WHEN AND IF ...

"IF EVER."

It was gallows humor, and it was not very funny.

XVIII

"Just possibly (Grimes read) somebody, somewhere, may stumble upon us. When we pushed off from Earth there was talk of an interstellar drive that would enable ships to take short cuts through sub-Space. I suppose that it's sub-Space that we're in now. But I don't know how we got here, and I don't know how we can get out. If I did know I would not have sanctioned the use of the Euthanol—and how was I to know that all but one of the containers had leaked?—and, in the case of the Gallaghers, the Nakamuras and ourselves, the rather messy substitutes. We could have finished our watch, of course, and then awakened Captain Mitchell and *his* staff so that they could have returned us to the state of suspended animation—but we talked it over and we decided against it. Our dreams, during our long sleep, our long watch below, would not have been happy ones. All the others are dreaming happily of the lives that they will lead on the new world to which we are bound, the lives of which their rationed vacations in Earth's fast dwindling Nature

Reserves were brief forecasts. But our dreams, now, would be full of anxiety, of cold and loneliness, of the black emptiness into which we have fallen.

"*But how?*

"*How?*

"It's the odd flotsam that we've sighted, from time to time, that has made up our minds. What laws of motion are valid in this Limbo we do not know. Perhaps there are no laws. But, appearing from nowhere, there was that corpse that orbited for some hours about the control sphere. It was that of a man. He was wearing archaic clothing: a gray top hat, a stock and cravat, a frock coat. Mary Gallagher, whose hobby is—*was*, I should say—history, said that his dress was that of the early Nineteenth Century. And then there was an aircraft, a flimsy affair of fabric and stays and struts. Centuries ago they must have fallen here—they and the other briefly glimpsed men and women, and a surface ship from the days of steam on Earth's seas, and a clumsy looking rocket (not that we can talk!) bearing on its side characters that bore no resemblance to any Earthly alphabet.

"But I feel that my time is running out. All the others are dead. Sarah asked me to dispose of her, giving as her reason her nervousness with firearms. But the others are dead. The Browns were lucky—when I dealt the cards she got the ace of spades, and with it the only intact bulb of Euthanol. The rest of us could have shared the pistol, but Nakamura preferred something more traditional (although, at the end, he didn't use the knife in a traditional way) and Gallagher was an engineer to the end. But my time is running out. When I have finished this I shall shut down the machinery and then come back here to use the pistol on myself.

"So here is the story—such as it is. If whoever finds it—and I feel that it will be some castaway like ourselves—can read it, it might be of value.

"Fully manned, provisioned and equipped, with a full load of passengers, we broke away from orbit on January 3, 2005. (Full details will be found in the Log Books.) Once we were on the trajectory for Sirius XIV, watches were set. First Captain Mitchell, as senior officer, did the first year, so that he and his staff could make any necessary minor adjustments. The rest of us, after the period of preparation, went into the Deep Freeze. First Captain Mitchell was succeeded by Second Captain von Spiedel, and he was succeeded by Third Captain Cleary. So it went on. It was a routine voyage, as much as any interstellar voyage is routine.

"We relieved Captain Cleary and his people.

"There was a period of three weeks, as measured by the chronometer, during which we were able to mingle socially with our predecessors, whilst Pamela Brown, in her capacity as Medical Officer, worked with Brian Kent, Cleary's M.O., to restore us to full wakefulness and to prepare the others for their long sleep. And then, after Cleary and his team had been tucked away, we were able to get ourselves organized. The control room watches, of course, were no more than a sinecure. Routine observations were taken and told us that we were exactly on course and that our speed of advance was as predicted. The last observation, made at 1200 hours on the day that it happened, gave our position as 1.43754 Light Years out from Earth, and our velocity as 300 m.p.s. Full details are in the Log Book.

"That night—we divided our time, of course, into twenty-four hour periods—all off-duty personnel were gathered in the wardroom. There was the usual rubber of bridge in progress, and the playmaster was providing light background music. Nakamura and Mary Gallagher were engaged in their habitual game of chess. Brown had the watch and his wife was keeping him company. It was typical, we all thought, of a quiet evening in Deep Space. Those of us who were on duty were keeping the machines running, those of us off duty were relaxing in our various ways.

"So the sudden ringing of the alarm bells was especially shocking.

"I was first in the control room, but only by a very short head. There was no need for Brown to tell us what was wrong; it was glaringly obvious. No, not *glaringly* obvious. It was the absence of glare, of light of any kind, that hit us like a blow. Outside the viewports there was only a featureless blackness.

"We thought at first that we had run into a cloud of opaque dust or gas, but we soon realized that this hypothesis was untenable. Until the very moment of black-out, Brown told us, the stars ahead had been shining with their usual brilliance, as had been the stars all around the ship. Furthermore, one cannot proceed through a cloud of dust or gas, however tenuous, at a speed of 300 m.p.s. without an appreciable rise in skin temperature. An appreciable rise? By this time the shell plating would have been incandescent and all of us incinerated.

"I'll not bore you, whoever you are (if there ever is anybody) with a full account of all that we did, of all that we tried, of all the theories that we discussed. Brown stuck to his story. At one microsecond the viewports had framed the blazing hosts of Heaven, at the next there had been nothing there but the unrelieved blackness. We thought that we might be able to learn something from the radio, but it was dead, utterly dead. We disassembled every receiver and transmitter in the control sphere, checked every component, reassembled. And still the radio was dead. There were no longer the faint signals coming in from Earth and from other interstellar ships. There were no longer the signals enamating from those vast broadcasting stations that are the stars.

"But there were no stars.

"There are no stars any more.

"And then, over the weeks, there were the—apparitions?

"No. Not apparitions. They were real enough. Solid. Brown and Nakamura took one of the tenders out, and ran right alongside an ocean-going ship out of Earth's past. Her name was *Anglo-Australian*, and on her funnel was a black swan on a yellow field. They were wearing their spacesuits, so they were able to board her. They found—but could it have been otherwise?—that all of her crew was dead. There were no entries in the Log Book to account for what had happened to her. As in our case, it must have been sudden.

"There was the flotsam—the bodies, some clothed in the fashions of bygone centuries, some not clothed at all. The sea-going ships and the aircraft—and some of them could have come from Earth. There was the huge affair that consisted of a long fuselage slung under what must have been an elongated balloon—but the balloon had burst—with a crew of insects not unlike giant bees. There was that other construction—a relatively small hull suspended amid a complexity of huge sails. We never found out who or what had manned her; as soon as we turned our searchlights on her she vanished into the distance. A sailing ship of Deep Space she must have been—and we, unwittingly, provided the photon gale that drove her out of our ken.

"And we worked.

"But there was no starting point. We had fallen somehow into sub-Space—as had all those others—but how? *How?*

"We worked, and then there were weeks of alcoholic, sexual debauch, a reaction from our days of wearisome, meaningless calculation and discussion. And when, sated, we returned to sobriety we were able to face the facts squarely. We were lost, and we did not possess the knowledge to find our way out of this desert of utter nothingness. We considered calling the other watches—and then, in the end, decided against it. They were happy in their sleep, with their dreams—but we, we knew, could never be happy. We knew too much—and too little—and our dreams would be long, long experiences of tortured anxiety. We could see no faintest gleam of hope.

"And so we have taken the only way out.

"But you, whoever you are (if there ever is anybody) will be able to help.

"The other watches are sleeping in their own compartments in the northern hemisphere of the main globe. The waking process is entirely automatic. Give First Captain Mitchell my best wishes and my apologies, and tell him that I hope he understands.

> John Carradine,
> Fourth Captain."

XIX

THEY LEFT the control sphere then, and made their way through an airlock to the tube that connected it with the large globe that was the main body of the ship. They found themselves in a cylindrical space with a domed deck head, in the center of which was the hatch through which they had entered. In the center of the deck there was a similar hatch.

There were doors equally spaced around the inside surface of the cylinder. All of them were labeled, having stenciled upon them names as well as rank. "First Captain Mitchell . . ." read Sonya Verrill. "Chief Officer Alvarez . . . Second Officer Mainbridge . . . . Third Officer Hannahan . . . Bio-Technician Mitchell . . ." She paused, then said, "I suppose that a husband-wife set-up is the best way of manning a ship like this . . ."

Grimes slid the door aside.

The helmet lanterns threw their beams onto eight tanks—a tier of four, and another tier of four. They looked, thought the Commodore, like glass coffins, and the people inside them like corpses. (*But corpses don't dream.*)

Four of the tanks held men, four held women. All of them were naked. All of them seemed to be in first-class physical condition. Mitchell—his name was on a metal tag screwed to the frame of his tank —was a rugged man, not young but heavily muscled, robust. He did not need a uniform as a professional identification. Even in repose, even in the repose that was almost death, he looked like a master of men and machines, a man of action with the training and intelligence to handle efficiently both great masses of complex apparatus and the mere humans that operated it.

Grimes looked at him, ignoring the other sleepers. He wondered if Mitchell were the fisherman whose pleasant dreams were being spoiled by the sense of anxiety, of urgency. It could be so. It probably was so. Mitchell had been overdue to be called for his watch for a matter of centuries, and his was the overall responsibility for the huge ship and her cargo of human lives.

Todhunter was speaking. There was a certain disappointment in his voice. "I don't have to do anything. I've been reading the instructions, such as they are. Everything is fully automated."

"All right, Doctor. You can press the button. I only want First Captain Mitchell awakened." He added softly, "After all, this is his ship. . . ."

"I've pressed the button," grumbled Todhunter. "And nothing has happened."

McHenry laughed. "Of course not. The dead Captain in the control sphere, in the wardroom, said that he'd shut down all the machinery."

"As I recall it," said Grimes, "these things were powered by a small reactor. It will be right aft, in the machinery sphere. Carradine was able to shut down by remote control, but we won't be able to restart the same way. The batteries must be dead."

"As long as the Pile is not," contributed McHenry.

"If it is, we shall send for power packs from the *Quest*. But I hope it's not."

So they left Mitchell and his staff in their deep, frozen sleep and made their way aft, through deck after deck of the glass coffins, the tanks of the motionless dreamers. Jones paused to look at a beautiful girl who seemed to be suspended in a web of her own golden hair, and murmured something about the Sleeping Beauty. Before Grimes could issue a mild reprimand to the officer, McHenry pushed him from behind, growling, "Get a move on! You're no Prince Charming!"

And Grimes, hearing the words, asked himself, *Have we the right to play at being Prince Charming? But the decision is not ours to make. It must rest with Mitchell . . .*

Then there was the airlocked tube leading to the machinery sphere, and there were the pumps and the generators that, said McHenry, must have come out of Noah's Ark. "But this *is* an Ark," said Jones. "That last deck was the storage for the deep-frozen, fertilized ova of all sorts of domestic animals. . . ."

There were the pumps, and the generators and then, in its own heavily shielded compartment, the Reactor Pile. McHenry consulted the counter he had brought with him. He grunted, "She'll do."

Unarmored, the people from *Faraway Quest* could not have survived in the Pile Room—or would not have survived for long after leaving it. But their spacesuits gave protection against radiation as well as against heat and cold and vacuum, and working with bad-tempered efficiency (some of the dampers resisted withdrawal and were subjected to the engineer's picturesque cursing) McHenry got the Pile functioning.

Suddenly the compartment was filled with an opaque mist, a fog that slowly cleared. With the return of heat the frozen air had thawed, had vaporized, although the carbon dioxide and water were still reluctant to abandon their solid state.

McHenry gave the orders—he was the Reaction Drive specialist, and as such was in charge, aboard his own ship, of all auxiliary machinery. McHenry gave the orders and Calhoun, assisted by the second Mate, carried them out. There were gauges and meters to watch and, finally, valves to open. Cooling fluid flashed into steam, and was bled carefully, carefully into piping that had been far too cold for far too long a time. And then hesitantly, complainingly, the first turbine was starting to turn, slowly, then faster and faster, and the throbbing whine of it was audible through their helmet diaphragms. Leaping from position to position like an armored monkey, McHenry tended his valves and then pounced on the switchboard.

Flickering at first, then shining with a steady brilliance, the lights came on.

They hurried back through the dormitory sphere to the compartment in which First Captain Mitchell and his staff were sleeping. There Todhunter took charge. He slid shut the door through which they had entered and then pulled another door into place, a heavier one with a thick gasket and dogs all around its frame. He borrowed a hammer from McHenry to drive these into place.

Grimes watched with interest. Obviously the

Surgeon knew what he was doing, had studied at some time the history of the "deep freeze" colonization ships, probably one written from a medical viewpoint. He remarked, "I can see the necessity for isolating this compartment, but what was that button you pressed when we first came in here? I thought that it was supposed to initiate the awakening process."

Todhunter laughed. "That was just the light switch, sir. But once we've got over these few preliminaries everything will be automatic. But, to begin with, I have to isolate the other bodies. Each tank, as you see, is equipped with its own refrigeration unit, although this transparent material is a highly efficient insulation. Even so, it will be as well to follow the instructions to the letter." He paused to consult the big, framed notice on the bulkhead, then went to a control console and pressed seven of a set of eight buttons. On seven of the eight coffins a green light glowed. "Now ... heat." Another button was pressed, and the frost and ice in the wedge-shaped compartment began to boil.

When the fog had cleared, the Surgen muttered, "So far, so good." He studied the tank in which lay the body of First Captain Mitchell, put out a tentative hand to touch lightly the complexity of wiring and fine piping that ran from its sides and base. He said, "You will have noticed, of course, that the arrangements here are far more elaborate than those in the main dormitory decks. When the passengers are awakened, they will be awakened *en masse* . . ."

"Get on with it, Doctor!" snapped Sonya Verrill.

"These things cannot be hurried, Commander. There is a thermostatic control, and until the correct temperature is reached the revivification process cannot proceed." He gestured towards a bulkhead thermometer. "But it should not be long now."

Suddenly there was the whine of some concealed machinery starting, and the stout body of the First Captain was hidden from view as the interior of his tank filled with an opaque, swirling gas, almost a liquid, that quite suddenly dissipated. It was replaced by a clear amber fluid that completely covered the body, that slowly lost its transparency as the pneumatic padding upon which Mitchell lay expanded and contracted rhythmically, imparting a gentle agitation to the frame of the big man. The massage continued while the fluid was flushed away and renewed, this process repeated several times.

At last it was over.

The lid of the coffin lifted and the man in the tank stretched slowly and luxuriously, yawned hugely.

He murmured in a pleasant baritone, "You know, I've been having the *oddest* dreams ... I thought that I hadn't been called, and that I'd overslept a couple or three centuries...." His eyes opened, and he stared at the spacesuited figures in the compartment. *"Who are you?"*

XX

GRIMES PUT up his hands to his helmet, loosened the fastenings and gave it the necessary half turn, lifted it from the shoulders of his suit. The air of the compartment was chilly still, and damp, and a sweet yet pungent odor made him sneeze.

"Gesundheit," muttered the big man in the coffin.

"Thank you, Captain. To begin with, we must apologize for having boarded your ship uninvited. I trust that you do not object to my breathing your atmosphere, but I dislike talking through a diaphragm when I don't have to."

"Never mind all that." Mitchell, sitting bolt upright in his tank, looked dangerously hostile. "Never mind all that. Who the hell are you?"

"My name is Grimes. Commodore. Rim Worlds Naval Reserve. These others, with the exception of the lady, are my officers. The lady is Commander Verrill of the Federation Survey Service."

"Rim Worlds? Federation?" He looked wildly at the other tanks, the transparent containers in which his own staff were still sleeping. "Tell me it's a dream, somebody. A bad dream."

"I'm sorry, Captain. It's not a dream. Your ship has been drifting for centuries," Sonya Verrill told him.

Mitchell laughed. It was a sane enough laugh, but bitter. "And while she's been drifting, the eggheads have come up with a practicable FTL drive. I suppose that we've fetched up at the very rim of the Galaxy." He shrugged. "Well, at least we've finally got some place. I'll wake my officers, and then we'll start revivifying the passengers." His face clouded. "But what happened to the duty watch? Was it von Spiedel? Or Cleary? Or Carradine?"

"It was Carradine." Grimes paused, then went on softly, "He and all his people are dead. But he asked to be remembered to you."

"Are you mad, Commodore whatever your name is? How did you know that it was Carradine? And how can a man who's been dead for centuries ask to be remembered to anybody?"

"He could write, Captain. He wrote before he died —an account of what happened. . . ."

"What did happen, damn you? And how did he die?"

"He shot himself," Grimes said gravely.

"*But what happened?*"

"He didn't know. I was hoping that you might be able to help us."

"To help you? I don't get the drift of this, Commodore. First of all you tell me that you've come to rescue us, and now you're asking for help."

"I'm deeply sorry if I conveyed the impression
that we were here to rescue you. At the moment
we're not in a position to rescue anybody. We're
castaways like yourselves."

"What a lovely, bloody mess to be woken up to!"
swore Mitchell. He pushed himself out of the tank,
floated to a tall locker. Flinging open the door he
took out clothing, a black, gold-braided uniform, a
light spacesuit. He dressed with seeming unhurried-
ness, but in a matter of seconds was attired save for
his helmet. He snapped to McHenry, who was hung
about with his usual assortment of tools, "You with
all the ironmongery, get ready to undog the door,
will you?" And to Grimes and Sonya Verrill, "Get
your helmets back on. I'm going out. I have to see for
myself . . ." And then he moved to the tank beside
the one that he had vacated, looked down at the still
body of the mature but lovely woman. He
murmured, "I'd like you with me, my dear, but
you'd better sleep on. I'll not awaken you to this
nightmare."

Mitchell read the brief account left by Carradine,
then went to the next level, the control room, to inspect the Log Book. He stared out through a port at
Faraway Quest, and Grimes, using his suit radio,
ordered Swinton to switch off the searchlights and
turn on the floods. He stared at the sleek, graceful
Quest, so very different from his own ungainly command, and at last turned away to look through the
other ports at the unrelieved emptiness. His suit had
a radio of sorts, but it was A.M. and not F.M. He
tried to talk with Grimes by touching helmets, but
this expedient was far from satisfactory. Finally the

Commodore told McHenry to seal off the control room and to turn on the heaters. When the frozen atmosphere had thawed and evaporated it was possible for them all to remove the headpieces of their suits.

"Sir, I must apologize for my lack of courtesy," said the First Captain stiffly.

"It was understandable, Captain Mitchell," Grimes told him.

"But Captain, Carradine should have called me," Mitchell went on.

"And if he had, Captain, what could you have done? In all probability you would have died as he died. As it is, you know now that you stand a chance."

"Perhaps, sir. Perhaps. But you haven't told me Commodore, how you come to be marooned in this Limbo."

"It's a long story," said Grimes doubtfully.

"And we've all the time in the Universe to tell it, John," put in Sonya Verrill. "Or all the time out of the Universe. What does it matter?"

"All right," said Grimes. "It's a long story, but you have to hear it, and it could well be that you might be able to make some suggestion, that there is some important point that has escaped us but that you, with a mind fresh to the problem, will seize upon."

"That's hardly likely," The First Captain said. "When I look at your ship out there, and envisage all the centuries of research that have gone into her building ... But go ahead, sir. At least I shall be privileged with a glimpse into the future—although it's not the future now."

Grimes told the story, trying to keep it as short as

possible, but obliged, now and again, to go into technical details. He told the story, asking his officers to supply their own amplifications when necessary. Mitchell listened attentively, asking an occasional question.

"So," he said when at last the Commodore was finished, "we are not the only ones to have fallen into this hole in Space-Time. There was the old surface ship that you boarded; there was the surface ship that Carradine's people boarded. There were the aircraft that Captain Carradine mentioned ... That dirigible airship, sir, with the crew of beelike beings. . . ?"

"The Shaara, Captain. They, too, have interstellar travel."

"There's some sort of a connection, Commodore. You got here, you think, by the use of your fantastic electronic gadgetry. But we didn't. And those old surface ships and aircraft didn't . . . And those people, sighted by Carradine, with no ships at all . . . These Shaara, Commodore, what are they like?"

"To all intents and purposes, Captain, they're highly evolved honey bees."

"H'm. But they have something that *we* have, otherwise they'd never have gotten here. Intelligence, of course. Technology. The airship that Carradine saw, and the spaceships that you say they have now . . . But there must be something else."

"There is," stated Calhoun flatly.

"And what is that, Commander?" asked Grimes.

"It's a matter of . . . Well, I suppose *you'd* call it Psionics, sir."

"But the Shaara are an utterly materialistic race."

"I agree, sir. But they still possess certain abilities,

certain talents that were essential to their survival before they started to climb the evolutionary ladder. Such as dowsing..."

"*Dowsing,* Commander Calhoun?"

"Yes. According to some authorities, the ability of the honey bee, on Earth, and on the other worlds to which it has been introduced, to find nectar-laden blossoms is akin to dowsing, for water or minerals, as practised by human beings."

"H'm. This is the first time that I've heard that theory."

"It's not a new one, sir."

Mitchell smiled for the first time since he had been awakened. It was not a happy smile, but it brought a momentary easing of the stern lines of his face. "Dowsing..." he whispered. "Yes. There could be a connection..."

"Such as?" asked Sonya Verrill.

The First Captain replied in a voice that was again doubtful, "I don't know. But..." He went on, "As you must know, this ship is one of the specialized vessels built for large scale colonization. I've no doubt that in your day, Commander Verrill, newly discovered worlds are thoroughly surveyed before the first shipment of colonists is made. But in my time this was not so. The big ships pushed out into the unknown, heading for sectors of Space recommended by the astronomers. If their first planetfall was disappointing, then they proceeded to an alternative objective. And so on. But the crews and the passengers of the ships were themselves the survey teams.

"I need hardly tell you what such a survey team would have to look for. Water, on worlds that were apparently completely arid. Necessary ores. Mineral oil. The necessary electronic divining apparatus could have been carried, but in many ways it was better to carry, instead, a certain number of men and women who, in addition to their other qualifications, possessed dowsing ability."

"I think I see what you're driving at, Captain," objected Sonya Verrill. "But those surface ships and aircraft would not have carried dowsers as an essential part of their crews."

"Perhaps not, Commander Verrill. But—"

Calhoun broke in. "Dowsing ability is far more widespread than is generally realized. Most people have it to some degree."

"So the Shaara can dowse, and we can dowse," said Grimes. "But what *is* the connection?"

"You know where the dowsers among your passengers are berthed, Captain?" asked Calhoun. "Or should I have said 'stowed?'"

"Stowed is the better word," Mitchell admitted. "I don't know at the moment where they are, but as soon as I've consulted the passenger list and the plans . . ."

"I'm sure that they've something to do with it," Calhoun stated firmly. Then, to the Commodore, "I suggest that you tell Commander Swinton to get Mr. Mayhew into a suit, and send him across here. As soon as possible."

"Who is Mr. Mayhew?" asked Mitchell.

"Our Psionic Radio Officer. A trained telepath."

"So that idea was developed after all. There was talk of it in my time. So you think he may be able to read the minds of my dowsers?"

"I hope so," said Grimes. Then, "I'll get Swinton to

send one of our suits across for you. It will make things easier if we're able to speak with each other when we're suited up again." He put his helmet back on, called his First Lieutenant aboard the *Faraway Quest* and gave him the orders.

XXI

THEY DID NOT have long to wait for Mayhew.

They watched him, accompanied by one of the junior engineers, jetting across the emptiness between the two ships. Jones squeezed through the sphincter airlock that sealed the hatch in the control room deck, and went down to the airlock proper in the after-hemisphere of the globe. He must have flashed his helmet lantern as a signal, as the two spacesuited figures veered abruptly in midflight and, shortly thereafter, were lost to view from the control room ports. Grimes, still wearing his helmet, heard Jones say, "Mr. Mayhew and Mr. Trent are aboard, sir."

"Good. Bring them up here, will you?"

The diaphragm in the deck bulged and developed a hole in its center, through which appeared the head of the Second Officer, and then his shoulders and finally, after a deal of squirming on his part, the rest of his body. The transparency of his helmet and the fabric of his suit were immediately bedewed with condensation. He stood there to help Mayhew through the Sphincter and, when he was in the control room, the junior engineer. They had been exposed to the cold for a longer period, and the congealing atmospheric moisture clothed them in glittering frost.

The three men put up their gloved hands to remove their helmets.

"You wanted me, sir?" asked Mayhew vaguely.

"Of course," Grimes bit back a sarcastic retort.

The telepath ignored him, turned his attention to First Captain Mitchell. "You're the fisherman. You were the one who was dreaming of sitting by a sun-lit stream with rod and line—"

"Never mind that now," snapped the Commodore. "Just listen to what we want, please."

"I already know, sir."

"H'm. Yes. I suppose you do. But isn't it rather against the Institute's Code of Ethics to eavesdrop?"

"Not in these circumstances, sir. My duty was to receive and to record every impression emanating from the minds of the boarding party."

"Well, it saves time. As you know, First Captain Mitchell, as soon as he's got himself into the spare suit you brought, is going to take us into the dormitory sphere, to where the team of dowsers is stowed. There may be some connection between them and the transference of ships and people to this . . . What did you call it, Captain? To this sub-Space."

Mitchell, out of his own spacesuit but not yet into the one from *Faraway Quest*, was standing by an open filing cabinet, had pulled from it a bulky folder. "C Level," he was muttering, "Sector 8. Tanks 18 to 23 inclusive . . ." He put the folder back into the cabinet and then was helped into the suit by Sonya Verrill.

With the Captain to guide them, it did not take them long to find the tanks in which the dowsers slept. There were six of them—two very ordinary looking men and four women, one of whom looked far from ordinary. The telepath stood by the first of the transparent containers, staring at the man inside it, his face behind the helmet viewplate wearing an expression of deep concentration.

"This man," he said at last, "is dreaming of food.... I can see a table, a table covered with a snow-white cloth, and an array of crystal goblets, and gleaming silverware. There are other people around the table, but they are blurred, indistinct. They are not important. But the waiter holding up the bottle of wine for my inspection is... He is an elderly, portly man, with a ruddy face and gray, muttonchop whiskers. He smiles as he pours a few drops from the bottle into my glass. I sip it. It is a white wine, very dry. I nod my approval.

"Another waiter is bringing in the first course: the oysters, the brown bread and butter, the lemon wedges..."

"Not much for us there," interrupted Grimes.

"Oh, all right. All right. But I was just beginning to enjoy it. It was the first time that I'd seen oysters —*me*, I mean, not the man who's having the dream —and I wanted to know what they taste like. But it's too late now. Time is accelerated in dreams, and he's polished them off...." He glowered moodily at the tank below the first one. "This man *works* in his dreams. He's striding up a hillside, over short, springy turf. He is holding a forked twig in his hands. I can feel the odd, soft roughness of it, the— the aliveness of it. There's a tension, a feeling of pleasurable anticipation, and it comes from the twig itself, and from the ground over which I am walk-

ing, and from me.... And I can feel the twig
twitching, and I know that it's water under my feet,
running water.... But I carry on. There's no urgency. I can *feel* all the mineral wealth beneath me,
around me—the metals, the radio-actives..."

"No," said Grimes. "That's not it."

"I wish you'd let me finish a dream, sir, even
though it's not my own."

Mayhew moved to the next tank.

In this one there was a woman, a tall, angular
woman with a narrow face, sharp features. There
was a drabness about her—a drabness, Grimes
somehow knew, that would still have been there
had she been awake and clothed, a coldness that
was more intense than the frigidity of her physical
environment.

The telepath stared at her, her face frightened. His
lips moved, but no sound came. He muttered at last,
"She's dead. She's dead, but..."

"But what?" demanded the Commodore sharply.

"There's... How shall I put it? There's a—a
record..."

"A ghost," said Calhoun.

"No. Not a ghost. There's the record of her last
thoughts still in her brain.... But I can't play it back.
There's the sense—no, not even the sense, just a hint
—of some orgasmic experience, something that was
too intense, something that was too much for her
mind...."

Todhunter said, "But there was no physical cause
of her death. In her condition there couldn't have
been. Perhaps we could still revivify her..." He
turned to Mitchell. "As I understand it, Captain, it
would be impossible to deal with people on these

dormitory decks individually. If we revive one, we revive them all."

"Yes," agreed the First Captain. "That is so."

"Then would you have any objection if we used the empty tank in your sleeping quarters for this woman?"

"Yes," replied Mitchell. "I most certainly should." His manner softened. "But there are eight empty tanks in Carradine's compartment, and neither he nor his officers are in any state to object."

"Good."

"Check the other dowsers first, Mr. Mayhew," said Grimes.

Mayhew did so. The three remaining women were all alive—if their state of suspended animation could be referred to as life—and all peacefully dreaming. The pictures in their minds were pleasant, humdrum pictures of husbands and homes and children.

The tank was opened, and the rectangular block of solid-frozen gas in which was the woman's body lifted out quite easily. Even so, it was an awkward burden, even under conditions of free fall. Todhunter and Jones maneuvered it through the tiers of containers to the cylinder that was the axis of the globe, and then it had to be carried from level to level until the final deck was reached, the deck on which were the crew dormitories.

The doctor left Jones in charge of the body, went with Mitchell and Grimes and Sonya Verrill into what had been the Fourth Captain's compartment. All the tanks, of course, were empty. Mitchell satisfied himself that Carradine's container was ready for occupancy, and the ice-encased corpse was brought in, lowered into the rectangular box. Then, when all members of the party were in the wedge-shaped room, the double door was dogged tight and the automatic revivification process initiated.

There was the gradual rise of temperature and the thawing and evaporation of the frozen gases, and there was the thawing of the frozen gas in the coffin. There was the influx and the drainage of the colored fluids, the rhythmic massaging action of the pneumatic padding. Slowly the skin of the woman changed from silvery gray to a yellowish pallor, and then was suffused with the faintest of pink flushes. The eyelids flickered, and one leg began to twitch.

"She's not dead," murmured Grimes.

"But she is," contradicted Mayhew. "And there's just a spark... Just a spark, no more. *And I don't like it.*"

The lid of the casket lifted, and as it did so the woman slowly assumed a sitting posture. Her eyes opened and she stared mindlessly. Her jaw hung slackly and saliva dribbled from her mouth. She was making a coarse, disgusting grunting noise.

"The blue sky..." Mayhew whispered. "The clear sky, and the aching blue of it... And it's rending, like a piece of cloth between two giant hands.... It's rending, and the noise of its tearing is louder than the loudest thunder.... And beyond it is the blackness, the dense blackness, and it's empty.... But it's not empty. They are there, company after company of them, robed in shining white and with great white wings that span the heavens.... And they raise their golden trumpets to their lips, and the sound is high and sweet, high and impossibly sweet, long, golden notes rolling down through that rent in the sky, and the voices, the golden voices and the silver voices, and the flaming swords lifted high to smite the unrighteous, and ... And ...

"And that was all," he concluded. "She's gone now, finally gone. What's in the box is no more than a mindless hunk of flesh. But she's gone ..."

"So that was what she dreamed?" asked Mitchell in an almost inaudible voice. "So that was what she dreamed, and with such intensity as almost to drag the ship with her through that rent in the blue sky.... But was it her? Could it possibly have been her?"

"Have you any better explanation?" countered the telepath.

"Is it an explanation?" asked Grimes tiredly.

XXII

IT WASN'T much of an explanation, but it was the only one that they had had. What *Faraway Quest's* people had achieved by a sophisticated juggling with the laws of physics (but the juggling had not been sufficiently sophisticated, or the laws not properly formulated) these others had achieved, inadvertently, by the function or malfunction of paraphysychological principles. Throughout human history—and the history of other intelligent beings in the Galaxy—dowsers had sought, and they had found. And some of these diviners, in dream states, had sought for things and places beyond the bounds of Space and Time. Perhaps some of them had attained their dream countries, but the majority must have fallen into this Limbo, this gulf between the Universes, dragging, in so many cases, their hapless shipmates with them.

"Commodore," whispered Mitchell, "that's how it must have been. Our ship isn't like yours. She's just an iron drive rocket, archaic by your standards. We've no fancy dimension-twisting gadgetry."

"That's how it could have been," admitted Grimes guardedly, but already he was considering ways and means, already he was trying to work out methods whereby both ships, his own as well as First Captain Mitchell's, could be saved. He was trying to recall all that he had read of the First Expansion, the Interstellar Arks. As in the Ark of Biblical legend the passengers had boarded two by two, an even distribution of the sexes being maintained. *So . . .* he thought. *So . . . there's just a chance that I may be able to salvage this hunk of ancient ironmongery and, at the same time, exact a fee for the operation. . . .* He saw that Sonya was looking at him, realized that already there was a strong bond between them, more than a hint of the telepathy that springs into being between people in love. She was looking at him, and an expression that could have been maternal pride flickered briefly over her face.

"Out with it, John," she murmured.

He smiled at her and then turned to the Psionic Radio Officer. "Mr. Mayhew, can you enter minds?"

"How do you mean, sir?" countered the telepath cautiously.

"To influence them."

"It's against the rules of the Institue, sir."

"Damn the Institute. Its rules may hold good throughout the Galaxy, but we're not in the Galaxy. As far as our own ship is concerned, I am the Law, just as Captain Mitchell is the Law in this vessel. Can you enter another person's mind to influence it?"

"Sometimes, sir."

"The mind of one of the sleepers aboard this ship. One of the dreamers."

"That would be easy, sir."

"Good. Now, Captain Mitchell, this is what I have in mind. You have five diviners, five dowsers, still dreaming happily in their tanks. Mr. Mayhew is

going to—to tamper with the dreams of four of them.
Mr. Mayhew is a very patriotic Rim Worlder and
thinks that Lorn is the next best place to Eden, and
he's going to use his talents to sell Lorn in a big way
to the dreaming dowsers. My idea is this. Each of
them will dream that he is lost in a dark emptiness
—as, in fact, we all are. Each of them will dream
that he has his rod in his hand—his hazel twig, or
his length of wire or whatever it is that he favors.
Each of them will dream that the wand is leading
him, pulling him towards a pearly globe set in the
black sky. He'll know the name of it, and Mayhew
will be able to supply details of the outlines of seas
and continents. The sky isn't always overcast, and
all of us have seen Lorn a few times from Outside
with all details visible.

"I'm not saying that this will work, Captain, but it
just might. If it doesn't work we shall none of us be any
worse off. And if it does work—well, you'd better get
your rockets warmed up before Mr. Mayhew goes to
work, so you'll be able to throw yourself into a safe
orbit."

"It sounds crazy, Commodore," Mitchell said. "It
sounds crazy, but no crazier than all of us being
here. I shall have to call my officers first so that all
stations are manned."

"Of course. Dr. Todhunter will lend you a hand."

Mitchell's expression was still dubious. "Tell me,
sir, why did you make it quite plain that four of the
dowsers are to be set to dreaming of Lorn? Why not
all five?"

"If this works out, Captain, it will be an act of
salvage. And I think that *Faraway Quest* will be entitled to some reward. I know how the crew and

passenger lists of these ships were made up. Male
and female, in equal numbers. Husbands and
wives. There's a hunch of mine that the husband of
the mindless woman, the religious fanatic who got
you into this mess, is one of the five remaining
dowsers."

"I'll check the passenger list, Commodore."

Mitchell went to the cabinet and pulled out the
files.

"So if it works," murmured Sonya, "we shall have
our own dowser to do the same for us."

"Yes."

Mitchell put the papers back into their file. He
said, "The mindless woman, as you have called her,
is—or was—Mrs. Carolyn Jenkins. Her husband,
John Jenkins, is also a member of the dowsing team.
And now, if you'll excuse me, I'll see about waking
my staff." His was somber. "I hope, for all our sakes,
that I'm not waking them for nothing."

They were down once more in the dormitory
sphere, on C Level, in Sector 8. There was Grimes,
and there was Sonya Verrill, and there was First
Captain Mitchell. There were Todhunter and
McHenry, and there was Mitchell's Medical Officer,
a woman whose hard, competent features were visible behind the transparency of her helmet and
who, when awakened and apprised of the situation,
had wished to discuss medical matters with her opposite number from *Faraway Quest*. And, of course,
there was Mayhew.

First of all there was the tank in which slept
Carolyn Jenkins' husband to disconnect from its fittings. Jenkins was the man who had been dreaming
about food, and who was now dreaming about oth-

er pleasures of the flesh. Grimes felt more than a little relieved. This dreamer would not object to his being press-ganged away from his own ship and would not feel the loss of his wife too deeply. The nature of his dreams told of years of hunger, of frustration.

McHenry and Todhunter maneuvered the clumsy tank through the cramped space, vanished with it in the direction of the control sphere. It was to be taken to the *Faraway Quest*, where the engineers would be able to set up the apparatus for maintaining the sleeper in his condition of suspended animation and for awakening him if Grimes' gamble paid off.

And then Mayhew went to the second of the male dowsers, the one who, in his dream, was still engaged in the exercise of his talent. The telepath vocalized his thoughts, and his voice was an eerie whisper in the helmet phones of his companions.

"You are lost. . . .

"You are lost. The sky is dark. There is no light anywhere. There is nothing anymore anywhere . . . Nothing . . . Nothing . . . Emptiness around you, emptiness underfoot . . . You are falling, falling, through the nothingness, and the rod is dead in your hands. . . .

"You are falling, falling . . .

"But not for always. The rod twitches. You feel it twitch. Feebly, but it twitches. That is all—now. That is all. But there will be more. In precisely one hundred and twenty minutes there will be more. The rod will twitch strongly, strongly, and pull you with it. You will see that it is pointing to a spark in the darkness—a golden spark. And the spark becomes a globe, becomes a fair world hanging there. There is the blue of seas, the green of continents, the gleaming white of the polar ice caps, and on the night hemisphere the sparking lights of great cities.... There is the blue of seas and the green of continents, and the great land mass, hourglass-shaped, that sprawls from pole to pole, with its narrow waist on the equator.... And the chain of islands that forms a natural breakwater to the great, eastern bay.... But you do not see it yet. The time must pass, and then you will see it. Then the rod will come alive in your hands and will draw you, pull you, to the fair world of Lorn, the world of your fresh start, to the sunny world of Lorn..."

Grimes thought, *I hope that they aren't too disappointed. But even Lorn's better than Limbo ...*

And so it went on.

Each of the four remaining dowsers was thoroughly indoctrinated, and by the time that the indoctrination was finished only thirty minutes remained before the posthypnotic command would take effect. Grimes and the others made their way back to the control sphere.

Mitchell's officers were in full charge now, and the pilot lights glowed over instrument consoles. With the exception of Grimes, Sonya Verrill and Mayhew, all of *Faraway Quest's* people were back aboard their own ship. The Commodore turned to Mitchell. "I'll leave you to it, Captain. If things work out for all of us, I'll see you on the Rim."

Mitchell grinned. "I hope so, sir. But tell me, are the Rim Worlds as marvelous as your Mr. Mayhew makes out?"

"You have to make allowances for local patriotism, Captain."

"But you needn't stay on the Rim," Sonya Verrill broke in. "I am sure that my own Service will be happy to assume responsibility for the settlement of your people on any world of their choice."

"The Federation's taxpapers have deep pockets," remarked Grimes.

"That joke is wearing a little thin, John."

"Perhaps it is, Sonya. But it's still true."

The Commodore shook hands with Mitchell and then pulled on the gloves of his spacesuit, snapping tight the connections. His helmet on, he watched Sonya Verrill and Mayhew resume their own armor and then, with one of Mitchell's officers in attendance, the party made its way to the airlock. They jetted across the emptiness to the sleek *Faraway Quest*, were admitted into their own ship. They lost no time in making their way to the control room.

And there they waited, staring at the contraption of globes and girders floating there in the nothingness, bright metal reflecting the glare of the *Quest's* searchlights. They waited, and watched the control room clock, the creeping minute hand and, towards the end, the sweep second pointer.

Grimes consulted his own watch.

Mayhew noticed the gesture. He said quietly, "I'm still in touch. They can see the spark in the darkness now. They can feel the rods stirring strongly in their hands. . . ."

"I don't see how it can work," muttered Renfrew.

"They got here without your gadgetry, Lieutenant," Calhoun told him sharply. "They should be able to get out the same way."

And then there was nothing outside the viewports.

Perhaps, thought Grimes, *our searchlights have failed. But even then we should see a dim glimmer from her control room ports, a faint flicker from her warmed-up drivers. . . .*

"The screens are dead," announced Swinton.

"She made it . . ." whispered Mayhew. "She made it. Somewhere."

XXIII

SO IT HAD worked for First Captain Mitchell and his Erector Set of an emigrant ship. It had worked for First Captain Mitchell, and so it should work for *Faraway Quest* and her people. The shanghaied dowser was sleeping in his tank, still dreaming orgiastic dreams, and Mayhew was working on him, entering his mind, trying to introduce the first faint elements of doubt, of discomfort, trying to steer his imaginings away from overpadded comfort to the cold and emptiness of the Limbo between the Universes.

But it was hard.

This was a man who had lived in his dreams, lived for his dreams. This was a man whose waking life was, at best, purgatorial—a man who never knew in his own home the sweet smoothness of flesh on flesh, a man who was denied even such simple pleasures as a glass of cold ale, a meal more elaborate than a spoiled roast and ruined, soggy vegetables. This was a man who lived in his dreams, and who loved his dreams, and who had fled to them as the ultimate refuge from an unspeakably drab reality.

Mayhew persisted, and his whispering voice, as he vocalized his thoughts, brought a chill of horror into the section of the auxiliary motor room in which the tank had been set up. He persisted, and he worked cunningly, introducing tiny, destructive serpents into the fleshly Eden—the tough steak and the blunt knife, the corked wine, the too-young cheese and the rolls with their leathery crusts. . . . The insufficiently chilled beer and the hot dog without the mustard. . . . The overdone roast of beef, and the underdone roast of pork. . . .

Small things, trivial things perhaps, but adding up to a sadistic needling.

And then there was the blonde who, when she smiled, revealed carious teeth and whose breath was foul with decay, and the voluptuous brunette who, undressed, was living proof of the necessity of foundation garments. . . .

So it went on.

The dream, perhaps, had not been a noble one, but it had been healthily hedonistic, with no real vice in it. And now, thanks to Mayhew's probing and tinkerings, it was turning sour. And now the man Jenkins, fleeing in disgust from the lewd embraces of a harridan in a decrepit hovel, was staggering over a dark, windy waste, oppressed by a sense of guilt and of shame, fearing even the vengeance of the harsh deity worshipped by his unloving wife. He was fleeing over that dark, windy waste, tripping on the tussocks of coarse grass, flail-

ing with his arms at the flapping sheets of torn, dis-
carded newspaper that were driven into his face by
the icy gusts.

The cold and the dark...

The cold and the dark, and the final stumble, and
the helpless fall into the pit that had somehow
opened beneath his feet, and fall into Absolute Nothingness, a negation worse than the fiery hell with
which his wife had, on more than one occasion,
threatened him.

The cold and the dark and the absolute emptiness, and the rod of twisted silver wire to which he
still clung desperately, the only proof of his identity,
the only link with sanity, the only guide back to
Space and Time...

The twisted wire, the twitching wire, and the insistent tug of it in his frozen hands, and ahead of
him in the darkness the faint yellow spark, but
brighter, brighter, golden now, no longer a spark
but a fair world hanging there in the blackness, a
world of beautiful, willing women, of lush gardens
in which glowed huge, succulent fruit, a world of
groaning tables and dim, dusty cellars in which
matured the stacked bottles of vintage years...

But not Lorn . . . thought Grimes.

"But not Lorn..." echoed Sonya.

"Lorn is hanging there in the darkness...."
Mayhew was whispering. "A fair world, a beautiful
world... And the divining rod is rigid in your
hands, a compass needle, pointing, pointing.... You
can cross the gulf.... You can bridge the gulf from
dream to reality.... Follow the rod.... Let the rod
guide you, draw you, pull you.... Follow the
rod...."

"But where?" interrupted Grimes. "But *where?*"

"To Lorn, of course," whispered Mayhew. And then, "To Lorn? But his dreams are too strong..."

Shockingly the alarm bells sounded, a succession of Morse "A"s.

Once again—Action Stations.

XXIV

THERE, TO PORT, was the lens of the Galaxy, and to starboard was the gleaming globe that was Lorn, the great, hourglass-shaped continent proof positive. From astern came the rumble of the gentle blasts fired by Swinton, intent on his instruments, that would put *Faraway Quest* into a stable orbit about the planet. From the speaker barked an oddly familiar voice, "What ship? What ship? Identify yourself at once." And at the controls of the transceiver Renfrew made the adjustments that would bring in vision as well as sound.

"What ship?" demanded the voice. "What ship?"

From his chair Grimes could see the screens of both radar and Mass Proximity Indicator. He could see the bright and brightening blob of light that gave range and bearing of another vessel, a vessel that was closing fast. She was not yet within visual range, but that would be a matter of minutes only.

"What ship? What ship?"

Grimes accepted the microphone on its wandering lead, said, *"Faraway Quest.* Auxiliary Cruiser, Rim Worlds Confederation Navy. *What ship?"*

The voice from the bulkhead speaker contrived to convey incredulity with an odd snorting sound.

"*Faraway Quest?* Rim Worlds Confederation? Never heard of you. Are you mad—or drunk?"

"No," Sonya Verrill was whispering. "No. It can't be...."

Grimes looked at her, saw that her face was white, strained.

The big screen over the transceiver was alive with swirling colors, with colors that eddied and coalesced as the picture hardened. It showed the interior of another control room, a compartment not unlike their own. It showed a uniformed man who was staring into the iconoscope. Grimes recognized him. In his, Grimes', Universe this man had been Master of *Polar Queen*, had smashed her up in a bungled landing at Fort Farewell, on Faraway. Grimes had been president of the Court of Inquiry. And this man, too, had been an officer of the Intelligence Branch of the Survey Service, his position as a tramp master being an excellent cover for his activities. And he and Sonya...

The Commodore swiveled in his chair. He rather prided himself on the note of gentle regret that he contrived to inject into his voice. He said to the woman, "Well, your quest is over. It's been nice knowing you."

She replied, "My quest was over some time ago. It's nice knowing *you.*"

"I've got their picture," Renfrew was saying unnecessarily. "But I don't think that they have ours yet."

"*Starfarer* to unknown ship. *Starfarer* to unknown ship. Take up orbit and prepare to receive boarding party."

"You'd better go and pretty yourself up," said

Grimes to Sonya. He thought, *It's a pity it had to end like this, before it got properly started even. But I mustn't be selfish.*

"You'll be meeting ... him. Again. Your second chance."

"*Starfarer* to unknown ship. Any hostile action will meet with instant retaliation. Prepare to receive boarders."

"Commander Swinton!" There was the authentic Survey Service crackle on Sonya Verrill's voice. "Stand by Mannschenn Drive. Random precession!"

"Ay, ay, sir." The young man flushed. "Ma'am." Then he swiveled to look at the Commodore. "*Your* orders sir?"

"John!" Sonya's voice and manner were urgent. "Get us out of here."

"No. This was the chance you were wanting, the second chance, and now you've got it."

She grinned. "A girl can change her mind. I want my own Universe, where there's only you ..." She laughed, pointing to the screen. A woman officer had come into *Starfarer's* control room, was standing behind the Captain's chair. He outranked her, but her attitude was obviously proprietorial. "Where there's only you," repeated Sonya, "and only one of me ..."

"Mannschenn Drive," ordered Grimes. "Random precession."

"Ay, ay, *sir,*" acknowledged Swinton, and with the thin, high keening of the precessing gyroscopes the screen blanked, the speaker went dead and, on the port hand, the Galactic lens assumed its familiar distortion, a Klein flask blown by a drunken glass blower.

*   *   *

"Sir," growled Renfrew, obviously in a mutinous mood, "they could have helped us to get back. And even if they couldn't, I'm of the opinion that the Rim Worlds under Federation Rule would have been somewhat better than those same planets under your Confederacy."

"That will do, Lieutenant," snapped Sonya, making it plain that she was capable of dealing with her own subordinates. "Both the Commodore and myself agreed upon our course of action."

"This was supposed to be a scientific expedition, Commander," protested Renfrew. "But it's been far from scientific. Seances, and dowsers . . ." He almost spat in his disgust.

"You can't deny that we got results," muttered Calhoun.

"Of a sort."

Grimes, seated at the table on the platform in the still unreconverted wardroom, regarded the squabbling officers with a tired amusement. He could afford to relax now. He had driven the ship down the warped Continuum in an escape pattern that had been partly random and partly a matter of lightning calculation. He had interrogated Maudsley—the other Maudsley—after the Polar Queen disaster and had not formed a very high opinion of that gentleman's capabilities as a navigator. And even if this Maudsley were brilliantly imaginative, a ship in Deep Space is a very small needle in a very big haystack. . . .

"Gentlemen," he said, "the purpose of this meeting is to discuss ways and means of getting back to our own Space-Time. Has anybody any suggestions?"

Nobody had.

"The trouble seems to be," Grimes went on, "that although the dowser technique works, Mayhew is far too liable to look at his home world through rose-colored spectacles. Unluckily he is the only one among us capable of influencing the dreams of the hapless Mr. Jenkins. No doubt the Rim Worlds are better off, in some respects, under Federation rule than under our Confederacy. Weather control (which is far from inexpensive) for example, and a much higher standard of living. But I've also no doubt that the loss of independence has been a somewhat high price to pay for these advantages. And, even you who are not Rim Worlders, would find it hard to get by in a Universe in which somebody else, even if it is *you*, has your job, your home, your wife."

"So—what are we to do?"

"We still have Jenkins," contributed Calhoun.

"Yes. We still have Jenkins. But how can we use him?"

"And you still have *your* talent," said Sonya.

"My talent?"

"Your hunches. And what is a hunch but a form of precognition?"

"My hunches," Grimes told her, "are more a case of extrapolation, from the past at that, than of precognition." And sitting there, held in his chair by the strap, he let his mind wander into the past, was only dimly conscious of the discussion going on around him. He recalled what had happened when *Faraway Quest* had been drawn into the first of the Alternative Universes before falling into Limbo. He remembered that odd sensation, the intolerable stretching, the sudden *snap*. Perhaps . . . "Mr. Mayhew!" he said.

"Yes? Sorry. Yes, sir?"

"What sort of feeling do you have for this ship?"

"She's just a ship."

"You don't, in your mind, overglamorize her?"

"Why the hell should I? Sir."

"Good. Please come with me again to this man Jenkins, the dowser. I want you to take charge of his dreams, the same way that you did before. I want you to lose him in nothingness again, and then to let his talent guide him out of the emptiness back to light and life and warmth."

"But you said that *my* vision of Lorn was too idealistic."

"It is. It is. I want you to envisage *Faraway Quest.*"

"*Us,* sir?"

"Who else?"

"The cold..." Mayhew was whispering. "The cold, and the dark, and the absolute emptiness. There's nothing, nothing. There's not anything, anywhere, but that rod of twisted silver wire that you hold in your two hands.... You feel it twitch. You feel the gentle, insistent tug of it.... And there's a glimmer of light ahead of you, faint, no more than a dim glow.... But you can make out what it is. It's the pilot lights of instrument panels, red and green, white and amber, and the flourescent tracings in chart tanks.... It's the control room of a ship, and the faint illumination shows through the big, circular ports. By it you can just read the name, in golden lettering, on her sharp stem, *Faraway Quest.*"

And Mayhew went on to describe the ship in detail, in amazing detail, until Grimes realized that he was drawing upon the knowledge stored in the brains of all the technical officers. He described the ship, and he described the personnel, and he contrasted the warmth and the light and the life of her interior with the cold, empty dream-Universe in which the dowser was floating. He described the ship and her personnel—and, Grimes thought wrily, some of his descriptions were far from flattering. But she was Home. She was a little world of men in the all-pervading emptiness.

She was Home, and Grimes realized that he, too, was feeling the emotions that Mayhew was implanting in the sleeping dowser's mind. She was Home, and she was close, and closer, an almost attained goal. She was Home, and Grimes knew that he could reach out to touch her, and he reached out, and felt the comforting touch of cool metal at his fingertips, the security of solidity in the vast, empty reaches of Deep Space....

She was Home, and he was home at last, where he belonged, and he was looking dazedly at the odd, transparent tank that had appeared from nowhere in the Auxiliary Machinery Room, the glass coffin with a complexity of piping and wiring extruded from its sides, the casket in which floated the nude body of a portly man.

He turned to Sonya Verrill, and he heard her say, "Your hunch paid off, John."

He remembered then. (But there were two sets of memories—separate and distinct. There were the memories of Limbo, and all that had happened there, and there were the memories of a boring, fruitless cruise after the first and only Rim Ghost sighting and the failure to establish even a fleeting contact.) He remembered then, and knew that some of the memories he must cling to, always. They were all that he would have, now. There were no longer any special circumstances. There was no longer the necessity for—how had she put it?—the political marriage of the heads of two potentially hostile tribes.

He muttered, unaware that he was vocalizing his thoughts, "Oh, well—it was nice knowing you. But now...."

"But now..." she echoed.

"If you'll excuse me, sir, and madam," broke in Mayhew, "I'll leave you alone. Now that we're back in our own Universe I'm bound by the Institute's rules again, and I'm not supposed to eavesdrop, let alone to tell either of you what the other one is thinking." He turned to the Commodore. "But I'll tell you this, sir. I'll tell you that all the guff about political marriages *was* guff. It was just an excuse. I'll tell you that the lady has found what she was looking for—or whom she was looking for—and that his name is neither Derek Calver nor Bill Maudsley."

"In the Survey Service," remarked Sonya Verrill softly, "he could be court martialed for that."

"And so he could be," Grimes told her, "in the Rim Confederacy Navy. But I don't think that I shall press any charges."

"I should be rather annoyed if you did. He told you what I should have gotten around to telling you eventually, and he has saved us a great deal of time."

They did not kiss, and their only gesture was a brief contact of hands. But they were very close together, and both of them knew it. Together they left the compartment, making for the control room.

Grimes supposed that it would be necessary to carry on the cruise for a while longer, to continue going through the motions of what young Swinton had termed a wild ghost chase, but he was no longer very interested. A long life still lay ahead of him, and there were pleasanter worlds than these planets of the far outer reaches on which to spend it.

For him, as for Sonya Verrill, the faraway quest was over.

Contraband from Otherspace

A. Bertram Chandler

SF

An ACE Book

This Ace printing: March 1979

Printed in U.S.A.

For who else but Susan?

They drift out to the Rim Worlds—the mis-
fits, the failures and the rebels. They make
their tortuous ways out to the very edge of the
Galaxy—the malcontents, the round pegs who,
even here, are foredoomed to the discovery of
an infinitude of square holes. And from all
Space they come—the displaced persons.

From all Space—and (for the skin of the ex-
panding Galaxy is stretched, in every
dimension, to the utmost flimsiness)—from all
Space-Time.

I

TO A CASUAL observer his seamed, deeply tanned face
would have appeared expressionless—but those
who knew him well could have read a certain regret
in the lines of his craggy features, in the almost im-
perceptible softening of the hard, slate-gray eyes.

The king had abdicated.

The Astronautical Superintendent of Rim Runners
had resigned from the service of the Rim Worlds
Confederacy—both as a senior executive of the government owned and operated shipping line and as
Commodore of the Rim Worlds Naval Reserve. His
resignations were not yet effective—but they would
be, so soon as Captain Trantor, in *Rim Kestrel*, came

dropping down through the overcast to be relieved of his minor command prior to assuming the greater one.

On a day such as this there was little for Grimes to see. Save for *Faraway Quest*, the Rim Worlds Government Survey Ship, and for *Rim Mamelute* the spaceport was deserted. Soon enough it would resume its normal activity, with units of the Rim Runners' fleet roaring in through the cloud blanket, from Faraway, Ultimo and Thule, from the planets of the Eastern Circuit, from the anti-matter systems to the Galactic West. (And among them would be Trantor's ship, inbound from Mellise.) But now there were only the old *Quest* and the little, battered space-tug in port, silent and deserted, the survey ship a squat, gray tower (that looked as though it should have been lichen-coated) half obscured by the snow squall, the *Mamelute* huddling at its base as though seeking shelter in the lee of the larger vessel.

Grimes sighed, only half aware that he had done so. But he was not (he told himself) a sentimental man. It was just that *Faraway Quest* had been his last spacegoing command, and would be his last command, ever, out on the Rim. In her he had discovered and charted the worlds of the Eastern Circuit, opened them up to trade. In her he had made the first contact with the people of the anti-matter systems. In her, only short weeks ago, with a mixed crew of Rim Worlds Naval Reserve officers and Federation Survey Service personnel, he had tried to solve the mystery of those weird, and sometimes frightening phenomena known as Rim Ghosts. And whilst on this Wild Ghost Chase (as his

second in command referred to it) he had found in
Sonya Verrill the cure for his loneliness—as she had
found, in him, the cure for hers. But his marriage to
her (as do all marriages) had brought its own problems, its own responsibilities. Already he was beginning to wonder if he would like the new life the
course of which Sonya had plotted so confidently.

He started as the little black box on his desk
buzzed. He heard a sharp female voice announce,
"Commander Verrill to see you, Commodore
Grimes."

Another voice, also female, pleasantly contralto
but with an underlying snap of authority, corrected
the first speaker. "*Mrs. Grimes* to see the Commodore, Miss Willoughby."

"Come in, Sonya," said Grimes, addressing the instrument.

She strode into the office, dramatic as always.
Melting snow crystals sparkled like diamonds on
her swirling, high-collared cloak of dull crimson
Altairian crystal silk, in the intricate coronet of her
pale blonde hair. Her face was flushed, as much by
excitement as by the warmth of the building after
the bitter cold outside. She was a tall woman, and a
splendid one, and many men on many worlds had
called her beautiful.

She reached out, grabbed Grimes by his slightly
protuberant ears, pulled his face to hers and kissed
him soundly.

After she had released him, he asked mildly,
"And what was that in aid of, my dear?"

She laughed happily. "John, I just had to come to
tell you the news in person. It wouldn't have been
the same over the telephone. I've just received two

Carlottigrams from Earth—one official, one personal. To begin with, my resignation's effective, as and from today. Oh, I can still be called back in an emergency, but that shouldn't worry us. And my gratuity has been approved..."

"How much?" he asked, not altogether seriously. She told him.

He whistled softly. "The Federation's more generous than the Confederacy. But, of course, your taxpayers are richer than ours, and there are so many more of them...."

She ignored this. "And that's not all, my dear. Admiral Salversen of the Bureau of Supply, is an old friend of mine. He sent a personal message along with the other. It seems that there's a little one ship company for sale, just a feeder line running between Montalbon and Carribea. The gratuity barely covers the down payment—but with *your* gratuity, and our savings, and the profits we're bound to make we shall be out of the red in no time at all. Just think of it, John! You as Owner-Master, and myself as your everloving Mate!"

Grimes thought of it as he turned to stare again out of the wide window, his mind's eye piercing the dismal overcast to the nothingness beyond. Light, and warmth, and a sky ablaze with stars instead of this bleak desolation...

Light and warmth... And a milk run.

And Sonya.

He said slowly, "We may find it hard to settle down. Even you. You're not a Rimworlder, but your life, in the Federation's Naval Intelligence, has been adventurous, and you've worked out on the Rim so much that you almost qualify for citizenship..."

"I qualified for citizenship when I married you. And I want to settle down, John. But not here."

The black box on the desk crackled, then said in Miss Willoughby's voice, "Port Control is calling, Commodore Grimes. Shall I put them through?"

"Yes, please," Grimes told her.

II

"Cassidy here," said the box.

"Yes, Captain Cassidy?"

"Orbital Station 3 reports a ship, sir."

"Isn't that one of the things they're paid for?" asked Grimes mildly.

"Yes, sir." Cassidy's voice was sulky. "But there's nothing due for almost a week, and . . ."

"Probably one of the Federation Survey Service wagons," Grimes told him, flashing a brief smile (which she answered with a glare) at Sonya. "They think they can come and go as they damn well please. Tell Station 3 to demand—*demand*, not request—identification."

"The Station Commander has already done that, Commodore. But there's no reply."

"And Station 3 doesn't run to a Psionic Radio Officer. I always said that we were ill advised to get rid of the telepaths as soon as our ships and stations were fitted with Carlotti equipment . . ." He paused, then asked, "Landing approach?"

"No, sir. Station 3 hasn't had time to extrapolate her trajectory yet, but the way she's heading now it looks as though she'll miss Lorn by all of a thousand miles and finish up in the sun. . . ."

"They haven't had time?" Grimes' voice was cold.

"What the hell sort of watch are they keeping?"

"A good one, sir. Commander Hall is one of our best men—as you know. It seems that this ship just appeared out of nothing—those were Hall's own words. There was no warning at all on the Mass Proximity Indicator. And then, suddenly, there she was—on both M.P.I. *and* radar. . . ."

"Any of your people loafing around these parts?" Grimes asked Sonya.

"No," she told him. "At least not that I know of."

"And you are—or were—an intelligence officer, so you should know. H'm." He turned again to the box. "Captain Cassidy, tell Station 3 that I wish direct communication with them."

"Very good, sir."

The Commodore strode to his desk, sat down in his chair, pulled out a drawer. His stubby fingers played over the console that was revealed. Suddenly the window went opaque, and as it did so the lights in the office dimmed to a faint glow. One wall of the room came alive, a swirl of light and color that coalesced to form a picture, three dimensional, of the Watch House of Station 3. There were the wide ports, beyond the thick transparencies of which was the utter blackness of Space as seen from the Rim Worlds, a blackness made even more intense by contrast with the faintly glimmering nebulosities, sparse and dim, that were the distant, unreachable island universes. Within the compartment were the banked instruments, the flickering screens, the warped, convoluted columns, each turning slowly on its axis, that were the hunting antennae of the Carlotti Beacon. Uniformed men and women busied themselves at control panels, stood tensely around the big plotting tank. One of them—the Station Commander—turned to face the camera. He asked, "Have you the picture, Commodore Grimes, sir?"

"I have, Commander," Grimes told him. "How is the extrapolation of trajectory?"

"You may have a close-up of the tank, sir."

The scene dissolved, and then only the plotting tank was in Grimes' screen. In the center of it was the dull-glowing (but not dull-glowing in reality) globe that represented the Lorn sun. And there was the curving filament of light that represented the orbit of the strange ship, the filament that extended itself as Grimes and Sonya watched, that finally touched the ruddy incandescence of the central sphere. This was only an extrapolation; it would be months before it actually occurred. There was still time, ample time, for the crew of the intruder to pull her out of the fatal plunge. And yet, somehow, there was a sense of urgency. If a rescue operation were to be undertaken, it must be done without delay. A stern chase is a long chase.

"What do you make of it?" Grimes asked Sonya.

She said, "I don't like it. Either they can't communicate, or they won't communicate. And I think they can't. There's something wrong with that ship. . . ."

"Something very wrong. Get hold of Cassidy, will you? Tell him that I want *Rim Mamelute* ready for Space as soon as possible." He stared at the screen, upon which Commander Hall had made a reappearance. "We're sending the *Mamelute* out after her, Hall. Meanwhile, keep on trying to communicate."

"We are trying, sir."

Cassidy's voice came from the black box. "Sir, Captain Welling, the skipper of the *Mamelute*, is in the hospital. Shall I . . . ?"

"No, Cassidy. Somebody has to mind the shop—and you're elected. But there's something you can do for me. Get hold of Mr. Mayhew, the Psionic Radio Officer. Yes, yes, I know that he's taking his Long Service Leave, but get hold of him. Tell him I want him here, complete with his amplifier, as soon as possible, if not before. And get *Mamelute* cleared away."

"But who's taking her out, sir?"

"Who do you think? Get cracking, Cassidy."

"You'll need a Mate," said Sonya.

He found time to tease her, saying, "Rather a come-down from the Federation Survey Service, my dear."

"Could be. But I have a feeling that this may be a job for an Intelligence Officer."

"You'll sign on as Mate," he told her firmly.

III

Rim Mamelute, as a salvage tug, was already in a
state of near-readiness. She was fully fueled and provisioned; all that remained to be done was the
mustering of her personnel. Her engineers, pottering
around in Rim Runners' workshop on the spaceport
premises, were easily located. The Port doctor was
conscripted from his office, and was pleased enough
to be pulled away from his boring paperwork. The
Port Signal Station supplied a radio officer and—for
Rim Mamelute's permanent Mate made it plain that
he would resent being left out of the party—Sonya
agreed to come along as Catering Officer.

Grimes could have got the little brute upstairs
within an hour of his setting the wheels in motion,
but he insisted on waiting for Mayhew. In any
salvage job, communication between the salvor and
the salved is essential—and to judge by the experience of Station 3, any form of electronic radio
communication was *out.* He stood on the concrete,
just outside the tug's airlock, looking up at the overcast sky. Sonya came out to join him.

"Damn the man!" he grumbled. "He's supposed
to be on his way. He was told it was urgent."

She said, "I hear something."

He heard it too, above the thin whine of the wind,

a deepening drone. Then the helicopter came into sight above the high roof of the Administration Building, the jet flames at the tip of its rotor blades a bright, blue circle against the gray sky. It dropped slowly, carefully, making at last a landing remarkable for its gentleness. The cabin door opened and the tall gangling telepath, his thin face pasty against the upturned collar of his dark coat, clambered to the ground. He saw Grimes, made a slovenly salute, then turned to receive the large case that was handed him by the pilot.

"Take your time," growled Grimes.

Mayhew shuffled around to face the Commodore. He set the case carefully down on the ground, patted it gently. He said, mild reproof in his voice, "Lassie's not as used to traveling as she was. I try to avoid shaking her up."

Grimes sighed. He had almost forgotten about the peculiar relationship that existed between the spacefaring telepaths and their amplifiers—the living brains of dogs suspended in their tanks of nutrient solution. It was far more intense than that existing between normal man and normal dog. When a naturally telepathic animal is deprived of its body, its psionic powers are vastly enhanced—and it will recognize as friend and master only a telepathic man. There is symbiosis, on a psionic level.

"Lassie's not at all well," complained Mayhew.

"Think her up a nice, juicy bone," Grimes almost said, then thought better of it.

"I've tried that, of course," Mayhew told him. "But she's not ... she's just not interested any more. She's growing old. And since the Carlotti system was introduced nobody is making psionic amplifiers any more."

"Is she functioning?" asked the Commodore coldly.

"Yes, sir. But . . ."

"Then get aboard, Mr. Mayhew. Mrs. Grimes will show you to your quarters. Prepare and secure for blast-off without delay."

He stamped up the short ramp into the airlock, climbed the ladders to the little control room. The Mate was already in the co-pilot's chair, his ungainly posture a match for his slovenly uniform. Grimes looked at him with some distaste, but he knew that the burly young man was more than merely competent, and that although his manner and appearance militated against his employment in a big ship he was ideally suited to service in a salvage tug.

"Ready as soon as you are, Skipper," the Mate said. "You takin' her up?"

"You're more used to this vessel than I am, Mr. Williams. As soon as all's secure you may blast off."

"Good-oh, Skip."

Grimes watched the indicator lights, listened to the verbal reports, aware that Williams was doing likewise. Then he said into the transceiver microphone, *"Rim Mamelute* to Port Control. Blasting off."

Before Port Control could acknowledge, Williams hit the firing key. Not for the *Mamelute* the relatively leisurely ascent, the relatively gentle acceleration of the big ships. It was, thought Grimes dazedly, like being fired from a gun. Almost at once, it seemed, harsh sunlight burst through the control room ports. He tried to move his fingers against the crushing weight, tried to bring one of them to the button set in the arm rest of his chair that controlled the polarization of the transparencies. The glare was beating full in his face, was painful even through his closed eyelids. But Williams beat him to it. When Grimes opened his eyes he saw that the Mate was grinning at him.

"She's a tough little bitch, the old *Mamelute*," announced the objectionable young man with pride.

"Yes, Mr. Williams," enunciated Grimes with difficulty. "But there are some of us who aren't as tough as the ship. And, talking of lady dogs, I don't think that Mr. Mayhew's amplifier can stand much acceleration. . . ."

"That pickled poodle's brain, Skip? The bastard's better off than we are, floatin' in its nice warm bath o' thick soup." He grinned again. "But I was forgettin'. We haven't the regular crew this time. What say we maintain a nice, steady one and a half Gs? That do yer?"

One G would be better, thought Grimes. *After all, those people, whoever they are, are in no immediate danger of falling into the sun. But perhaps even a few minutes' delay might make all the difference between life and death to them . . . Even so, we must be capable of doing work, heavy, physical work, when we catch them.*

"Yes, Mr. Williams," he said slowly. "Maintain one and a half gravities. You've fed the elements of the trajectory into the computer, of course?"

"Of course, Skip. Soon as I have her round I'll put her on auto. She'll be right."

When the tug had settled down on her long chase,

Grimes left Williams in the control room, went down into the body of the ship. He made his rounds, satisfied himself that all was well in engine room, surgery, the two communications offices and, finally, the galley. Sonya was standing up to acceleration as though she had been born and bred on a high gravity planet. He looked at her with envy as she poured him a cup of coffee, handing it to him without any obvious compensation for its increased weight. Then she snapped at him, "Sit down, John. If you're as tired as you look you'd better lie down."

He said, "I'm all right."

"You're not," she told him. "And there's no need for you to put on the big, tough space captain act in front of me."

"If you can stand it..."

"What if I can, my dear? I haven't led such a sheltered life as you have. I've knocked around in little ships more than I have in big ones, and I'm far more used to going places in a hurry than you."

He lowered himself to a bench and she sat beside him. He sipped his coffee, then asked her, "Do you think, then, that we should be in more of a hurry?"

"Frankly, no. Salvage work is heavy work, and if we maintain more than one and a half Gs over a quite long period we shall all of us be too tired to function properly, even that tough Mate of yours." She smiled. "I mean the Mate who's on Articles as such, not the one you're married to."

He chuckled. "But she's tough, too."

"Only when I have to be, my dear."

Grimes looked at her, and thought of the old proverb which says that there is many a true word spoken in jest.

IV

THE STRANGE VESSEL was a slowly expanding speck of light in the globular screen of the Mass Proximity Indicator; it was a gradually brightening blip on *Mamelute's* radar display that seemed as though it were being drawn in towards the tug by the ever decreasing spiral of the range marker. Clearly it showed up on the instruments, although it was still too far distant for visual sighting, and it was obvious that the extrapolation of trajectory made by Station 3 was an accurate one. It was falling free, neither accelerating nor decelerating, its course determined only by the gravitational forces within the Lorn Star's planetary system, and left to itself must inevitably fall into the sun. But long before its shell plating began to heat it would be overhauled by the salvage ship and dragged away and clear from its suicide orbit.

And it was silent. It made no reply to the signals beamed at it from *Rim Mamelute's* powerful transmitter. Bennett, the Radio Officer, complained to Grimes, "I've tried every frequency known to civilized man, and a few that aren't. But, so far, no joy."

"Keep on trying," Grimes told him, then went to the cabin that Mayhew, the telepath, shared with his organic amplifier.

The Psionic Radio Officer was slumped in his chair, staring vacantly at the glass tank in which, immersed in its cloudy nutrient fluid, floated the obscenely naked brain. The Commodore tried to ignore the thing. It made him uneasy. Every time that he saw one of the amplifiers he could not help wondering what it would be like to be, as it were, disembodied, to be deprived of all external stimuli but the stray thoughts of other, more fortunate (or less unfortunate) beings—and those thoughts, as like as not, on an incomprehensible level. What would a man do, were he so used, his brain removed from his skull and employed by some race of superior beings for their own fantastic purpose? Go mad, probably. And did the dogs sacrificed so that Man could communicate with his fellows over the light years ever go mad?

"Mr. Mayhew," he said.

"Sir?" muttered the telepath.

"As far as electronic radio is concerned, that ship is dead."

"Dead?" repeated Mayhew in a thin whisper.

"Then you think that there's nobody alive on board her?"

"I ... I don't know. I told you before we started that Lassie's not a well dog. She's old, Commodore. She's old, and she dreams most of the time, almost all of the time. She ... she just ignores me ..." His voice was louder as he defended his weired pet against the implied imputation that he had made himself. "It's just that she's old, and her mind is getting very dim. Just vague dreams and ghostly memories, and the past more real than the present, even so."

"What sort of dreams?" asked Grimes, stirred to pity for the naked canine brain in its glass cannister.

"Hunting dreams, mainly. She was a terrier, you know, before she was ... conscripted. Hunting dreams. Chasing small animals, like rats. They're good dreams, except when they turn to nightmares. And then I have to wake her up—but she's in such a state of terror that she's no good for anything."

"I didn't think that dogs have nightmares," remarked Grimes.

"Oh, but they do, sir, they do. Poor Lassie always has the same one—about an enormous rat that's just about to kill her. It must be some old memory of her puppy days, when she ran up against such an animal, a big one, bigger than she was...."

"H'm. And, meanwhile, nothing from the ship."

"Nothing at all, sir."

"Have you tried transmitting, as well as just maintaining a listening watch?"

"Of course, sir." Mayhew's voice was pained. "During Lassie's lucid moments I've been punching out a strong signal, strong enough even to be picked up by non-telepaths. You must have felt it yourself, sir. *Help is on the way.* But there's been no indication of mental acknowledgement."

"All we know about the ship, Mayhew, is that she seems to be a derelict. We don't know who built her. We don't know who mans her—or manned her."

"Anybody who builds a ship, sir, must be able to think."

Grimes, remembering some of the unhandier vessels in which he had served in his youth, said, "Not necessarily."

Mayhew, not getting the point, insisted, "But they

must be able to think. And, in order to think, you must have a brain to think with. And any brain at all, emits psionic radiation. Furthermore, sir, such radiation sets up secondary radiation in the in- animate surroundings of the brain. What is the aver- age haunt but a psionic record on the walls of a house in which strong emotions have been let loose? A record that is played back given the right condi- tions."

"H'm. But you say that the derelict is psionically dead, that there's not even a record left by her builders, or her crew, to be played back to you."

"The range is still extreme, sir. And as for this secondary psionic radiation, sir, sometimes it fades rapidly, sometimes it lingers for years. There must be laws governing it, but nobody has yet been able to work them out."

"So there could be something . . ."

"There could be, sir. And there could not."

"Just go on trying, Mr. Mayhew."

"Of course, sir. But with poor Lassie in her pres- ent state I can't promise anything."

Grimes went along to the galley. He seated himself on the bench, accepted the cup of coffee that Sonya poured for him. He said, "It looks, my dear, as though we shall soon be needing an Intelligence Of- ficer as well as a Catering Officer."

"Why?" she asked.

He told her of his conversation with Mayhew. He said, "I'd hoped that he'd be able to find us a few short cuts—but his crystal ball doesn't seem to be functioning very well these days . . . If you could call that poodle's brain in aspic a crystal ball."

"He's told me all about it," she said. "He's told everybody in the ship all about it. But once we get the derelict in tow, and opened up, we shall soon be able to find out what makes her tick. Or made her tick."

"I'm not so sure, Sonya. The way in which she suddenly appeared from nowhere, not even a trace on Station 3's M.P.I. beforehand, makes me think that she could be very, *very* alien."

"The Survey Service is used to dealing with aliens," she told him. "The Intelligence Branch especially so."

"I know, I know."

"And now, as I'm still only the humble galley slave, can I presume to ask my lord and master the E.T.C.?"

"Unless something untoward fouls things up, E.T.C. should be in exactly five Lorn Standard Days from now."

"And then it will be *Boarders Away!*" she said, obviously relishing the prospect.

"Boarders Away!" he agreed. "And I, for one, shall be glad to get out of this spaceborne sardine can."

"Frankly," she said, "I shall be even gladder to get out of this bloody galley so that I can do the real work for which I was trained."

V

SLOWLY THE RANGE closed, until the derelict was visible as a tiny, bright star a few degrees to one side of the Lorn Sun. The range closed, and *Rim Mamelute's* powerful telescope was brought into play. It showed very little; the stranger ship appeared to be an almost featureless spindle, the surface of its hull unbroken by vanes, sponsons or antennae. And still, now that the distance could be measured in scant tens of miles, the alien construction was silent, making no reply to the signals directed at it by both the salvage tug's communications officers.

Grimes sat in the little control room, letting Williams handle the ship. The Mate crouched in his chair, intent upon his tell-tale instruments, nudging the tug closer and closer to the free-falling ship with carefully timed rocket blasts, matching velocities with the skill that comes only from long practice. He looked up briefly from his console to speak to Grimes. "She's hot, Skipper. Bloody hot."

"We've radiation armor," said Grimes. The words were question rather than statement.

"O' course. The *Mamelute's* ready for anything. Remember the *Rim Eland* disaster? Her pile went critical. We brought her in. I boarded her when we

186

took her in tow, just in case there was anybody still living. There wasn't. It was like bein' inside a radio-active electric fryin' pan ..."

A charming simile . . . thought Grimes.

He used the big, mounted binoculars to study the derelict. They showed him little more than had the telescope at longer range. So she was hot, radio-active. It seemed that the atomic blast that had initiated the radiation had come from outside, not inside. There were, after all, protuberances upon that hull, but they had been melted and then re-hardened, like guttering candle wax. There were the remains of what must have been vaned landing gear. There was the stump of what could have been, once, a mast of some kind, similar to the retractable masts of the spaceships with which Grimes was familiar, the supports for Deep Space radio antennae and radar scanners.

"Mr. Williams," he ordered, "we'll make our approach from the other side of the derelict."

"You're the boss, Skipper."

Brief accelerations crushed Grimes down into the padding of his chair, centrifugal force, as *Mamelute's* powerful gyroscopes turned her about her short axis, made him giddy. Almost he regretted having embarked upon this chase in person. He was not used to small ships, to the violence of their motions. He heard, from somewhere below, a crash of kitchenware. He hoped that Sonya had not been hurt.

She had not been—not physically, at any rate. Somehow, even though the tug was falling free once more, she contrived to stamp into the control room. She was pale with temper, and the smear of some rich, brown sauce on her right cheek accentuated her pallor. She glared at her husband and demanded, "What the hell's going on? Can't you give us some warning before indulging in a bout of astrobatics?"

Williams chuckled to himself and made some remark about the unwisdom of amateurs shipping out in space tugs. She turned on him, then, and said that she had served in tugs owned by the Federation Survey Service, and that they had been, like all Federation star ships, taut ships, and that any officer who failed to warn all departments of impending maneuvers would soon find himself busted down to Spaceman, Third Class.

Before the Mate could make an angry reply Grimes intervened. He said smoothly, "It was my fault, Sonya. But I was so interested in the derelict that I forgot to renew the alarm. After all, it was sounded as we began our approach...."

"I know that. But I was prepared for an approach, not this tumbling all over the sky like a drunken bat."

"Once again, I'm sorry. But now you're here, grab yourself the spare chair and sit down. This is the situation. All the evidence indicates that there's been some sort of atomic explosion. That ship is *hot*. But I think that the other side of the hull will be relatively undamaged."

"It is," grunted Williams.

The three of them stared out of the viewports. The shell plating, seen from this angle, was dull, not bright, pitted with the tiny pores that were evidence of frequent passages through swarms of micrometeorites. At the stern, one wide vane stood out sharp and clear in the glare of *Mamelute's* searchlights. Forward, the armor screens over the control room ports were obviously capable of being retracted, were not fused to the hull. There were sponsons from which projected the muzzles of weapons—they could have been cannon or laser projectors, but what little was visible was utterly unfamiliar. There was a telescopic mast, a-top which was a huge, fragile-seeming radar scanner, motionless.

And just abaft the sharp stem there was the name.

No, thought Grimes, studying the derelict through the binoculars, *two names.*

It was the huge, sprawling letters, crude daubs of black paint, that he read first. *Freedom,* they spelled. Then there were the other symbols, gold-embossed, half obscured by the dark pigment. There was something wrong about them, a subtle disproportion, an oddness of spacing. But they made sense—after a while. They did not belong to the alphabet with which Grimes was familiar, but they must have been derived from it. There was the triangular "D", the "I" that was a fat, upright oblong, the serpentine "S" . . .

"Distriyir . . ." muttered Grimes. *"Destroyer?"* He passed the glasses, on their universal mount, to Sonya. "What do you make of this? What branch of the human race prints like that? What people have simplified their alphabet by getting rid of the letter 'E'?"

She adjusted the focus to suit her own vision. She said at last, "That painted-on-name is the work of human hands all right. But the other . . . I don't know. I've never seen anything like it before. There's a certain lack of logicality—human logicality, that is. Oh, that stylized 'D' is logical enough. But the substitution of 'I' for 'E'—if it *is* a substitution . . . And then, as far as *we* are concerned, a destroyer is a class of ship—not a ship's name . . ."

"I seem to recall," Grimes told her, "that there was once a warship called *Dreadnought*—and the dreadnoughts have been a class of warship ever since the first ironclads were launched on Earth's seas."

"All right, Mr. amateur naval historian—but have you ever, in the course of your very wide reading on your favorite subject, come across mention of a ship called *Destroyer*—and spelled without a single 'E'? There are non-humans mixed up in this somewhere —and highly intelligent non-humans at that."

"And humans," said Grimes.

"But we'll never find out anything just by talking about it," grumbled the Mate. "An' the sooner we take this bitch in tow, the shorter the long drag back to Port Forlon. I'd make fast alongside—but even here, in the blast shadow, that hull is too damn' hot. It'll have to be tow wires from the outriggers—an' keep our fingers crossed that they don't get cut by our exhaust . . ."

"Take her in tow, then board," said Sonya.

"O' course. First things first. There'll be nobody alive inside that radio-active can . . ."

The intercommunication telephone was buzzing furiously. Grimes picked up the instrument. "Commodore here."

"Mayhew, sir." The telepath's voice was oddly muffled. He sounded as though he had been crying. "It's Lassie, sir. She's dead. . . ."

A happy release, thought Grimes. *But what am I supposed to do about it?*

"One of her nightmares, sir," Mayhew babbled on. "I was inside her mind, and I tried to awaken her. But I couldn't. There was this huge rat—and there were the sharp yellow teeth of it, and the stink of it.... It was so ... it was so real, so vivid. And it was the fear that killed her—I could feel her fear, and it was almost too much for me...."

"I'm sorry, Mr. Mayhew," said Grimes inadequately. "I'm sorry. I will see you later. But we are just about to take the derelict in tow, and we are busy."

"I ... I understand, sir."

And then Grimes relaxed into the padding of his chair, watching, not without envy, as Williams jockeyed the salvage tug into position ahead of the derelict, then carefully matched velocity. The outriggers were extruded, and then there was the slightest shock as the little missiles, each with a powerful magnetic grapnel as its warhead, were fired.

Contact was made, and then Williams, working with the utmost care, eased *Rim Mamelute* around in a great arc, never putting too much strain on the towing gear, always keeping the wires clear of the tug's incandescent exhaust. It was pretty to watch.

Even so, when at last it was over, when at last the Lorn Star was almost directly astern, he could not resist the temptation of asking, "But why all this expenditur of reaction mass and time to ensure a bows-first tow, Mr. Williams?"

"S.O.P., Skipper. It's more convenient if the people in the towed ship can see where they're going."

"But it doesn't look as though there are any people. Not live ones, that is."

"But we could be putting a prize crew aboard her, Skipper."

Grimes thought about saying something about the radio-activity, then decided not to bother.

"You just can't win, John," Sonya told him.

VI

In theory one can perform heavy work while clad in radiation armor. One can do so in practice—provided that one has been through a rigorous course of training. Pendeen, Second Engineer of *Rim Mamelute*, had been so trained. So, of course, had been Mr. Williams—but Grimes had insisted that the Mate stay aboard the tug while he, with Sonya and the engineer, effected an entry into the hull of the derelict. Soon, while the boarding party was making its exploratory walk over the stranger ship's shell plating, he had been obliged to order Williams to cut the drive; sufficient velocity had been built up so that both vessels were now in Free Fall away from the sun.

Even in Free Fall it was bad enough. Every joint of the heavy suit was stiff, every limb had so much mass that great physical effort was required to conquer inertia. Weary and sweating heavily, Grimes forced himself to keep up with his two companions, by a great effort of will contrived to maintain his side of the conversation in a voice that did not betray his poor physical condition.

He was greatly relieved when they discovered, towards the stern, what was obviously an airlock door. Just a hair-thin crack in the plating it was, outlining a circular port roughly seven feet in diameter. There were no signs of external controls, and the crack was too thin to allow the insertion of any tool.

"Send for the bell, sir?" asked Pendeen, his normally deep voice an odd treble in Grimes' helmet phones.

"The bell? Yes, yes. Of course. Carry on, Mr. Pendeen."

"Al to Bill," Grimes heard. "Do you read me? Over."

"Bill to Al. Loud an' clear. What can I do for you?"

"We've found the airlock. But we want the bell."

"You would. Just stick around. It'll be over."

"And send the cutting gear while you're about it."

"Will do. Stand by."

"Had any experience with the Laverton Bell, sir?" asked Pendeen, his voice not as respectful as it might have been.

"No. No actual working experience, that is."

"I have," said Sonya.

"Good. Then you'll know what to do when we get it."

Grimes, looking towards *Rim Mamelute,* could see that something bulky was coming slowly towards them along one of the tow wires, the rocket that had given the packet its initial thrust long since burned out. He followed the others towards the stem of the derelict, but stood to one side, held to the plating by the magnetic soles of his boots, as they unclipped the bundle from the line. He would have helped them to carry it back aft, but they ignored him.

Back at the airlock valve, Sonya and Pendeen worked swiftly and competently, releasing the fastenings, unfolding what looked like a tent of tough white plastic. This had formed the wrapper for other things—including a gas bottle, a laser torch and a thick tube of adhesive. Without waiting for instructions Sonya took this latter, removed the screw cap and, working on her hands and knees, used it to describe a glistening line just outside the crack that marked the door. Then all three of them, standing in the middle of the circle, lifted the fabric above their heads, unfolding it as they did so. Finally, with Grimes and Pendeen acting as tent poles, Sonya neatly fitted the edge of the shaped canopy to the ring of adhesive, now and again adding a further gob of the substance from the tube.

"Stay as you are, sir," the engineer said to Grimes, then fell to a squatting position. His gloved hands went to the gas cylinder, to the valve wheel. A white cloud jetted out like a rocket exhaust, then faded to invisibility. Around the boarding party the walls of the tent bellied outwards, slowly tautened, distended to their true shape by the expanding helium. Only towards the end was the hiss of the escaping gas very faintly audible.

Pendeen shut the valve decisively, saying, "That's that. Is she all tight, Sonya?"

"All tight, Al," she replied.

"Good." With a greasy crayon he drew a circle roughly in the center of the airlock door, one large enough to admit a spacesuited body. He picked up the laser torch, directed its beam downwards, thumbed the firing button. The flare of vaporizing metal was painfully bright, outshining the helmet lights, reflected harshly from the white inner surface of the plastic igloo. There was the illusion of suffocating heat—or was it more than only an illusion? Pendeen switched off the torch and straightened, looking down at the annulus of still-glowing metal. With an effort he lifted his right foot, breaking the contact of the magnetized sole with the plating. He brought the heel down sharply. The *clang*, transmitted through the fabric of their armor, was felt rather than heard by the others.

And then the circular plate was falling slowly, into the darkness of the airlock chamber, and the rough manhole was open so that they could enter.

Grimes was first into the alien ship, followed by Sonya and then Pendeen. It was light enough in the little compartment once they were into it, the beams of their helmet lights reflected from the white-painted walls. On the inner door there was a set of manual controls that worked—once Grimes realized that the spindle of the wheel had a left handed thread. Beyond the inner door there was an alleyway, and standing there was a man.

The Commodore whipped the pistol from his holster, his reflexes more than compensating for the stiffness of the joints of his suit. Then, slowly, he returned the weapon to his belt. This man was dead. Radiation may have killed him, but it had not killed all the bacteria of decay present in his body. Some freak of inertial and centrifugal forces, coming into play when the derelict had been taken in tow, had flung him to a standing posture, and the magnetic soles of his rough sandals—Grimes could see the gleam of metal—had held him to the deck.

So he was dead, and he was decomposing, his skin taut and darkly purple, bulging over the waist-band of the loincloth—it looked like sacking—that was his only clothing. He was dead—and Grimes was suddenly grateful for the sealed suit that he was wearing, the suit that earlier he had been cursing, that kept out the stench of him.

Gently, with pity and pointless tenderness, he put his gloved hands to the waist of the corpse, lifted it free of the deck, shifted it to one side.

"We must be just above engineroom level," said Sonya, her voice deliberately casual.

"Yes," agreed Grimes. "I wonder if this ship has an axial shaft. If she has, it will be the quickest way of getting to the control room."

"That will be the best place to start investigations," she said.

They moved on through the alleyway, using the Free Fall shuffle that was second nature to all of them, letting the homing instinct that is part of the nature of all spacemen guide them. They found more bodies, women as well as men, sprawled in untidy attitudes, hanging like monstrous mermen and merwomen in a submarine cave. They tried to ignore them, as they tried to ignore the smaller bodies, those of children, and came at last, at the end of a short, radial alleyway, to the stout pillar of the axial shaft.

There was a door in the pillar, and it was open, and one by one they passed through it and then began pulling themselves forward along the central guide rod, ignoring the spiral ramp that lined the tunnel. Finally they came to a conventional enough hatchway, but the valve sealing the end of the shaft was jammed. Grimes and Sonya fell back to let Pendeen use the laser torch. Then they followed him into the control room.

VII

THERE WERE MORE bodies in the control room. There were three dead men and three dead women, all of them strapped into acceleration chairs. Like all the others scattered throughout the ship they were clad only in rough, scanty rags, were swollen with decomposition.

Grimes forced himself to ignore them. He could do nothing for them. Perhaps, he thought, he might some day avenge them (somehow he did not feel that they had been criminals, pirates)—but that would not bring them back to life. He looked past the unsightly corpses to the instruments on the consoles before their chairs. These, at first glance, seemed to be familiar enough—white dials with the black calibrations marked with Arabic numerals; red, green, white and amber pilot lights, dead now, but ready to blossom with glowing life at the restoration of a power supply. Familiar enough they were, at first glance. But there were the odd differences, the placement of various controls in positions that did not tally with the construction and the articulation of the normal human frame. And there was the lettering: MINNSCHINN DRIVI, RIMITI CINTRIL. Who, he asked himself, were the builders of this ship, this vessel that was almost a standard

Federation Survey Service cruiser? What human race had jettisoned every vowel in the alphabet but this absurdly fat "I?"

"John," Sonya was saying, "give me a hand, will you?"

He turned to see what she was doing. She was trying to unbuckle a seat belt that was deeply embedded in the distended flesh at the waist of one of the dead men.

He conquered his revulsion, swallowed the nausea that was rising in his throat. He pulled the sharp sheath knife from his belt, said, "This is quicker," and slashed through the tough fabric of the strap. He was careful not to touch the gleaming, purple skin. He knew that if he did so the dead man would ... burst.

Carefully, Sonya lifted the body from its seat, set it down on the deck so that the magnetized sandal soles were in contact with the steel plating. Then she pointed to the back of the chair. "What do you make of that?" she asked.

That was a vertical slot, just over an inch in width, that was continued into the seat itself, half bisecting it.

It was Pendeen who broke the silence. He said simply, "They had tails."

"But they haven't," objected Grimes. It was obvious that the minimal breech-clouts of the dead people could not conceal even a tiny caudal appendage.

"My dear John," Sonya told him in an annoyingly superior voice, "these hapless folk are neither the builders nor the original crew of this ship. Refugees? Could be. Escapees? A slave revolt? Once again—

could be. Or must be. This is a big ship, and a fighting ship. You can't run a vessel of this class without uniforms, without marks of rank so you can see at a glance who is supposed to be doing what. Furthermore, you don't clutter up a man-o-war with children."

"She's not necessarily a man-o'-war," demurred Grimes. "She could be a defensively armed merchantman..."

"With officers and first class passengers dressed in foul rags? With a name like DESTROYER?"

"We don't *know* that that grouping of letters on the stern does spell DESTROYER."

"We don't *know* that this other grouping of letters"—she pointed to the control panel that Grimes had been studying—"spells MANNSCHENN DRIVE, REMOTE CONTROL. But I'm willing to bet my gratuity that if you trace the leads you'll wind up in a compartment full of dimension-twisting gyroscopes."

"All right," said Grimes. "I'll go along with you. I'll admit that we're aboard a ship built by some humanoid—but possibly non-human race that, even so, uses a peculiar distortion of English as its written language...."

"A humanoid race with tails," contributed Pendeen.

"A humanoid race with tails," agreed Sonya. "But *what* race? Look at this slot in the chair back. It's designed for somebody—or something—with a thin tail, thin at the root as well as at the extremity. And the only tailed beings we know with any technology comparable to our own have thick tails—and, furthermore, have their own written languages. Just imagine one of our saurian friends trying to get out of that chair in a hurry, assuming that he'd ever been able to get into it in the first place. He'd be trapped."

"You're the Intelligence Officer," said Grimes rather nastily.

"All right. I am. Also, I hold a Doctorate in Xenology. And I tell you, John, that what we've found in this ship, so far, doesn't add up to any kind of sense at all."

"She hasn't made any sense ever since she was first picked up by Station 3," admitted Grimes.

"That she hasn't," said Pendeen. "And I don't like her. Not one little bit."

"Why not, Mr. Pendeen?" asked Grimes, realizing that it was a foolish question to ask about a radioactive hull full of corpses.

"Because ... because she's *wrong*, sir. The proportions of all her controls and fittings—just wrong enough to be scary. And left-handed threads, and gauges calibrated from right to left."

"So they are," said Grimes. "So they are. But that's odder still. Why don't they write the same way? From Right to Left?"

"Perhaps they do," murmured Sonya. "But I don't think so. I think that the only difference between their written language and ours is that they have an all-purpose 'I', or an all-purpose symbol that's used for every vowel sound." She was prowling around the control room. Damn it all, there *must* be a Log Book. ..."

"There should be a Log Book," amended Grimes.

"All right. There should be a Log Book. Here's an obvious Log Desk, complete with stylus, but empty.

I begin to see how it must have been. The ship safe in port, all her papers landed for checking, and then her seizure by these people, by these unfortunate humans, whoever they were . . . H'm. The Chart Tank might tell us something . . ." She glared at the empty globe. "It would have told us something if it hadn't been in close proximity to a nuclear blast. But there will be traces. Unfortunately we haven't the facilities here to bring them out." She resumed her purposeful shuffle. "And what have we here? SIGNIL LIG? SIGNAL LOG? A black box that might well contain quite a few answers when we hook it up to a power supply. And that, I think, will lie within the capabilities of our Radio Officer back aboard *Rim Mamelute.*"

The thing was secured by simple enough clips to the side of what was obviously a transceiver. Deftly, Sonya disengaged it, tucked it under her arm.

"Back to the *Mamelute,*" said Grimes. It was more an order than a suggestion.

"Back to the *Mamelute,*" she agreed.

The Commodore was last from the control room, watched first Pendeen and then Sonya vanish through the hatch into the axial shaft. He half-wished that enough air remained in their suit tanks for them to make a leisurely examination of the accommodation that must be situated abaft Control— and was more than half-relieved that circumstances did not permit such a course of action. He had seen his fill of corpses. In any case, the Signal Log might tell them far more than the inspection of decomposing corpses ever could.

He felt far easier in his mind when the three of them were standing, once more, in the plastic igloo that covered the breached airlock, and almost happy when, one by one, they had squeezed through the built-in spincter valve back to the clean emptiness of Space. The harsh working lights of *Rim Mamelute* seemed soft somehow, mellow almost, suggested the lights of Home. And the cramped interior of the tug, when they were back on board, was comforting. If one has to be jostled, it is better to be jostled by the living than by dead men and women, part-cremated in a steel coffin tumbling aimlessly between the stars.

VIII

It was very quiet in the radio office of *Rim Mamelute*. Grimes and Sonya stood there, watching chubby little Bennett make the last connections to the black box that they had brought from the control room of the derelict. "Yes," the Electronic Radio Officer had told them, "it *is* a Signal Log, and it's well shielded, so whatever records it may contain probably haven't been wiped by radiation. Once I get it hooked up we'll have the play-back."

And now it was hooked up. "Are hou sure you won't burn it out?" asked the Commodore, suddenly anxious.

"Almost sure, sir," answered Bennett cheerfully. "The thing is practically an exact copy of the Signal Logs that were in use in some ships of the Federation Survey Service all of fifty years ago. Before my time. Anyhow, my last employment before I came out to the Rim was in the Lyran Navy, and their wagons were all Survey Service cast-offs. In many of them the original communications gear was still in place, and still in working order. No, sir, this isn't the first time that I've made one of these babies sing. Reminds me of when we picked up the wreck of the old *Minstrel Boy*; I was Chief Sparks of the *Tara's Hall* at the time, and got the gen from her Signal Log that put us on the trail of Black Bart"—he added un-necessarily—"the pirate."

"I have heard of him," said Grimes coldly.

Sonya remarked, pointing towards the box, "But it doesn't look old."

"No, Mrs. Grimes. It's not old. Straight from the maker, I'd say. But there's no maker's name, which is odd. . . ."

"Switch on, Mr. Bennett," ordered the Commodore.

Bennett switched on. The thing hummed quietly to itself, crackled briefly and thinly as the spool was rewound. It crackled again, more loudly, and the play-back began.

The voice that issued from the speaker spoke English—of a sort. But it was not human. It was a thin, high, alien squeaking—and yet, somehow, not alien enough. The consonants were ill-defined, and there was only one vowel sound.

"*Eeveengeer* tee *Deestreeyeer. Eeveengeer* tee *Deestreeyeer.* Heeve tee. Heeve tee!"

The voice that answered was not a very convincing imitation of that strange accent. "*Deestreeyer tee Eeveenger.* Reepeet, pleese. Reepeet . . ."

"A woman," whispered Sonya. "Human . . ."

"Heeve tee, *Deestreeyeer.* Heeve tee, eer wee ee-peen feer!"

A pause, then the woman's voice again, the imitation even less convincing, a certain desperation all too evident: "*Deestreeyer* tee *Avenger. Deestreeyeer tee Eeveengeer* . . . Eer Dreeve ceentreels eer eet eef eerdeer!"

Playing for time, thought Grimes. *Playing for time, while clumsy hands fumble with unfamiliar armament. But they tried. They did their best. . . .*

"Dee!" screamed the inhuman voice. "Heemeen sceem, dee!"

"And that must have been it," muttered Grimes.

"It was," said Sonya flatly, and the almost inaudible whirring of what remained on the spool bore her out.

"That mistake she made," said Grimes softly, "is the clue. For *Eeveengeer,* read *Avenger.* For every 'E' sound substitute the vowel that makes sense. But insofar as the written language is concerned, that fat 'I' is really an 'E'. . . ."

"That seems to be the way of it," agreed Sonya.

" 'Die,' " repeated the Commodore slowly. " 'Human scum, die!' " He said, "Whoever those people are, they wouldn't be at all nice to know."

"That's what I'm afraid of," Sonya told him. "That we might get to know them. Whoever they are—and wherever, and whenever. . . ."

IX

THE DERELICT HUNG in orbit about Lorn, and the team of scientists and technicals continued the investigations initiated by *Rim Mamelute's* people during the long haul to the tug's home planet. Grimes, Sonya and the others had been baffled by what they had found—and now, with reluctance, the experts were admitting their own bafflement.

This ship, named *Destroyer* by her builders, and renamed *Freedom* by those who had not lived long to enjoy it, seemed to have just completed a major refit and to have been in readiness for her formal recommissioning. Although her magazines and some of her storerooms were stocked, although her hydroponics tanks and tissue culture vats had been operational at the time of her final action, her accommodation and working spaces were clean of the accumulation of odds and ends that, over the years, adds appreciably to the mass of any vessel. There were no files of official correspondence, although there was not a shortage of empty filing cabinets. There were no revealing personal possessions such as letters, photographs and solidographs, books, recordings, magazines and pin-up girl calendars. (The hapless humans who had been killed by the blast seemed to have brought aboard only the rags that they were wearing.) There were no log books in either control or engine rooms.

The cabins were furnished, however, and in all of them were the strange chairs with the slotted backs and seats, the furniture that was evidence of the existence of a race—an unknown race, insisted the xenologists—of tailed beings, approximating the human norm in stature. Every door tally was in place, and each one made it clear that the creatures who had manned the ship, before her seizure, used the English language, but a version of it peculiarly their own: KIPTIN ... CHIIF INGINIIR ... RIICTIIN DRIVI RIIM ... HIDRIPINICS RIM. . . .

Even so she was, apart from the furniture and the distortion of printed English and—as the engineers pointed out—the prevalence of left-handed threads, a very ordinary ship, albeit somewhat old fashioned. There was, for example, no Carlotti navigational and communications equipment. And the signal log was a model the use of which had been discontinued by the Survey Service for all of half a standard century. And she lacked yet another device, a device of fairly recent origin, the Mass Proximity Indicator.

She was, from the engineering viewpoint, a very ordinary ship; it was the biologists who discovered the shocking abnormality.

They did not discover it at once. They concentrated, at first, upon the cadavers of the unfortunate humans. These were, it was soon announced, indubitably human. They had been born upon and had lived their lives upon an Earth-type planet, but their lives had not been pleasant ones. Their physiques exhibited all the signs of undernourishment, of privation, and they almost all bore scars that told an ugly story of habitual maltreatment. But they were men, and they were women, and had they lived and had they enjoyed for a year or so normal living conditions they would have been indistinguishable from the citizens of any man-colonized world.

And there was nothing abnormal in the hydroponics tanks. There were just the standard plants that are nutured in ships' farms throughout the Galaxy—tomatoes and cucumbers, potatoes and carrots, the Centaurian umbrella vine, Vegan mossfern.

It was the tissue culture vats that held the shocking secret.

The flesh that they contained, the meat that was the protein supply for the tailed beings who should have manned the ship, was human flesh.

"I was right," said Sonya to Grimes. "I was right. Those people—whoever, wherever (and whenever?) they are—are our enemies. But *where* are they? And when?"

"From ... from Outside ... ?" wondered the Commodore.

"Don't be a bloody fool, John. Do you think that a race could wander in from the next galaxy but three, reduce a whole planet of humans to slavery, and worse than slavery, without our knowing about it? And why should such a race, if there were one, have to borrow or steal our shipbuilding techniques, our language even? Damn it all, it doesn't make sense. It doesn't even begin to make sense."

"That's what we've all been saying ever since this blasted derelict first appeared."

"And it's true." She got up from her chair and began to pace up and down Grimes' office. "Meanwhile, my dear, we've been left holding the baby. You've been asked to stay on in your various capacities until the mystery has been solved, and my resignation from the Intelligence Branch of the Survey Service has been rescinded. I've been empowered by the Federation Government to co-opt such Confederacy personnel to assist me in my investigations as I see fit. (That means you—for a start.) Forgive me for thinking out loud. It helps sometimes. Why don't you try it?"

"All we know," said Grimes slowly, "is that we've been left holding the baby."

"All we know," she countered, "is that we're supposed to carry the can back."

"But why shouldn't we?" he demanded suddenly. "Not necessarily this can, but one of our own."

She stopped her restless motion, turned to stare at him. She said coldly, "I thought that you had made a study of archaic slang expressions. Apparently I was wrong."

"Not at all, Sonya. I know what 'to carry the can back' means. I know, too, that the word 'can' is still used to refer to more and bigger things than containers of beer or preserved foods. Such as . . ."

"Such as ships," she admitted.

"Such as ships. All right. How do we carry the can, or *a* can back? Back to where the can came from?"

"But where? Or when?"

"That's what we have to find out."

She said, "I think it will have to be *the* can. That is if you're thinking what I think you're thinking:

that this *Destroyer* or *Freedom* or whatever you care
to call her drifted in from one of the alternative universes. She'll have that built-in urge, yes, urge. She'll
have that built-in urge to return to her own continuum."

"So you accept the alternative universe theory?"

"It seems to fit the facts. After all, out here on the
Rim, the transition from one universe to another has
been made more than once."

"As we should know."

"If only we knew how the derelict did drift in...."

"Did she *drift* in?" asked Grimes softly. And then,
in spoken answer to his wife's unspoken query, "I
think that she was blown in."

"Yes ... yes. Could be. A nuclear explosion in
close, very close proximity to the ship. The very fabric of the continuum strained and warped ..." She
smiled, but it was a grim smile. "That could be it."

"And that could be the way to carry the can back."

"I don't want to be burned, my dear. And, oddly
enough, I shouldn't like to see you burned."

"There's no need for anybody to be burned. Have
you ever heard of lead shielding?"

"Of course. But the weight! Even if we shielded
only a small compartment, the reaction drive'd be
working flat out to get us off the ground, and we'd
have damn all reaction mass to spare for any maneuvers. And the rest of the ship, as we found when
we boarded the derelict, would be so hot as to be
unihhabitable for months."

He gestured towards the wide window to the
squat tower that was *Faraway Quest*. "I seem to
remember, Sonya, that you shipped with me on our
Wild Ghost Chase. Even though you were aboard as

an officer of the Federation's Naval Intelligence you should remember how the *Quest* was fitted. That sphere of anti-matter—now back in safe orbit—that gave us anti-gravity... We can incorporate it into *Freedom's* structure as it was incorporated into Quest's. With it functioning, we can afford to shield the entire ship and still enjoy almost negative mass."

"So you think we should take *Freedom*, or *Destroyer*, and not *Faraway Quest?*"

"I do. Assuming that we're able to blow her back into the continuum she came from, she'll be a more convincing Trojan horse than one of our own ships."

"Cans," she said. "Trojan horses. Can you think of any more metaphors?" She smiled again, and her expression was not quite so grim. "But I see what you mean. Our friends with the squeaky voices and the long, thin tails will think that their own lost ship has somehow wandered back to them, still manned by the escaped slaves." Her face hardened. "I almost feel sorry for them."

"Almost," he agreed.

X

THE BOFFINS WERE reluctant to release *Freedom*, but Grimes was insistent, explaining that disguise of *Faraway Quest*, no matter how good, might well be not good enough. A small, inconspicuous but betraying feature of her outward appearance could lead to her immediate destruction. "Then what about the crew, Commodore?" asked one of the scientists. "Surely those tailed beings will soon realize that the ship is not manned by the original rebels."

"Not necessarily," Grimes told the man. "In fact, I think it's quite unlikely. Even among human beings all members of a different race tend to look alike. And when it comes to members of two entirely different species ..."

"I'm reasonably expert," added Sonya, "but even I find it hard until I've had time to observe carefully the beings with whom I'm dealing."

"But there's so much that we could learn from the ship!" protested the scientist.

"Mr. Wales," Grimes said to the Rim Runners' Superintending Engineer, "how much do you think there is to be learned from the derelict?"

"Not a damn thing, Commodore. But if we disguise one of our own ships, and succeed in blowing her into whatever comic alternative universe she came from, there's far too much that could be learned from *us*. As far as shipbuilding is concerned, we're pratically a century ahead."

"Good enough. Well, gentlemen?"

"I suggest, Commodore, that we bring your *Freedom's* armament up to scratch," said Admiral Hennessey, but the way that he said it made it more of an order than a suggestion.

Grimes turned to face the Admiral, the Flag Officer Commanding the Naval Force of the Confederacy. Bleak stare clashed with bleak stare, almost audibly. As an officer of the Reserve, Grimes considered himself a better spaceman than his superior, and was inclined to resent the intrusion of the Regular Navy into what he was already regarding as his own show.

He replied firmly, "No, sir. That could well give the game away."

He was hurt when Sonya took the Admiral's side —but, after all, she was regular Navy herself, although Federation and not Confederacy. She said, "But what about the lead sheathing, John? What about the sphere of anti-matter?"

Grimes was not beaten. "Mr. Wales has already made a valid point. He thinks that it would be imprudent to make the aliens a present of a century's progress in astronautical engineering. It would be equally imprudent to make them a present of a century's progress in weaponry."

"You have a point there, Grimes," admitted the Admiral. "But I do not feel happy in allowing my personnel to ship in a vessel on a hazardous mission without the utmost protection that I can afford them."

"Apart from the Marines, sir, my personnel rather

than yours. Practically every officer will be a reservist."

The Admiral glared at the Commodore. He growled, "Frankly, if it were not for the pressure brought to bear by our Big Brothers of the Federation, I should insist on commissioning a battle squadron." He smiled coldly in Sonya's direction. "But the Terran Admiralty seems to trust Commander Verrill—or Mrs. Grimes—and have given her on-the-spot powers that would be more fitting to a holder of Flag Officer's rank. And my own instructions from Government House are to afford her every assistance."

He made a ritual of selecting a long, black cigar from the case that he took from an inside pocket of his uniform, lit it, filled the already foul air of the derelict's control room with wreathing eddies of acrid blue smoke. He said in a voice that equaled in acridity the fumes that carried it, "Very well, Commodore. You're having your own way. Or your wife is having her own way; she has persuaded the Federation that you are to be in full command. (But will you be, I wonder . . .) May I, as your Admiral, presume to inquire just what are your intentions, assuming that the nuclear device that you have commandeered from my arsenal does blow you into the right-continuum?"

"We shall play by ear, sir."

The Admiral seemed to be emulating the weapon that he had just mentioned, but he did not quite reach critical mass. "Play by ear!" he bellowed at last, when coherent speech was at last possible. "Play by ear! Damn it all, sir, that's the sort of fatuous remark one might expect from a Snotty making his first training cruise, but not from an allegedly responsible officer."

"Admiral Hennessey," Sonya's voice was as cold as his had been. "This is not a punitive expedition. This is not a well organized attack by naval forces. This is an Intelligence operation. We do not know what we are up against. We are trying to find out." Her voice softened slightly. "I admit that the Commodore expressed himself in a rather unspacemanlike manner, but playing by ear is what we shall do. How shall *I* put it? We shall poke a stick into the ants' nest and see what comes out. . . ."

"We shall hoist the banner of the Confederacy to the masthead and see who salutes," somebody said in one of those carrying whispers. The Admiral, the Commodore and Sonya Verrill turned to glare at the man. Then Sonya laughed. "That's one way of putting it. Only it won't be the black and gold of the Confederacy—it'll be the black and silver of the Jolly Roger. A little judicious piracy—or privateering. Will Rim Worlds Letters of Marque be valid wherever we're going, Admiral?"

That officer managed a rather sour chuckle. "I think I get the drift of your intentions, Commander. I hate to have to admit it—but I wish that I were coming with you." He transferred his attention to Grimes. "So, Commodore, I think that I shall be justified in at least repairing or renewing the weapons that were damaged or destroyed by the blast—as long as I don't fit anything beyond the technology of the builders of this ship."

"Please do that, sir."

"I shall. But what about small arms for your officers and the Marines?"

Grimes pondered the question. There had been no pistols of any kind aboard the derelict when he had boarded her. It could be argued that this was a detail that did not much matter—should the ship be boarded and seized herself there would be both the lead sheathing *and* the sphere of anti-matter that would make it obvious to the boarding party that she had been ... elsewhere. Assuming, that is, that the last survivors of her crew did not trigger the explosive charge that would shatter the neutronium shell and destroy the magnets, thus bringing the sphere of anti-iron into contact with the normal matter surrounding it. Then there would be nobody to talk about what had been found.

But *Freedom*—as a pirate or a privateer—would be sending boarding parties to other ships. There was the possibility that she might have to run before superior forces, unexpectedly appearing, leaving such a boarding party to its fate. Grimes most sincerely hoped that he would never have to make such a decision. And if the boarding party possessed obviously alien hand weapons the tailed beings would be, putting it very mildly, suspicious.

"No hand weapons," he said at last, reluctantly. "But I hope that we shall be able to capture a few, and that we shall be able to duplicate them in the ship's workshop. Meanwhile, I'd like your Marines to be experts in unarmed combat—both suited and unsuited."

"And expert knife fighters," added Sonya.

"Boarding axes and cutlasses," contributed the Admiral, not without relish.

"Yes, sir," agreed Grimes. "Boarding axes and cutlasses."

"I suggest, Commodore," said Hennessey, "that you do a course at the Personal Combat Center at Lorn Base."

"I don't think there will be time, sir," said Grimes hopefully.

"There will be, Commodore. The lead sheathing and the anti-matter sphere cannot be installed in five minutes. And there are weapons to be repaired and renewed."

"There will be time," said Sonya.

Grimes sighed. He had been in one or two minor actions in his youth, but they had been so ... impersonal. It was the enemy ship that you were out to get, and the fact that a large proportion of her crew was liable to die with her was something that you glossed over. You did not see the dreadful damage that your missiles and beams did to the fragile flesh and blood mechanisms that were human beings. Or if you did see it—a hard frozen corpse is not the same as one still warm, still pumping blood from severed arteries, still twitching in a ghastly semblance to life.

"There will be time, Commodore," repeated the Admiral.

"There will be time," repeated Sonya.

"And what about you, Mrs. Grimes?" asked Hennessey unkindly.

"You forget, sir, that in my branch of the Federation's service we are taught how to kill or maim with whatever is to hand any and every life form with which we may come into contact."

"Then I will arrange for the Commodore's course," Hennessey told her.

*   *   *

It was, for Grimes, a grueling three weeks. He was fit enough, but he was not as hard as he might have been. Even wearing protective armor he emerged from every bout with the Sergeant Instructor badly bruised and battered. And he did not like knives, although he attained fair skill with them as a throwing weapon. He disliked cutlasses even more. And the boarding axes, with their pike heads, he detested.

And then, quite suddenly, it came to him. The Instructor had given him a bad time, as usual, and had then called a break. Grimes stood there, sagging in his armor, using the shaft of his axe as a staff upon which to lean. He was aching and he was itching inside his protective clothing, and his copious perspiration was making every abrasion on his skin smart painfully.

Without warning the Instructor kicked Grimes' support away with a booted foot and then, as the Commodore sprawled on the hard ground, raised his own axe for the simulated kill. Although a red haze clouded his vision, Grimes rolled out of the path of the descending blade, heard the blunted edge thud into the dirt a fraction of an inch from his helmeted head. He was on his feet then, moving with an agility that he had never dreamed that he possessed, he was on his feet, crouching, and his pike head thrusting viciously at the Instructor's crotch. The man squealed as the blow connected; even the heavy cod piece could not save him from severe pain. He squealed, but brought his own axe around in a sweeping, deadly arc. Grimes parried, blade edge to shaft, to such good effect that the lethal head of the other's weapon was broken off, clattering to the ground many feet away. He parried and followed through, his blade clanging on the Instructor's shoulder armor. Yet another blow, this time to the man's broad back, and he was down like a felled ox.

Slowly the red haze cleared from the commodore's vision as he stood there. Slowly he lowerd his axe, and as he did so he realized that the Instructor had rolled over, was lying there, laughing up at him, was saying, "Easy, sir. Easy. You're not supposed to kill me, sir. Or to ruin my matrimonial prospects."

"I'm sorry, Sergeant," Grimes said stiffly. "But that was a dirty trick *you* played."

"It was meant to be dirty, sir. Never trust nobody —that's Lesson One."

"And Lesson Two, Sergeant?"

"You've learned that too, sir. You gotta *hate*. You officers are all the same—you don't really hate the poor cows at the other end of the trajectory when you press a firing button. But in this sort of fighting you *gotta* hate."

"I think I see, Sergeant," said Grimes.

But he was not sorry when he was able to return to his real business—to see *Freedom* (or *Destroyer*) readied for her expedition into the Unknown.

XI

Freedom was commissioned as a cruiser of the Navy of the Rim Worlds Confederacy, but the winged wheel of the Rim Worlds had not replaced the embossed lettering of her original name or the crude, black-painted characters that had partially obscured it. *Freedom* was manned by spacemen and spacewomen of the Reserve and a company of Marines. But there was no display of gold braid and brass buttons—marks of rank and departmental insignia had been daubed on the bare skin of wrists and upper arms and shoulders in an indelible vegetable dye. Apart from this crude attempt at uniform, the ship's complement was attired in scanty, none too clean rags. The men were shaggily beareded, the roughly hacked hair of the women was unkempt. All of them bore unsightly cicatrices on their bodies —but these were the result of plastic surgery, not of ill-treatment.

Outwardly, *Freedom* was just as she had been when she suddenly materialized in her suicidal orbit off Lorn. Internally, however, there had been changes made. On the side that had been scarred by the blast, the weapons—the laser projectors and the missile launchers—had been repaired, although this had been done so as not to be apparent to an ex-

222

ternal observer. In a hitherto empty storeroom just forward of the enginerooms the sphere of anti-matter had been installed—the big ball of anti-iron, and the powerful magnets that held it in place inside its neutronium casing. And within the shell plating was the thick lead sheathing that would protect the ship's personnel from lethal radiation when the nuclear device was exploded, the bomb that, Grimes hoped, would blow the vessel back to where she had come from. (The physicists had assured him that the odds on this happening were seven to five, and that the odds on the ship's finding herself in a habitable universe were almost astronomical.)

There was one more change insofar as the internal fittings were concerned, and it was a very important one. The tissue culture vats now contained pork, and not human flesh. "After all," Grimes had said to a Biologist who was insisting upon absolute verisimilitude, "there's not all that much difference between pig and long pig. . . ."

The man had gone all technical on him, and the Commodore had snapped, "Pirates we may have to become, but not cannibals!"

But even pirates, thought Grimes, surveying the officers in his control room, *would be dressier than this mob.* He was glad that he had insisted upon the painted badges of rank—the beards made his male officers hard to recognize. With the female ones it was not so bad, although other features (like the men, the women wore only breech clouts) tended to distract attention from their faces.

Clothes certainly make the man, the Commodore admitted wryly to himself. *And the women—although this very undress uniform suits Sonya well enough, even though her hair-do does look as though she's been dragged through a hedge backwards.* And it felt all wrong for him to be sitting in the chair of command, the seat of the mighty, without the broad gold stripes on his epaulettes (and without the epaulettes themselves, and without a shirt to mount them on) and without the golden comets encrusting the peak of his cap. But the ragged, indigo band encircling each hairy wrist would have to do, just as the coarse, burlap kilt would have to substitute for the tailored, sharply creased shorts that were his normal shipboard wear.

He was concerning himself with travialities, he knew, but it is sometimes helpful and healthy to let the mind be lured away, however briefly, from consideration of the greater issues.

Williams—lately Mr. Williams, Mate of *Rim Mamelute,* now Commander Williams, Executive Officer of *Freedom*—had the con. Under his control the ship was riding the beam from Lorn back to the position in which she had first been picked up by Orbital Station 3. It was there, the scientists had assured Grimes, that she would stand the best change of being blown back into her own continuum. The theory seemed to make sense, although the mathematics of it were far beyond the Commodore, expert navigator though he was.

The ship was falling free now, her reaction drive silent, dropping down the long, empty miles towards a rendezvous that would be no more (at first) than a flickering of needles on dials, an undulation of the glowing traces on the faces of monitor tubes. She was falling free, and through the still unshuttered ports there was nothing to be seen ahead but the dim, ruddy spark that was the Eblis sun, and nothing to port but a faint, far nebulosity that was one of the distant island universes.

To starboard was the mistily gleaming galactic lens, a great ellipse of luminosity in which there were specks of brighter light, like jewels in the hair of some dark goddess.

Grimes smiled wryly at his poetic fancies, and Sonya, who had guessed what he had been thinking, grinned at him cheerfully. She was about to speak when Williams' voice broke the silence. "Hear this! Hear this! Stand by for deceleration. Stand by for deceleration!"

Retro-rockets coughed, then shrieked briefly. For a second or so seat belts became almost intolerable bonds. The Executive Officer emitted a satisfied grunt, then said, "spot on, Skipper. Secure for the Big Bang?"

"You know the drill, Commander Williams. Carry on, please."

"Good-oh, Skipper." Williams snapped orders, and the ship shivered a little as the capsule containing the nuclear device was launched. Grimes saw the thing briefly from a port before the shutters—armor plating and thick lead sheathing—slid into place. It was just a dull-gleaming metal cylinder. It should have looked innocuous, but somehow it didn't. Grimes was suddenly acutely conscious of the craziness of this venture. The scientists had been sure that everything would work as it should, but they were not here to see their theories put to the test. *But I must be fair,* Grimes told himself. *After all, it was our idea. Mine and Sonya's. . . .*

"Fire!" he heard Williams say.

But nothing happened.

There was no noise—but, of course, in the vacuum of Deep Space there should not have been. There was no sense of shock. There was no appreciable rise of the control room temperature.

"A missfire?" somebody audibly wondered.

"Try to raise Lorn," Grimes ordered the Radio Officer. "Orbital Station 3 is maintaining a listening watch on our frequency."

There was a period of silence, broken only by the hiss and crackle of interstellar static, then the voice of the operator saying quietly, *"Freedom* to Station Three. *Freedom* to Station Three. Do you hear me? Come in, please."

Again there was silence.

"Sample the bands," said Grimes. "Listening watch only."

And then they knew that the bomb had exploded, that the results of the explosion had been as planned. There was an overhead dialogue between two beings with high, squeaky voices, similar to the voice that had been recorded in *Freedom's* signal log. There was a discussion of Estimated Time of Arrival and of arrangements for the discharge of cargo—hard to understand at first, but easier once ear and brain became attuned to the distortion of vowel sounds.

When the ports were unscreened, the outside view was as it had been prior to the launching of the bomb, but Grimes and his people knew that the worlds in orbit around those dim, far suns were not, in this Universe, under human dominion.

XII

"WHAT'S THEIR radar like?" asked Grimes.

"Judging by what's in this ship, not too good," replied Williams. "Their planet and station-based installations will have a longer range, but unless they're keepin' a special lookout they'll not pick us up at this distance."

"Good," said Grimes. "Then swing her, Commander. Put the Lorn sun dead ahead. Then calculate what deflection we shall need to make Lorn itself our planetfall."

"Reflection Drive, sir?"

"No. Mannshenn Drive."

"But we've no Mass Proximity Indicator, Skipper, and a jump of light minutes only."

"We've slipsticks, and a perfectly good computer. With any luck we shall be able to intercept that ship coming in for a landing."

"You aren't wasting any time, John," said Sonya, approval in her voice. The Commodore could see that she was alone in her sentiments. The other officers, including the Major of Marines, were staring at him as though doubtful of his sanity.

"Get on with it, Commander," snapped Grimes. "Our only hope of intercepting that ship is to make a fast approach, and one that cannot be detected. And make it Action Stations while you're about it."

"And Boarding Stations?" asked the Major. The spacegoing soldier had recovered his poise and was regarding his superior with respect.

"Yes. Boarding Stations. Get yourself and your men into those adapted spacesuits." He added, with a touch of humor, "And don't trip over the tails."

He sat well back in his chair as the gyroscopes whined, as the ship's transparent nose with its cobweb of graticules swung slowly across the almost empty sky. And then the yellow Lorn sun was ahead and Sonya, who had taken over the computer, was saying, "Allowing a time lag of exactly one hundred and twenty seconds from ... *now*, give her five seconds of arc left deflection."

"Preliminary thrust?" asked Williams.

"Seventy-five pounds, for exactly 0.5 second."

"Mannschenn Drive ready," reported the officer at the Remote Control.

Grimes was glad that he had ordered the time-varying device to be warmed up before the transition from one universe to the other had been made. He had foreseen the possibility of flight; he had not contemplated the possibility of initiating a fight. But, as he had told the Admiral, he was playing by ear.

He said to Sonya, "You have the con, Commander Verrill. Execute when ready."

"Ay, ay, sir. Stand by all. Commander Williams—preliminary thrust on the word 'Fire!' Mr. Cavendish, Mannschenn Drive setting 2.756. Operate for exactly 7.5 seconds immediately reaction drive has been cut. Stand by all. Ten ... Nine ... Eight ... Seven ... Six ... Five ..."

Like one of the ancient submarines, Grimes was thinking. *An invisible approach to the target, and not even a periscope to betray us. But did those archaic warships ever make an approach on Dead*

Reckoning? I suppose that they must have done, but only in their infancy.

"Four ... Three ... Two ... One ... *Fire!*"

The rockets coughed briefly, diffidently, and the normally heavy hand of acceleration delivered no more than a gentle pat. Immediately there was the sensation of both temporal and spatial disorientation as the ever-precessing gyroscopes of the Drive began to spin—a sensation that faded almost at once. And then the control room was flooded with yellow light—light that dimmed as the ports were polarized. But there was still light, a pearly radiance of reflected illumination from the eternal overcast, the familiar overcast of Lorn. That planet hung on their port beam, a great, featureless sphere, looking the same as it had always looked to the men and women at the controls of the ship.

But it was not the same.

There was that excited voice, that shrill voice spilling from the speaker: *"Whee eere yee? Wheet sheep? Wheet sheep? Wee sheell reepeert yee. Yee knee theer eet ees feerbeedeen tee eese thee Dreeve weetheen three reedeei!"*

"Almost rammed the bastards," commented Williams. "That was close, Skip."

"It was," agreed Grimes, looking at the radar repeater before his chair. "Match trajectory, Commander." He could see the other ship through the ports now. Like *Freedom*, she was in orbit about Lorn. The reflected sunlight from her metal skin was dazzling and he could not make out her name or any other details. But Sonya had put on a pair of polaroids with telescopic lenses. She reported, "Her name's *Weejee*. Seems to be just a merchantman.

No armament that I can see."

"Mr. Carter!"

"Sir!" snapped the Gunnery Officer.

"See if your laser can slice off our friend's main venturi. And then the auxiliary ones."

"Ay, ay, sir."

The invisible beams stabbed out from *freedom's* projectors. In spite of the dazzle of reflected sunlight from the other's hull the blue incandescence of melting, vaporizing metal was visible. And then Grimes was talking into the microphone that somebody had passed to him, *"Freedom* to *Weejee. Freedom* to *Weejee.* We are about to board you. Offer no resistance and you will not be harmed."

And then the shrill voice, hysterical now, was screaming to somebody far below on the planet's surface. "Heelp! Heelp! Eet ees thee *Deestreeyeer!* Eet ees the sleeves! Heelp!"

"Jam their signals!" ordered Grimes. How long would it be before a warship came in answer to the distress call? Perhaps there was already one in orbit, hidden by the bulk of the planet. And there would be ground to space missiles certainly—but Carter could take care of them with his laser.

Somebody came into the control room, a figure in bulky space armor, a suit that had been designed to accommodate a long, prehensile tail. For a moment Grimes thought that it was one of the rightful owners of the ship, that somehow a boarding had been effected. And then the Major's voice, distorted by the diaphragm in the snouted helmet, broke the spell. "Commodore Grimes, sir," he said formally, "my men are ready."

Grimes told him, "I don't think that our friends

out there are going to open up." He added regretfully, "And we have no laser pistols."

"There are cutting and burning tools in the engineering workshop, sir. I have already issued them to my men."

"Very good, Major. You may board."

"Your instructions, sir?"

"Limit your objectives. I'd like the log books from her Control, and any other papers, such as manifests, that could be useful. But if there's too much resistance, don't bother. We may have to get out of here in a hurry. But I shall expect at least one prisoner."

"We shall do our best, sir."

"I know you will, Major. But as soon as I sound the Recall, come a-running."

"Very good, sir." The Marine managed a smart salute, even in the disguising armor, left the control room.

"Engaging ground to space missiles," announced the Gunnery Officer in a matter of fact voice. Looking out through the planetward ports Grimes could see tiny, distant, intensely brilliant sparks against the cloud blanket. There was nothing to worry about—yet. Carter was picking off the rockets as soon as they came within range of his weapons.

And then he saw the Marines jetting between the two ships, each man with a vapor trail that copied and then surpassed the caudal appendage of his suit. They carried boarding axes, and the men in the lead were burdened with bulky cutting tools. He watched them come to what must have been a clangorous landing on the other vessel's shell plating and then, with an ease that was the result of many drills, disperse themselves to give the tool-bearers room to work. Metal melted, flared and exploded into glowing vapor. The ragged-edged disc that had been the outer valve of the airlock was pried up and clear and sent spinning away into emptiness. There was a slight delay as the inner door was attacked— and then the armored figures were vanishing rapidly into the holed ship.

From the speaker of the transceiver that was tuned to spacesuit frequency Grimes heard the Major's voice, "Damn it all, Bronsky, that's a tool, not a weapon! Don't waste the charge!"

"He'd have got you, sir..."

"Never mind that. I want that airtight door down!"

And there were other sounds—clanging noises, panting, a confused scuffling. There was a scream, a human scream.

In the control room the radar officer reported. "Twelve o'clock low. Two thousand miles. Reciprocal trajectory. Two missiles launched."

"Carter!" said Grimes.

"In hand, sir," replied that officer cheerfully. "So far."

"Recall the Marines," ordered Grimes. "Secure control room for action."

The armored shutters slid over the ports. Grimes wondered how much protection the lead sheathing would give against laser, if any. But if the Major and his men were caught between the two ships their fate would be certain, unpleasantly so. And it was on the planetary side of the ship, the side from which the boarding party would return, that the exterior television scanner had been destroyed by the

blast that had thrown the ship into Grimes' universe.
That scanner had not been renewed. The Commodore could not tell whether or not the Major had
obeyed his order; by the time that the Marines were
out of the radar's blind spot they would be almost in
Freedom's airlock.

Not that the radar was of much value now, at
short range; *Freedom* was enveloped in a dense
cloud of metallic motes. This would shield her from
the enemy's laser, although not from missiles. And
the floating screen would render her own anti-mis-
sile laser ineffective. Missile against missile was all
very well, but the other warship was operating from
a base from which she could replenish her magazines.

"Reporting on board, sir." It was the Major's
voice, coming from the intercom speaker. "With cas-
ualties—none serious—and prisoner."

Wasting no time, Grimes sized up the navigational situation. The ship would be on a safe trajectory if the reaction drive were brought into operation at once. He so ordered and then, after a short
blast from the rockets, switched to Mannschenn
Drive. He could sort out the ship's next destination
later.

"Secure all for interstellar voyage," he ordered.
Then, into the intercom microphone: "Take your
prisoner to the wardroom, Major. We shall be along
in a few minutes."

XIII

THE PRISONER, still with his guards, was in the wardroom when Grimes, Sonya and Mayhew got there. He was space-suited still, and manacled at wrists and ankles, and six Marines, stripped to the rags that were their uniforms aboard this ship, were standing around him, apparently at ease but with their readiness to spring at once into action betrayed by a tenseness that was felt rather than seen. But for something odd about the articulation of the legs at the knee, but for the unhuman eyes glaring redly out through the narrow transparency of the helmet, this could have been one of the Major's own men, still to be unsuited. And then Grimes noticed the tail. It was twitching inside its long, armored sheath.

"Mr. Mayhew?" asked Grimes.

"It ... He's not human, sir," murmured the telepath. Grimes refrained from making any remarks about a blinding glimpse of the obvious. "But I can read ... after a fashion. There is hate, and there is fear—dreadful, paralyzing fear."

The fear, thought Grimes, *that any rational being will know when his maltreated slaves turn on him, gain the upper hand.*

"Strip him, sir?" asked the Major briskly.

"Yes," agreed Grimes. "Let's see what he really looks like."

"Brown! Gilmore! Get the armor off the prisoner."

"We'll have to take the irons off him first, sir," pointed out one of the men dubiously.

"There are six of you, and only one of him. But if you want to be careful, unshackle his wrists first, then put the cuffs back on as soon as you have the upper half of his suit off."

"Very good, sir."

"I think that we should be careful," said Sonya.

"We are being careful, ma'am," snapped the Major.

Brown unclipped a key ring from his belt, found the right key and unlocked the handcuffs, cautiously, alert for any hostile action on the part of the prisoner. But the being still stood there quietly, only that twitching tail a warning of potential violence. Gilmore attended to the helmet fastenings, made a half turn and lifted the misshapen bowl of metal and plastic from the prisoner's head. All of the humans stared at the face so revealed—the gray-furred visage with the thin lips crinkled to display the sharp, yellow teeth, the pointed, bewhiskered snout, the red eyes, the huge, circular flaps that were the ears. The thing snarled shrilly, wordlessly. And there was the stink of it, vaguely familiar, nauseating.

Gilmore expertly detached air tanks and fittings, peeled the suit down to the captive's waist while Brown, whose full beard could not conceal his unease, pulled the sleeves down from the long, thin arms, over the clawlike hands. The sharp click as the handcuffs were replaced coincided with his faint sigh of relief.

And when we start the interrogation, Grimes was wondering, *shall we be up against the name, rank and serial number convention?*

Gilmore called another man to help him who, after Brown had freed the prisoner's ankles, lifted one foot after the other from its magnetic contact with the deck plating. Gilmore continued stripping the captive, seemed to be getting into trouble as he tried to peel the armor from the tail. He muttered something about not having enlisted to be a valet to bleeding snakes.

Yes, it was like a snake, that tail. It was like a snake, and it whipped up suddenly, caught Gilmore about the throat and tightened, so fast that the strangling man could emit no more than a frightened grunt. And the menacled hands jerked up and then swept down violently, and had it not been for Brown's shaggy mop of hair he would have died. And a clawed foot ripped one of the other men from throat to navel.

It was all so fast, and so vicious, and the being was fighting with a ferocity that was undiminished by the wounds that he, himself was receiving, was raging through the compartment like a tornado, a flesh and blood tornado with claws and teeth. Somebody had used his knife to slash Gilmore free, but he was out of the fight, as were Brown and the Marine with the ripped torso. Globules of blood from the ragged gash mingled with the blood that spouted from the stump of the severed tail, were dispersed by the violently agitated air to form a fine, sickening mist.

Knives were out now, and Grimes shouted that he wanted the prisoner alive, not dead. Knives were out, but the taloned feet of the captive were as effective as the human weapons, and the manacled hands were a bone-crushing club.

"Be careful!" Grimes was shouting. "Careful! Don't kill him!"

But Sonya was there, and she, of all those present, had come prepared for what was now happening. She had produced from somewhere in her scanty rags a tiny pistol, no more than a toy it looked. But it was no toy, and it fired anaesthetic darts. She hovered on the outskirts of the fight, her weapon ready, waiting for the chance to use it. Once she fired—and the needle-pointed projectile sank into glistening human skin, not matted fur. Yet another of the Marines was out of action.

She had to get closer to be sure of hitting her target, the target that was at the center of a milling mass of arms and legs, human and non-human. She had to get closer, and as she approached, sliding her magnetized sandals over the deck in a deceptively rapid slouch, the being broke free of his captors, taking advantage of the sudden lapse into unconsciousness of the man whom Sonya had hit with her first shot.

She did not make a second one, the flailing arm of one of the men hit her gun hand, knocking the weapon from her grasp. And then the blood-streaked horror was on her, and the talons of one foot were hooked into the waistband of her rags and the other was upraised for a disembowelling stroke.

Without thinking, without consciously remembering all that he had been taught, Grimes threw his knife. But the lessons had been good ones, and, in this one branch of Personal Combat, the Commodore had been an apt pupil. Blood spurted from a severed caratoid artery and the claws—bloody themselves, but with human blood—did not more, in their last spasmodic twitch, than inflict a shallow scratch between the woman's breasts.

Grimes ran to his wife but she pushed him away, saying, "Don't mind me. There are others more badly hurt."

And Mayhew was trying to say something to him, was babbling about his dead amplifier, Lassie, about her last and lethal dream.

It made sense, but it had made sense to Grimes before the telepath volunteered his explanation. The Commodore had recognized the nature of the prisoner, in spite of the size of the being, in spite of the cranial development. In his younger days he had boarded a pest-ridden grain ship. He had recalled the vermin that he had seen in the traps set up by the ship's crew, and the stench of them.

And he remembered the old adage—that a cornered rat will fight.

XIV

Freedom was falling down the dark dimensions, so far with no course set, so far with her destination undecided.

In Grimes' day cabin there was a meeting of the senior officers of the expedition to discuss what had already been learned, to make some sort of decision on what was to be done next. The final decision would rest with the Commodore, but he had learned, painfully, many years ago, that it is better to ask some of the questions than to know all the answers.

The Major was telling his story again: "It wasn't all that hard to get into the ship, sir. But they were waiting for us, in spacesuits, in the airlock vestibule. Some of them had pistols. As you know, we brought one back."

"Yes," said Grimes. "I've seen it. A not very effective laser weapon. I think that our workshop can turn out copies—with improvements."

"As you say, sir, not very effective. Luckily for us. And I gained the impression that they were rather scared of using them. Possibly it was the fear of doing damage to their own ship." He permitted himself a slight sneer. "Typical, I suppose, of merchant spacemen."

"It's easy to see, Major, that you've never had to write to Head Office to explain a half inch dent in the shell plating. But carry on."

"There were hordes of them, sir, literally choking the alleyways. We tried to cut and burn and bludgeon our way through them, to get to the control room, and if you hadn't recalled us we'd have done so..."

"If I hadn't recalled you you'd be prisoners now—or dead. And better off dead at that. But tell me, were you able to notice anything about the ship herself?"

"We were rather too busy, sir. Of course, if we'd been properly equipped, we'd have had at least two cameras. As it was..."

"I know. I know. You had nothing but spacesuits over your birthday suits. But surely you gained some sort of impression."

"Just a ship, sir. Alleyways, airtight doors and all the rest of it. Oh, yes... Fluorescent strips instead of luminescent panels. Old-fashioned."

"Sonya?"

"Sounds like a mercantile version of this wagon, John. Or like a specimen of Rim Rummers' vintage tonnage."

"Don't be catty. And you, Doctor?"

"So far," admitted the medical officer, "I've made only a superficial examination. But I'd say that our late prisoner was an Earth-type mammal. Male. Early middle age."

"And what species?"

"I don't know, Commodore. If we had thought to bring with us some laboratory white rats I could run a comparison of tissues."

"In other words, you smell a rat. Just as we all do." He was speaking softly now. "Ever since the first ship rats have been stowaways—in surface vessels, in aircraft, in spaceships. Carried to that planet in shipments of seed grain they became a major pest on Mars. But, so far, we have been lucky. There have been mutations, but never a mutation that has become a real menace to ourselves."

"Never?" asked Sonya with an arching of eyebrows.

"Never, so far as we know, in *our* Universe."

"But in this one ..."

"Too bloody right they are," put in Williams. "Well, we know what's cookin' now, Skipper. We still have one nuclear thunderflash in our stores. I vote that we use it and blow ourselves back to where we came from."

"I wish it were as simple as all that, Commander," Grimes told him. "When we blew ourselves here, the chances were that the ship would be returned to her own Space-Time. When we attempt to reverse the process there will be, I suppose, a certain tendency for ourselves and the machinery and materials that we have installed to be sent back to our own Universe. But no more than a tendency. We shall be liable to find ourselves anywhere—or anywhen." He paused. "Not that it really worries any of us. We're all volunteers, with no close ties left behind us. But we have a job to do, and I suggest that we at least try to do it before attempting a return."

"Then what do we try to do, Skip?" demanded Williams.

"We've made a start, Commander. We know now

what we're up against. Intelligent, oversized rats who've enslaved man at least on the Rim Worlds.

"Tell me, Sonya, you know more of the workings of the minds of Federation top brass, both military and political, than I do. Suppose this state of affairs had come to pass in our Universe, a hundred years ago, say, when the Rim Worlds were no more than a cluster of distant colonies always annoying the Federation by demanding independence?"

She laughed bitterly. "As you know, there are planets whose humanoid inhabitants are subjects of the Shaara Empire. And on some of those worlds the mammalian slaves of the ruling arthropods are more than merely humanoid. They are human, descendents of ships' crews and passengers cast away in the days of the Ehrenhaft Drive vessels, the so-called gaussjammers. But we'd never dream of going to war against the Shaara to liberate our own flesh and blood. It just wouldn't be ... expedient. And I guess that in this Space-Time it just wouldn't be expedient to go to war against these mutated rats. Too, there'll be quite a large body of opinion that will say that the human Rim Worlders should be left to stew in their own juice."

"So you, our representative of the Federation's armed forces, feel that we should accomplish nothing by making for Earth to tell our story."

"Not only should we accomplish nothing, but, in all probability, our ship would be confiscated and taken apart to see what makes her tick insofar as dimension hopping is concerned. And it would take us all a couple of lifetimes to break free of the red tape with which we should be festooned."

"In other words, if we want anything done we have to do it ourselves."

"Yes."

"Then do we want anything done?" asked Grimes quietly.

He was almost frightened by the reaction provoked by his question. It seemed that not only would he have a mutiny on his hands, but also a divorce. Everybody was talking at once, loudly and indignantly. There was the Doctor's high-pitched bray: "And it was *human* flesh in the tissue culture vats!" and William's roar: "You saw the bodies of the sheilas in this ship, an' the scars on 'em!" and the Major's curt voice: "The Marine Corps will carry on even if the Navy rats!" Then Sonya, icily calm: "I thought that the old-fashioned virtues still survived on the Rim. I must have been mistaken."

"Quiet!" said Grimes. "Quiet!" he shouted. He grinned at his officers. "All right. You've made your sentiments quite clear, and I'm pleased that you have. The late owners of this ship are intelligent beings—but that does not entitle them to treat other intelligent beings as they treat their slaves. Sonya mentioned the human slaves on the worlds of the Shaara Empire, but those so-called slaves are far better off than many a free peasant on Federation worlds. They're not mistreated, and they're not livestock. But we've seen the bodies of the men, women and children who died aboard this ship. And if we can make their deaths not in vain..."

Sonya flashed him an apologetic smile. "But how?" she asked. "But how?"

"That's the question." He turned to Mayhew. "You've been maintaining a listening watch. Do these people have psionic radio?"

"I'm afraid they do, sir," the telepath told him unhappily. "I'm afraid they do. And ..."

"Out with it, man."

"They use amplifiers, just as we do. But ..."

"But what?"

"They aren't dogs' brains. They're human ones!"

XV

SONYA ASKED SHARPLY, "And what else have you to report?"

"I . . . I have been listening."

"That's what you're paid for. And what have you picked up?"

"There's a general alarm out. To all ships, and to Faraway Ultimo and Thule, and to the garrisons on Tharn, Mellise and Grollor . . ."

"And to Stree?"

"No. Nothing at all to Stree."

"It makes sense," murmured the woman. "It makes sense. Tharn, with its humanoids living in the equivalent of Earth's Middle Ages. Grollor, with just the beginnings of an industrial culture. Mellise, with its intelligent amphibians and no industries, no technology at all. Our mutant friends must have found the peoples of all those worlds a push-over."

"But Stree . . . *We* don't know just what powers—psychic? psionic?—those philosophical lizards can muster, and we're on friendly terms with them. So . . ."

"So we might get help there," said Grimes. "It's worth considering. Meanwhile, Mr. Mayhew, has there been any communication with the anti-matter worlds to the Galactic West?"

"No, sir."

"And any messages to our next door neighbors— the Shakesperian Sector, the Empire of Waverly?"

"No, sir."

Grimes smiled—but it was a cold smile. "Then this is, without doubt, a matter for the Confederacy. The legalities of it all are rather fascinating..."

"The illegalities, Skipper," said Williams. "But I don't mind being a pirate in a good cause."

"You don't mind being a pirate. Period," said Sonya.

"Too bloody right I don't. It makes a change."

"Shall we regard ourselves as liberators?" asked Grimes, but it was more an order than a question. "Meanwhile, Commander Williams, I suggest that we set course for Stree. And you, Mr. Mayhew, maintain your listening watch. Let me know at once if there are any other vessels in our vicinity—even though they haven't Mass Proximity Indicators they can still pick up our temporal precession field, and synchronize."

And what are your intentions when you get to Stree, sir?" asked the Major.

"As I told the Admiral, I play by ear." He unstrapped himself from his chair and, closely followed by Sonya, led the way to the control room. He secured himself in his seat and watched Williams as the Commander went through the familiar routine of setting course—Mannschenn Drive off, directional gyroscopes brought into play to swing the ship to

her new heading, the target star steadied in the
cartwheel sight, the brief burst of power from the
reaction drive. Mannschenn Drive cut in again. The
routine was familiar, and the surroundings in
which it was carried out were familiar, but he still
found it hard to adjust to the near nudity of himself
and his officers. But Williams, with only three bands
of indigo dye on each thick, hairy wrist to make his
rank, was doing the job as efficiently as he would
have done had those bands been gold braid on black
cloth.

"On course, Skipper," he announced.

"Thank you, Commander Williams. All off duty
personnel may stand down. Maintain normal deep
space watches." Accompanied by his wife, he returned to his quarters.

It was, at first and in some respects, just another
voyage.

In the Mannschenn Drive Room the complexity of
spinning gyroscopes precessed, tumbled, quivered
on the very edge of invisibility, pulling the ship and
all her people with them down the dark
dimensions, through the warped continuum, down
and along the empty immensities of the rim of
space.

But, reported Mayhew, they were not alone.
There were other ships, fortunately distant, too far
away for *Freedom's* wake through Space-Time to
register on their instruments.

It was more than just another voyage. There was
the hate and the fear with which they were surrounded, said Mayhew. He, of course, was listening
only—the other operators were sending. There were

warships in orbit about Lorn, Faraway, Ultimo and Thule; there were squadrons hastening to take up positions off Tharn, Mellise, Grollor and Stree. And the orders to single vessels and to fleets were brutally simple: *Destroy on sight.*

"What else did you expect?" said Sonya, when she was told.

"I thought," said Grimes, "that they might try to capture us."

"Why should they? As far as they know we're just a bunch of escaped slaves who've already tried their hand at piracy. In any case, I should hate to be captured by those ... things."

"Xenophobia—from *you*, of all people?"

"No ... not Xenophobia. Real aliens one can make allowances for. But these aren't real aliens. They're a familiar but dangerous pest, a feared and hated pest that's suddenly started fighting us with our own weapons. We have never had any cause to love them —human beings have gotten, at times, quite sentimental over mice, but never rats—and they've never had any cause to love us. A strong, mutual antipathy...." Absently she rubbed the fading scar between her breasts with her strong fingers.

"What do you make of this squadron dispatched to Stree?"

"A precautionary measure. *They* think that we might be making for there, and that they might be able to intercept us when we emerge into normal Space-Time. But according to Mayhew, there have been no psionic messages to planetary authorities, as there have been to the military governments on Tharn, Mellise and Grollor." She said, a note of query in her voice, "We shall make it before they do?"

"I think so. I hope so. Our Mannschenn Drive unit is running flat out. It's pushed to the safety limits. And you know what will happen if the governor packs up."

"I don't know," she told him. "Nobody knows. I do know most of the spacemen's fairy stories about what *might* happen."

"Once you start playing around with Time, anything might happen," he said. "The most important thing is to be able to take advantage of what happens."

She grinned. "I think I can guess what's flitting through your apology for a mind."

"Just an idea," he said. "Just an idea. But I'd like to have a talk with those saurian philosophers before I try to do anything about it."

"If we get there before that squadron," she said.

"If we don't, we may try out the idea before we're ready to. But I think we're still leading the field."

"What's that?" she demanded suddenly.

That was not a noise. *That* was something that is even more disturbing in any powered ship traversing any medium—a sudden cessation of noise.

The buzzer that broke the tense silence was no proper substitute for the thin, high keening of the Mannschenn Drive.

It was the officer of the watch, calling from Control. "Commodore, sir, O.O.W. here. Reporting breakdown of interstellar drive."

Grimes did not need to be told. He had experienced the uncanny sensation of temporal disorientation when the precessing gyroscopes slowed, ceased to precess. He said, "Don't bother the engineers—every second spent answering the telephone means delay in effecting repairs. I'll be right up."

"Looks as though our friends might beat us to Stree after all, remarked Sonya quietly.

"That's what I'm afraid of," said Grimes.

XVI

THE BREAKDOWN OF *Freedom's* Mannschenn Drive unit
was a piece of bad luck—but, Grimes admitted, the
luck could have been worse, much worse. The ship
had made her reentry into the normal continuum
many light years from any focal point and well
beyond the maximum range of the radar installations of the enemy war vessels. She had Space—or, at
any rate, a vast globe of emptiness—all to herself in
just this situation. But, as an amateur of naval history, Grimes knew full well what an overly large
part is played by sheer, blind mischance in warfare.
Far too many times a hunted ship has blundered
into the midst of her pursuers when all on board
have considered themselves justified in relaxing
their viligance—not that viligance is of great avail
against overwhelming fire power. And fire power,
whether it be the muzzle loading cannon of the days
of sail or the guided missile and laser beam of today,
is what makes the final decision.

But, so far, there was no need to worry about fire
power. A good look-out, by all available means, was
of primary importance. And so, while *Freedom* fell
—but slowly, slowly, by the accepted standards of
interstellar navigation—towards the distant Stree
sun the long fingers of her radar pulses probed the

emptiness about her and, in the cubby hole that he shared with the naked canine brain that was a poor and untrained substitute for his beloved Lassie, Mayhew listened, alert for the faintest whisper of thought that would offer some clue as to the enemy's whereabouts and intentions.

After a while, having received no reports from the engineers, Grimes went along to the Mannschenn Drive Room. He knew that the engineroom staff was working hard, even desperately, and that the buzz of a telephone in such circumstances can be an almost unbearable irritation. Even so, as Captain of the ship he felt that he was entitled to know what was going on.

He stood for a while in the doorway of the compartment, watching. He could see what had happened—a seized bearing of the main rotor. That huge flywheel, in the gravitational field of an Earth type planet, would weigh at least five tons and, even with *Freedom* falling free, it still possessed considerable mass. Its spindle had to be eased clear of the damaged bearing, and great care had to be taken that it did not come into contact with and damage the smaller gyroscopes surrounding it. Finally Bronson, the Chief Engineer, pausing to wipe his sweating face, noticed the Commodore and delivered himself of a complaint.

"We should have installed one of our own units, sir."

"Why, Commander?"

"Because ours have a foolproof system of automatic lubrication, that's why. Because the bastards who built this ship don't seem to have heard of such a thing, and must rely on their sense of smell to warn them as soon as anything even starts to run hot."

"And that's possible," murmured Grimes, thinking that the mutants had not been intelligent long enough for their primitive senses to become dulled. Then he asked, "How long will you be?"

"At least two hours. At least. That's the best I can promise you."

"Very good." He paused. "And how long will it take you to modify the lubrication system, to bring it up to our standards?"

"I haven't even thought about that, Commodore. But it'd take days."

"We can't afford the time," said Grimes as much to himself as to the engineer. "Just carry on with the repairs to the main rotor, and let me know as soon as the unit is operational. I shall be in Control." As he turned to go he added, half seriously, "And it might be an idea to see that your watchkeepers possess a keen sense of smell!"

Back in the control room he felt more at home, even though this was the nerve center of a crippled ship. Officers sat at their posts and there was the reassuring glow from the screens of navigational instruments—the chart tank and the radarscopes. Space, for billions of miles on every hand, was still empty, which was just as well.

He went to stand by Sonya and Williams, told them what he had learned.

"So they beat us to Stree," commented the Executive Officer glumly.

"I'm afraid that they will, Commander."

"And then what do we do?"

"I wish I knew just what the situation is on Stree,"

murmured Grimes. "*They* don't seem to have taken over, as they have on the other Rim Worlds. Should we be justified in breaking through to make a landing?"

"Trying to break through, you mean," corrected Sonya.

"All right. Trying to break through. Will it be a justified risk?"

"Yes," she said firmly. "As far as I can gather from Mayhew, our rodent friends are scared of Stree —and its people. They've made contact, of course, but that's all. The general feeling seems to be one of you leave us alone and we'll leave you alone."

"I know the Streen," said Grimes. "Don't forget that it was I that made the first landing on their planet when I opened up the Eastern Circuit to trade. They're uncanny brutes—but, after all, mammals and saurians have little in common, psychologically speaking."

"Spare us the lecture, John. Furthermore, while you were nosing around in the engineroom, Mayhew rang Control. He's established contact with the squadron bound for Stree."

"What! Is the man mad? Send for him at once."

"Quietly, John, quietly. Our Mr. Mayhew may be a little round the bend, like all his breed, but he's no fool. When I said that he had made contact with the enemy I didn't mean that he had been nattering with the officer commanding the squadron. Oh, he's made contact—but with the underground."

"Don't talk in riddles."

"Just a delaying action, my dear, to give you time to simmer down. I didn't want you to order that Mayhew be thrown out of the airlock without a spacesuit. The underground, as I have referred to it, is made up of the human brains that our furry friends use as psionic amplifiers."

"But it's still criminal folly. *They* will employ telepaths as psionic radio officers, just as we do. And those telepaths will read the thoughts of their amplifiers, just as Mayhew reads the thoughts of his dog's brain in aspic."

"But will they? Can they? Don't forget that our telepaths employ as amplifiers the brains of creatures considerably less intelligent than Man. Whoever heard of a dog with any sort of mental screen? *They* will be using the brains of humans who have been unlucky enough to be born with telepathic ability. And any human telepath, any trained human telepath, is able to set up a screen."

"But why should *They* use human brains? The risk of sabotage of vital communications . . ."

"What other brains are available for their use? As far as *They* are concerned, both dogs and cats are out—repeat, out!"

"Why?"

"Far too much mutual antipathy."

"Wouldn't that also apply in the case of themselves and human beings?"

"No. I doubt if they really hate us. After all, we have provided their ancestors with food, shelter and transportation for many centuries. The rats would have survived if they hadn't had the human race to bludge upon, but they wouldn't have flourished, as they have, traps and poisons notwithstanding. Oh, all right. With the exception of the occasional small boy with his albino pets, every human being has this hatred of rats. But hate isn't the only mainspring of human behavior."

"What do you mean?"

"Look at it this way. Suppose you're a telepath, born on one of the Rim Worlds in this continuum. By the time that your talent has been noted, by the time that you're ... conscripted, you will have come to love your parents and the other members of your family. You will have made friends outside the family circle. Without being overly precocious you may even have acquired a lover."

"I think I see. Play ball, or else."

"Yes."

"Then why should the poor bastards risk the 'or else' now?"

"Because Mayhew's peddled them a line of goods. Very subtly, very carefully. Just induced dreams at first, just dreams of life as it is on the Rim Worlds in *our* Universe—but a somewhat glamorized version."

"I can imagine it. Mayhew's a very patriotic Rim Worlder."

"First the dreams, and then the hints. The whisper that all that they have dreamed is true, that all of it could become the way of life of their own people. The story of what actually happened to *Freedom* and to the escaped slaves. The message that we have come to help them—and the request for help for ourselves."

"But I don't understand how he could have done all this in so short a time."

"How long does a dream take? It is said that a man can dream of a lifetime's happenings in a few seconds."

Already Grimes' active mind was toying with ideas, with ruses and stratagems. Deceit, he knew, has always been a legitimate technique of warfare. Not that legalities counted for overmuch in this here-

and-now. Or did they? If the Federation got dragged into the mess, he and his people might well find themselves standing trial for piracy. It was unlikely —but, bearing in mind the Federation's pampering of various unpleasant nonhuman races on his time track, possible.

He grinned. The legal aspects of it all were far too complicated—and, at the moment, far too unimportant.

He said, "Send for Mr. Mayhew."

XVII

GRIMES WENT INTO conference with Mayhew and certain others of his officers. There was Sonya, of course, and there was Williams, and there was Dangerford, the Chief Reaction Drive Engineer. Also present was one Ella Kubinsky, who held the rank of Lieutenant in the Rim Worlds Volunteer Naval Reserve. She was not a spacewoman. She was a specialist officer, and in civilian life she was an instructor at the University of Lorn, in the Department of Linguistics. Looking at her, Grimes could not help thinking that she was ideally suited for the part that she would be called upon to play. Her straggling hair was so pale as to be almost white; her chin and forehead receded sharply from her pointed nose. Her arms and legs were scrawny, her breasts meager. She had been nicknamed "The White Rat."

To begin with, Grimes and Sonya questioned Mayhew closely, with Sonya playing the major part in the interrogation. They wished that they could have subjected the bodiless human telepaths aboard the enemy ships to a similar interrogation—but that, of course, was impossible. However, Mayhew said that they were sincere in their desire to help—and sincerity is almost impossible to simulate when you have thrown your mind open to another skilled, trained intelligence.

Then other, less recondite matters were discussed with Williams and Dangerford. These concerned the efficiency of various detergents and paint removers and, also, the burning off from the hull plating of certain lettering and its replacement with other letters, these characters to be fabricated in the Engineers' workshop by Dangerford and his juniors who, of course, were not involved in the repair work to the Mannschenn Drive unit. Mayhew was called upon to supply the specifications for these characters.

And then tapes were played to Ella Kubinsky. These were records of signals received from the mutants' ships. She repeated the words, imitating them in a thin, high, squeaking voice that exactly duplicated the original messages. Even Sonya expressed her satisfaction.

While this was being done, Mayhew retired to his cabin for further consultations with his fellow telepaths. There was so much that they could tell him. There was so much that they knew, as all psionic signals had to pass through their brains. When he came back to Grimes' cabin he was able to tell the Commodore what name to substitute for both *Freedom* and *Distriyir* when these sets of characters had been removed from the forward shell plating.

While Williams and his working party were engaged outside the ship, and Dangerford and his juniors were fabricating the new characters, Grimes, Sonya and Ella Kubinsky accompanied Mayhew to his quarters. It was more convenient there to rehearse and to be filled in with the necessary background details. It seemed, at times, that the disembodied presences of the human psionic amplifiers were crowded with them into the cramped compartment, bringing with them the mental stink of their hates and fears. It has been said that to know is to love—but, very often, to know is to hate. Those brains, bodiless, naked in their baths of nutrient solution, must know their unhuman masters as no intelligence clothed in flesh and blood could ever know them. And Grimes found himself pitying Mayhew's own psionic amplifier, the brain of the dog that possessed neither the knowledge nor the experience to hate the beings who had deprived it of a normal existence.

Bronson had finished the repairs to the Mannschenn before Williams and Dangerford were ready. He was glad enough to be able to snatch a brief rest before his machinery was restarted.

And then the new name was in place.

Grimes, Sonya and Williams went back to Control where, using the public address system, the Commodore told his ship's company of the plan for the landing on Stree. He sensed a feeling of disappointment. Carter, the Gunnery Officer, and the Major and his Marines had been looking forward to a fight. Well, they could be ready for one, but if all went as planned they would not be getting it.

*Cirsir—Corsair—*as she had been renamed, set course for the Stree sun. The real *Cosair* had been unable to join the squadron, being grounded for repairs on Tharn. The real *Corsair's* psionic amplifier knew, by this time, what was happening, but would not pass on the information to the unhuman psionic radio officer who was his lord and master. And the psionic amplifier aboard the other ships would let it be known that *Corsair* was hastening to join the blockade of Stree.

It was all so simple. The operation, said Sonya, was an Intelligence Officer's dream of Heaven—to know everything that the enemy was thinking, and to have full control over the enemy's communications. The pseudo *Corsair*—and Grimes found that he preferred that name to either *Freedom* or *Destroyer*—was in psionic touch with the squadron that she was hurrying to overtake. Messages were passing back and forth, messages that, from the single ship, were utterly bogus and that, from the fleet, were full of important information. Soon Grimes knew every detail of tonnage, manning and armament, and knew that he must avoid any sort of showdown. There was enough massed fire-power to blow his ship into fragments in a microsecond, whereupon the laser beams, in another microsecond, would convert those fragments into puffs of incandescent vapor.

As *Corsair* closed the range the squadron ahead was detected on her instruments, the slight flickering of needles on the faces of gauges, the shallow undulation of the glowing traces in monitor tubes, showed that in the vicinity were other vessels using the interstellar drive. They were not yet visible, of course, and would not be unless temporal precession rates were synchronized. And synchronization was what Grimes did not want. As far as he knew, his *Corsair* was typical of her class (as long as her damaged side was hidden from view) but the humans (if bodiless brains could still be called human) aboard the ships of the squadron were not spacemen, knew nothing of subtle differences that can be picked up immediately by the trained eye.

Grimes wished to be able to sweep past the enemy, invisible, no more than interference on their screens, and to make his landing on Stree before the squadron fell into its orbits. That was his wish, and that was his hope, but Bronson, since the breakdown, did not trust his Mannschenn Drive unit and dare not drive the machine at its full capacity. He pointed out that, even so, they were gaining slowly upon the enemy, and that was evidence that the engineers of those vessels trusted their interstellar drives even less than he, Bronson did. The Commodore was obliged to admit that his engineer was probably right in this assumption.

So it was when *Corsair*, at last, cut her Drive and reentered normal Space-Time that the blockading cruisers were already taking up their stations. Radar and radio came into play. From the transceiver in *Corsair's* control room squeaked an irritable voice: "*Heenteer tee Ceerseer, Heenteer tee Ceerseer,* teeke eep steeteen ees eerdeered."

Ella Kubinsky, who had been throughly rehearsed for just this situation, squeaked the acknowledgement.

Grimes stared out of the viewports at the golden globe that was Stree, at the silver, flitting sparks that were the other ships. He switched his regard to Williams, saw that the Executive Officer was going through the motions of maneuvering the ship into a closed orbit—and, as he had been ordered, making a deliberate botch of it.

"*Heenteer* tee *Ceerseer*. Whee ees neet yeer veeseen screen een?"

Ella Kubinsky squeaked that it was supposed to have been overhauled on Tharn, and added some unkind remarks about the poor quality of humanoid labor. Somebody—Grimes was sorry that he did not see who it was—whispered unkindly that if Ella did switch on the screen it would make no difference, anyhow. The ugly girl flushed angrily, but continued to play her part calmly enough.

Under Williams' skilled handling, the ship was falling closer and closer to the great, expanding globe of the planet. But this did not go unnoticed for long. Again there was the enraged squeaking, but in a new voice. "Thees ees thee Eedmeereel. Wheet thee heell eere yee plee-eeng et, *Ceerseer?*"

Ella told her story of an alleged overhaul of reaction drive controls and made further complaints about the quality of the dockyard labor on Tharn.

"Wheere ees yeer Cepteen? Teell heem tee speek tee mee."

Ella said that the Captain was busy, at the controls. The Admiral said that the ship would do better by herself than with such an illegitimate son of a human female handling her. Williams, hearing this, grinned and muttered, "I did *not* ride to my parents' wedding on a bicycle."

"Wheere ees thee Ceepteen?"

And there was a fresh voice: "*Heeveec* tee *Heenteer*. Wheere deed shee geet theet deemeege?"

"All right," said Grimes. "Action stations. And get

her downstairs, Williams, as fast as Christ will let
you!"

Gyroscopes whined viciously and rockets
screamed, driving the ship down to the exosphere in
a powered dive. From the vents in her sides puffed
the cloud of metallic particles that would protect her
from laser—until the particles themselves were destroyed by the stabbing beams. And her launching
racks spewed missiles, each programmed for random action, and to seek out and destroy any target
except their parent ship. Not that they stood much
chance of so doing—but they would, at least, keep
the enemy laser gunners busy.

Corsair hit the first, tenuous fringes of the Streen
atmosphere and her internal temperature rose fast,
too fast. Somehow, using rockets only, taking advantage of her aerodynamic qualities, such as they
were, Williams turned her, stood her on her tail.
Briefly she was a sitting duck—but Carter's beams
were stabbing and slicing, swatting down the
swarm of missiles that had been loosed at her.

She was falling then, stern first, falling fast but
under control, balanced on her tail of incandescence, the rocket thrust that was slowing her,
that would bring her to a standstill (Grimes hoped)
when her vaned landing gear was only scant feet
above the surface of the planet.

She was dropping through the overcast—blue-sil-
ver at first, then gradually changing hue to gold. She
was dropping through the overcast, and there was
no pursuit, although when she entered regions of
denser atmosphere she was escorted, was surrounded by great, shadowy shapes that wheeled

about them on wide wings, that glared redly at them through the control room ports.

Grimes recornized them. After all, in his own continuum he had been the first human to set foot on Stree. They were the huge flying lizards, not unlike the pterosauria of Earth's past—but in Grimes' Space-Time they had never behaved like this. They had avoided spaceships and aircraft. These showed no inclination towards doing so, and only one of the huge brutes colliding with the ship, tipping her off balance, could easily produce a situation beyond even Williams' superlative pilotage to correct.

But they kept their distance, more or less, and followed *Corsair* down, down, through the overcast and through the clear air below the cloud blanket. And beneath her was the familiar landscape—low, rolling hills, broad rivers, lush green plains that were no more than wide clearings in the omnipresent jungle.

Yes, it was familiar, and the Commodore could make out the site of his first landing—one of the smaller clearings that, by some freak of chance or nature, had the outline of a great horse.

Inevitably, as he had been on the occasion of his first landing, Grimes was reminded of a poem that he had read as a young man, that he had tried to memorize—*The Ballad of the White Horse*, by Chesterton. How did it go?

> *For the end of the world was long ago*
> *And all we stand today*
> *As children of a second birth*
> *Like some strange people left on Earth*
> *After a Judgment Day.*

Yes, the end of their world had come for the Rim colonists, in this Universe, long ago.

And could Grimes and his crew of outsiders reverse the Judgment?

XVIII

SLOWLY, CAUTIOUSLY *Corsair* dropped to the clearing, her incandescent rocket exhaust incinerating the grasslike vegetation, raising great, roiling clouds of smoke and steam. A human-built warship would have been fitted with nozzles from which, in these circumstances, a fire-smothering foam could be ejected. But *Corsair's* builders would have considered such a device a useless refinement. Slowly she settled, then came to rest, rocking slightly on her landing gear. Up and around the control room ports billowed the dirty smoke and the white steam, gradually thinning. Except for a few desert areas, the climate of Stree was uniformly wet and nothing would burn for long.

Grimes asked Mayhew to—as he phrased it—take psionic soundings, but from his past experience of this planet he knew that it would be a waste of time. The evidence indicated that the Streen practiced telepathy among themselves but that their minds were closed to outsiders. But the saurians must have seen the ship land, and the pillar of cloud that she had created would be visible for many miles.

Slowly the smoke cleared and those in the control room were able to see, through the begrimed ports, the edge of the jungle, the tangle of lofty, fern-like growths with, between them, the interlacing entanglement of creepers. Something was coming through the jungle, its passage marked by an occasional eruption of tiny flying lizards from the crests of the tree ferns. Something was coming through the jungle, and heading towards the ship.

Grimes got up from his chair and, accompanied by Sonya, made his way down to the airlock. He smiled with wry amusement as he recalled his first landing on this world. *Then* he had been able to do things properly, had strode down the ramp in all the glory of gold braid and brass buttons, had even worn a quite useless ceremonial sword for the occasion. *Then* he had been accompanied by his staff, as formally attired as himself. *Now* he was wearing scanty, dirty rags and accompanied by a woman as nearly naked as he was. (But the Streen, who saw no need for clothing, had been more amused than impressed by his finery.)

The airlock door was open and the ramp was out. The Commodore and his wife did not descend at once to the still slightly smoking ground. One advantage of his dress uniform, thought Grimes, was that it had included half-Wellington boots. The couple watched the dark tunnel entrance in the cliff of solid greenery that marked the end of the jungle track.

A Streen emerged. He would have passed for a small dinosaur from Earth's remote past, although the trained eye of a paleontologist would have detected differences. There was one difference that was obvious even to the untrained eye—the cranial development. This being had a brain, and not a small one. The little, glittering eyes stared at the humans. A voice like the hiss of escaping steam said, "Greetings."

"Greetings," replied the Commodore.

"You come again, man Grimes." It was a statement of fact rather than a question.

"I have never been here before," said Grimes, adding, "Not in this Space-Time."

"You have been here before. The last time your body was covered with cloth and metal, trappings of no functional value. But it does not matter."

"How can you remember?"

"I cannot, but our Wise Ones remember all things. What was, what is to come, what might have been and what might be. They told me to greet you and to bring you to them."

Grimes was less than enthusiastic. On the occasion of his last visit the Wise Ones had lived not in the jungle but in a small, atypical patch of rocky desert, many miles to the north. Then he had been able to make the journey in one of *Faraway Quest's* helicopters. Now he had no flying machines at his disposal, and a spaceship is an unhandy brute to navigate in a planetary atmosphere. He did not fancy a long, long journey on foot, or even riding one of the lesser saurians that the Streen used as draught animals, along a rough track partially choken with thorny undergrowth. Once again he was acutely conscious of the inadequacy of his attire.

The native cackled. (The Streen was not devoid of a sense of humor.) He said, "The Wise Ones told me that you would not be clad for a journey. The Wise Ones await you in the village."

"Is it far?"

"It is where it was when you came before, when you landed your ship in this very place."

"No more than half an hour's walk," began Grimes, addressing Sonya, then fell suddenly silent as an intense light flickered briefly, changing and brightening the green of the jungle wall, the gaudy colors of the flowering vines. Involuntarily he looked up, but the golden overcast was unbroken. There was another flare behind the cloud blanket, blue-white, distant, and then, belatedly, the thunder of the first explosion drifted down, ominous and terrifying.

"Missiles ... whispered the Commodore. "And my ship's a sitting duck..."

"Sir," hissed the saurian, "you are not to worry. The Wise Ones have taken adequate steps for your—and our—protection."

"But you have no science, no technology!" exclaimed Grimes, realizing the stupidity of what he had said when it was too late.

"We have science, man Grimes. We have machines to pit against the machines of your enemies. But our machines, unlike yours, are of flesh and blood, not of metal—although our anti-missiles, like yours, possess only a limited degree of intelligence."

"These people," exclaimed Grimes to Sonya, "are superb biological engineers."

"I know," she said. "And I have little doubt that their air umbrella of pterodactyls will last longer than our furry friends' supply of missiles. So I suggest that we leave them to it and go to see the Wise Ones." She looked dubiously at the jungle, then turned to call to a woman inside the ship, "Peggy! Bring us out a couple of machetes!"

"You will not need them," commented the Streen, "even though your skins are too soft."

They did need them, even though their guide

went ahead like a tank clearing the way for infantry. The vines and brambles were springy, reaching out with taloned tentacles as soon as the saurian had passed. Grimes and Sonya slashed until their arms were tired, but even so, their perspiration smarted painfully in the fresh scratches all over their bodies. They were far from sorry when they emerged into another clearing, a small one, almost completely roofed over with the dense foliage of the surrounding trees.

There were the usual huts, woven from still-living creepers. There was the steaming compost pile that was the hatchery. There were the domesticated lizards, large and small, engaged in their specialized tasks—digging the vegetable plots, weeding and pruning. There were the young of the Streen, looking absurdly like plucked chickens, displaying the curiosity that is common to all intelligent beings throughout the Galaxy, keeping a respectful distance from the visitors, staring at them from their black, unwinking eyes. There were the adults, equally curious, some of whom hustled the community's children out of the path of the humans, clearing a way to the door of a hut that, by Streen standards, was imposing. From the opening drifted blue eddies of smoke—aromatic, almost intoxicating. Grimes knew that the use of the so-called sacred herbs, burned in a brazier and the smoke inhaled, was confined to the Wise Ones.

There were three of the beings huddled there in the semi-darkness, grouped around the tripod from the top of which was suspended the cage in which the source of the smoke smoldered ruddily. The Commodore sneezed. The vapor, as far as he could gather, was mildly euphoric and, at the same time, hallucinogenic—but to human beings it was only an irritant to the nasal membranes. In spite of his efforts to restrain himself he sneezed again, loudly.

The Streen around the tripod cackled thinly. The Commodore, his eyes becoming accustomed to the dim lighting, could see that they were old, their scales shabby and dulled with a lichenous growth, their bones protuberant beneath their armored skins. There was something familiar about them— sensed rather than visually recognized. One of them cackled, "Our dream smoke still makes you sneeze, man Grimes."

"Yes, Wise One."

"And what do you here, man Grimes? Were you not happy in your own here-and-now? Were you not happy with the female of your kind whom you acquired since last we met, otherwhen-and-where?"

"You'd better say 'yes' to that!" muttered Sonya.

Again the thin cackling. "We are lucky, man Grimes. We do not have the problems of you mammals, with your hot blood...." A pause. "But still, we love life, just as you do. And we know that out there, falling about our world, are those who would end our lives, just as they would end yours. *Now* they have not the power, but it is within their grasp."

"But would it matter to you?" asked Sonya. "I thought that you were—how shall I put it?—co-existent with yourselves in all the alternative universes. You must be. You remember John's first landing on this planet—but that was never in *this* here-and-now."

"You do not understand, woman Sonya. You cannot understand. But we will try to explain. Man Grimes—in *your* here-and-now what cargoes do your ships bring to Stree?"

"Luxuries like tea and tobacco, Wise One. And books...."

"What sort of books, man Grimes?"

"History. Philosophy. Novels, even ... poetry."

"And your poets say more in fewer words than your philosophers. There is one whom I will quote to you:

And he who lives more lives than one
More deaths than one shall die.

Does that answer your question, woman Sonya?"

"I can *feel* it," she murmured. "But I can't understand it."

"It does not matter. And it does not matter if you do not understand what you are going to do—as long as you understand how to do it."

"And what is that?" asked Grimes.

"To destroy the egg before it hatches," was the reply.

XIX

ANYBODY MEETING the seemingly primitive Streen for the first time would never dream that these saurians, for all their obvious intelligence, are engineers. Their towns and villages are, to the human way of thinking, utterly innocent of machines. But what is a living organism but a machine—an engine that derives its motive power from the combustion of hydro-carbons in an oxygen atmosphere? On Stree, a variety of semi-intelligent lizards perform the tasks that on man-colonized worlds are performed by mechanisms of metal and plastic.

Yes, the Streen *are* engineers—biological and psychological engineers—of no mean calibre.

In their dim hut, what little light there was further obscured by the acrid fumes from the brazier, the Wise Ones talked and Grimes and Sonya listened. Much of what they were told was beyond them—but there was emotional rather than intellectual acceptance. They would not altogether understand—but they could *feel*. And, after all, the symbiosis of flesh-and-blood machine and machine of metal and plastic was not too alien a concept. Such symbiosis, to a limited extent, has been known ever since the first seaman handled the first ship, learning to make that clumsy contraption of wood and fiber an extension of his own body.

Then, convinced although still not understanding, the Commodore and his wife returned to the ship. With them—slowly, creakingly—walked Serressor, the most ancient of the Wise Ones, and ahead of them their original guide did his best, as before, to clear a way for them through the spiny growths.

They came to the clearing, to the charred patch of ground already speckled with the pale green sprouts of new growth. And already the air ferns had begun to take root upon protuberances from the ship's shell plating, from turrets and sponsons and antennae; already the vines were crawling up the vaned tripod of the landing gear. Williams had a working party out, men and women who were hacking ill-humoredly at the superfluous and encroaching greenery.

From the corner of his eye the Executive Officer saw the approach of the Commodore, ceased shouting directions to his crew and walked slowly to meet his superior. He said, "The game's crook, Skipper. What with lianas an' lithophytes we'll be lucky to get off the ground. An' if we do, we've had it, like as not."

"Why, Commander Williams?"

"Mayhew tells me that *They* have cottoned on to what their psionic amplifiers have been doing. So— no more psionic amplifiers. Period."

"So we can't give them false information through their own communications system," said Sonya.

"You can say that again, Mrs. Grimes."

Serressor croaked, "So you depend upon misdirection to make your escape from our world."

"That is the case, Wise One," Grimes told him.

"We have already arranged that, man Grimes."

"You have?" Williams looked at the ancient saurian, seeing him for the first time. "*You* have? Cor stone the bleedin' lizards, Skipper, what *is* this?"

"This, Commander Williams," said Grimes coldly, "is Serressor, Senior Wise One of the Streen. He and his people are as interested in disposing of the mutants as we are. They have told us a way in which it may be done, and Serressor will be coming with us to play his part in the operation."

"An' how will you do it?" demanded Williams, addressing the saurian.

Serressor hissed, "Destroy the egg before it is hatched."

Surprisingly, Williams did not explode into derision. He said quietly, "I'd thought o' that myself. We could do it—but it's iffy, iffy. Too bloody iffy. There're all the stories about what happens when the Drive gets out o' kilter, but nobody's ever come back to tell us if they're true."

"If we're going to use the Drive as Serressor suggests, it will have to be fitted with a special governor."

"That makes sense, Skipper. But where're we gettin' this governor from?"

"We have it—or him—right here."

"Better him than me. There're better ways o' dyin' than bein' turned inside out." He shifted his regard to the working party, who had taken the opportunity to relax their efforts. "Back to yer gardenin', yer bunch o' drongoes! I want this hull clean as a baby's bottom!"

"Shouldn't you have said 'smooth', Commander?" asked Sonya sweetly.

Before an argument could start Grimes pulled her up the ramp and into the ship. Following them slowly came the aged and decrepit saurian.

Grimes and his officers were obliged to admit that the Streen had planned well and cunningly. When *Corsair* was ready for blasting off a veritable horde of the winged lizards assembled above her, most of them carrying in their talons fragments of metal. Obedient to the command of their masters—it seemed that the Streen were, after all, telepathic, but only insofar as their own kind were concerned—the pterosaurs grouped themselves into a formation resembling a spaceship, flapped off to the eastward. To the radar operators of the blockading squadron it would appear that *Corsair* had lifted, was navigating slowly and clumsily within the planetary atmosphere.

There were missiles, of course.

Some were intercepted by the suicidal air umbrella above the decoys, some, whose trajectory would take them into uninhabited jungle regions, were allowed to continue their fall to the ground. They had been programmed to seek and to destroy a spaceship, winged lizards, even metal-bearing lizards, they ignored.

Meanwhile, but cautiously, cautiously, with frequent and random shifts of frequency, *Corsair's* radio was probing the sky. It seemed that the mutants' squadron had swallowed the bait. Ship after ship broke from her orbit, recklessly expending her reaction mass so as to be advantageously situated when

Corsair, the pseudo-*Corsair,* emerged from the overcase into space.

And then the way out was as clear as ever it would be. The mutants' cruisers were hull down, dropping below the round shoulder of the world. Aboard *Corsair* all hands were at their stations, and the firing chambers were warmed up in readiness.

Grimes took her upstairs himself. With a deliberately dramatic flourish he brought his hand down to the keys, as though he were smacking a ready and willing steed on the rump. It was more like being fired from a gun than a conventional blast-off. Acceleration thrust all hands deep into the padding of their chairs. The Commodore was momentarily worried by a thin, high whistling that seemed to originate inside the ship rather than outside her hull. Then, had it not been for the brutal down-drag on his facial muscles, he would have smiled. He remembered that the Streen, normally coldly unemotional, had always expressed appreciation of a trip in a space-vessel and had enjoyed, especially, violent maneuvers such as the one that he was now carrying out. If Serressor was whistling, then he was happy.

Corsair whipped through the cloud blanket as though it had been no more than a chiffon veil, and harsh sunlight beat through the control room viewports like a physical blow. From the speaker of the transceiver came a shrill gabble of order and counter-order—evidently some alert radar operator had spotted the break-out. But *Corsair* was out of laser range from the blockading squadron, was almost out of missile range. And by the time the enemy were able to close her, she would be well clear of the Van Allens, would be falling into and through the dark, twisted dimensions created about herself by her own interstellar drive.

It was time to get Serressor along to the Mannschenn Drive room. Grimes handed over to Williams, waited until he saw the Commander's capable hands resting on his own control panel, and then, slowly and painfully, levered himself out of his seat. He found it almost impossible to stand upright under the crushing pseudo-gravity—but speed had to be maintained, otherwise the ship would be englobed by her enemies. Already Carter was picking off the first missiles with his laser. The Commodore watched two burly Marines struggle to get the aged saurian to his feet. They were big men, and strong, but the task was almost beyond them.

Then, with every shuffling step calling for an almost superhuman effort, Grimes led the way to the interstellar drive compartment. There—and how long had it taken him to make that short journey?— he found Bronson, Chief Interstellar Drive Engineer, with his juniors. And there was the ship's Doctor, and the telepath Mayhew. Extending from the complexity of rotors, now still and silent, was a tangle of cables, each one of which terminated in a crocodile clip.

The wall speaker crackled: "Commander to M.D. room. Calling the Commodore."

"Commodore here, Commander Williams."

"Clear of Van Allens. No immediate danger from enemy fire."

"Then carry on, Commander. You know what you have to do."

"Stand by for Free Fall. Stand by for course correction."

The silence, as the rocket drive was cut, fell like a blow. Then, as the whining directional gyroscopes took over, the Doctor, assisted by Bronson's juniors, began to clip the cable ends to various parts of Serressor's body.

The old saurian hissed gently, "You cannot hurt me, man Doctor. My scales are thick."

And then it was Mayhew's turn, and a helmet of metal mesh was fitted over his head. The telepath was pale, frightened-looking. Grimes sympathized with him, and admired him. He, as had every space-man, heard all the stories of what happened to those trapped in the field of a malfunctioning Drive—and even though this would be (the Commodore hoped) a controlled malfunction, it would be a malfunction nonetheless. The telepath, when the situation had been explained to him, had volunteered. Grimes hoped that the decoration for which he would rec-ommend him would not be a posthumous one.

The gentle, off-center gravitational effect of cen-trifugal force abruptly ceased, together with the humming of the directional gyroscope. Then the ship trembled violently and suddenly, and again. A hit? No, decided the Commodore, it was Carter fir-ing a salvo of missiles. But the use of these weapons showed that the enemy must be getting too close for comfort.

Williams' voice from the bulkhead speaker was loud, with a certain urgency.

"On course for Lorn, Skipper!"

"Mannschenn Drive on remote control," ordered Grimes. "Serressor will give the word to switch on."

Already the Doctor and the junior engineers had left the Mannschenn Drive room, making no secret of their eagerness to be out of the compartment before things started to happen. Bronson was making some last, finicking adjustments to his machinery, his heavily bearded face worried.

"Hurry up, Commander," Grimes snapped.

The engineer grumbled, "I don't like it. This is an interstellar drive, not a Time Machine. . . ."

Again came the violent trembling, and again, and again.

Bronson finished what he was doing, then reluctantly left his domain. Grimes turned to Serressor, who now looked as though he had become enmeshed in the web of a gigantic spider. He said, "You know the risk. . . ."

"I know the risk. If I am . . . everted, it will be a new experience."

And not a pleasant one, thought the Commodore, looking at Mayhew. The telepath was paler than ever, and his prominent Adam's apple wobbled as he swallowed hard. And not a pleasant one. And how could this . . . this non-human philosopher, who had never handled a metal tool in his long life, be so sure of the results of this tampering with, to him, utterly alien machinery? Sure, Serressor had read all the books (or his other-self in Grimes' own continuum had read all the books) on the theory and practice of Mannschenn Drive operation—but book knowledge, far too often, is a poor substitute for working experience.

"Good luck," said Grimes to the saurian and to Mayhew.

He left the compartment, carefully shut the door behind him.

He heard the whine, the wrong-sounding whine,

as the Drive started up.

And then the dream-filled darkness closed about him.

XX

IT IS SAID that a drowning man relives his life in the seconds before final dissolution.

So it was with Grimes—but he relived his life in reverse, experienced backwards the long history of triumphs and disasters, of true and false loves, of deprivations and shabby compromises, of things and people that it was good to remember, of things and people that it had been better to forget. It was the very unreality of the experience, vivid though it was, that enabled him to shrug it off, that left him, although badly shaken, in full command of his faculties when the throbbing whine of the ever-precessing gyroscopes ceased at last.

The ship had arrived.

But where?

When?

Ahead in Space and Astern in Time—that was the principle of the Mannschenn Drive. But never Full Astern—or, never *intentionally* Full Astern. Not until now. And what of the governors that had been fitted to the machine, the flesh-and-blood governors—the human telepath and the saurian philosopher, with his intuitive grasp of complexities that had baffled the finest mathematical brains of mankind?

What of the governors? Had they broken under the strain?

And what of himself, Grimes? (And what of Sonya?)

He was still Grimes, still the Commodore, with all his memories (so far as he knew) intact. He was not a beardless youth (his probing hand verified this). He was not an infant. He was not a tiny blob of protoplasm on the alleyway deck.

He opened the door.

Serressor was still there, still entangled in the shining filaments. But his scales gleamed with the luster of youth, his bright eyes were unfilmed. His voice, as he said, "Man Grimes, we were successful!" was still a croak, but no longer a senile croak. "We did it!" confirmed Mayhew, in an oddly high voice.

The telepath was oddly shrunken. The rags that had been his loin clout were in an untidy bundle about his bare feet. No, shrunken was not the word. He was smaller, younger. Much younger.

"That was the hardest part," he said. "That was the hardest part—to stop the reversal of biological time. Serressor and I were right in the field, so we were affected. But the rest of you shouldn't be changed. You sill have your long, gray beard, Commodore."

But my beard wasn't gray, thought Grimes, with the beginning of panic. *Neither was it long.* He pulled a hair from it, wincing at the sudden pain, examined the evidence, (still dark brown) while Serressor cackled and Mayhew giggled.

"All right," he growled. "You've had your joke. What now?"

"We wait," Mayhew told him. "We wait, here and now, until *Sundowner* shows up. Then it's up to you, sir."

Sundowner, thought Grimes. *Jolly Swagman . . . Waltzing Matilda.* Names that belonged to the early history of the Rim Worlds. The battered star tramps of the Sundowner Line that had served the border planets in the days of their early colonization, long before accession from the Federation had been even dreamed of, long before the Rim Worlds government had, itself, become a shipowner with the Rim Runners fleet.

Sundowner . . . She had been (Grimes remembered his history) the first ship to bring a cargo of seed grain to Lorn. And that was when this alternative universe, this continuum in which Grimes and his people were invaders, had run off the historical rails. *Sundowner* . . . Serressor knew his history too. The Wise One had planned this rendezvous in Space and Time, so that Grimes could do what, in his universe, had been accomplished by plague or traps, or, even, cats or terrier dogs.

"I can hear her. . . ." murmured Mayhew distantly. "She is on time. Her people are worried. They want to get to port before their ship is taken over by the mutants."

"In this here-and-now," said Serressor, "she crashed—will crash?—in the mountains. Most of the mutants survived. But go to your control room, man Grimes. And then you will do what you have to do."

They were all very quiet in the control room, all

shaken by the period of temporal disorientation through which they had passed. Grimes went first to Williams, hunched in his co-pilot's chair. He said softly, "You are ready, Commander?"

"Ready," answered the Executive Officer tonelessly.

Then the Commodore went to sit beside his wife. She was pale, subdued. She looked at him carefully, and a faint smile curved her lips. She murmured, "You aren't changed, John. I'm pleased about that. I've remembered too much, things that I thought I'd forgotten, and even though it was all backwards it was ... shattering. I'm pleased to have you to hold on to, and I'm pleased that it *is* you, and not some puppy...."

"I shouldn't have minded losing a few years in the wash," grunted Grimes.

He looked at the officers at their stations—radar, gunnery, electronic radio. He stared out of the ports at the Lorn sun, its brightness dimmed by polarization, at the great, dim-glowing Galactic lens. Here, at the very edge of the Universe, the passage of years, of centuries was not obvious to a casual glance. There were no constellations in the Rim sky that, by their slow distortions, could play the part of clocks.

"Contact," announced the radar officer softly.

The Commodore looked into his own repeater screen, saw the tiny spark that had appeared in the blackness of the tank.

The radio officer was speaking into his microphone. "*Corsair* to Sundowner. *Corsair* to *Sundowner*. Do you read me? Over."

The voice that answered was that of a tired man, a man who had been subjected to considerable strain. It was unsteady, seemed on the edge of hysteria. "I hear you, whoever you are. What the hell did you say your name was?"

"*Corsair*. This is *Corsair*, calling *Sundowner*. Over."

"Never heard of you. What sort of name is that, anyhow?" And there was another, fainter voice, saying, "*Corsair*? Don't like the sound of it, Captain. Could be a pirate."

"A pirate? Out here, on the Rim? Don't be so bloody silly. There just aren't the pickings to make it worth while." A pause. "If she *is* a pirate, she's welcome to *our* bloody cargo."

"*Corsair* to *Sundowner*. *Corsair* to *Sundowner*. Come in, please. Over."

"Yes, *Corsair*. I hear you. What the hell do you want?"

"Permission to board."

"Permission to board? Who the bloody hell do you think you are?"

"R.W.C.S. *Corsair* . . ."

"R.W.C.S.?" It was obvious that *Sundowner*'s Captain was addressing his Mate without bothering either to switch off or to cover his microphone. "What the hell is *that*, Joe?" "Haven't got a clue," came the reply.

Grimes switched in his own microphone. He did not want to alarm *Sundowner*, did not want to send her scurrying back into the twisted continuum generated by her Mannschenn Drive. He knew that he could blow the unarmed merchantman to a puff of incandescent vapor, and that such an action would have the desired result. But he did not want to play it that way. He was acutely conscious that he was about to commit the crime of genocide—and who could say that the mutated rats were less deserving of life than the humans whom, but for Grimes' intervention, they would replace?—and did not wish, also, to have the murder of his own kind on his conscience.

"Captain," he said urgently, "this is Commodore Grimes speaking, of the naval forces of the Rim Worlds Confederacy. It is vitally important that you allow us to board your ship. We know about the trouble you are having. We wish to help you."

"You wish to help us?"

"If we wished you ill," said Grimes patiently, "we could have opened fire on you as soon as you broke through into normal Space-Time." He paused. "You have a cargo of seed grain. There were rats in the grain. And these rats have been multiplying. Am I correct?"

"You are. But how do you know?"

"Never mind that. And these rats—there are mutants among them, aren't there? You've been coming a long time from Elsinore, haven't you? Mannschenn Drive breakdowns ... and fluctuations in the temporal precession fields to speed up the rate of mutation."

"But, sir, how do you *know*? We have sent no messages. Our psionic radio officer was killed by the ... the mutants."

"We know, Captain. And now—may we board?"

From the speaker came the faint voice of *Sundowner's* Mate. "Rim Ghosts are bad enough—but when they take over Quarantine it's a bit rough."

"Yes," said Grimes. "You may regard us as Rim Ghosts. But we're solid ones."

XXI

HIS BIG HANDS playing over his console like those of a master pianist, Williams, with short, carefully timed bursts from the auxiliary jets, jockeyed *Corsair* into a position only yards from *Sundowner,* used his braking rockets to match velocities. Grimes and his people stared out through the ports at the star tramp. She was old, old. Even now, at a time that was centuries in the past of *Corsair's* people, she was obsolete. Her hull plating was dull, pitted by years of exposure to micrometeorites. Two of the embossed letters of her name had been broken off and never replaced, although somebody had replaced the missing U and W with crudely painted characters. Grimes could guess what conditions must be like on board. She would be one of those ships in which, to give greater lift for cargo, the pile shielding had been cut to a minimum, the contents of her holds affording, in theory, protection from radiation. And her holds were full of grain, and this grain supported pests that, through rapid breeding and mutation, had become a menace rather than a mere nuisance.

"Boarders away, sir?" asked the Marine officer.

"Yes, Major. Yourself and six men should do. I and Mrs. Grimes will be coming with you."

"Side arms, sir?"

"No. That crate'll have paper-thin bulkheads and shell plating, and we can't afford any playing around with laser."

"Then knives and clubs, sir?"

"It might be advisable. Yes."

Grimes and Sonya left Control for their quarters. There, helping each other, they shrugged into their modified spacesuits. These still had the tail sheaths and helmets designed to accommodate a long-muzzled head. This had its advantages, providing stowage for a full beard. But Grimes wondered what *Sundowner's* people would think when they saw a party of seeming aliens jetting from *Cosair* to their airlock. Anyhow, it was their own fault. They should have had their vision transmitter and receiver in order.

The boarding party assembled at the main airlock which, although it was cramped, was big enough to hold all of them. The inner door slowly closed and then, after the pumps had done their work *(Corsair* could not afford to throw away atmosphere) the outer door opened, Grimes could see, then, that an aperture had appeared in the shell plating of the other ship, only twenty feet or so distant. But it was small. It must be only an auxiliary airlock. The Captain of *Sundowner,* thought Grimes, must be a cautious man: must have determined to let the boarding party into his ship one by one instead of in a body. *And he'll be more cautious still,* thought Grimes, *when he sees these spacesuits.*

He shuffled to the door sill. He said into his helmet microphone, "There's room for only one at a time in that airlock of theirs. I'll go first."

He heard the Major acknowledge, and then he jumped, giving himself the slightest possible push-off from his own ship. He had judged well and did not have to use his suit reaction unit. Slowly, but not too slowly, he drifted across the chasm between the two vessels, extended his arms to break his fall and, with one hand, caught hold of the projecting rung above *Sundowner*'s airlock door.

As he had assumed, the compartment was large enough to hold only one person—and he had to act quickly to pull his dummy tail out of the way of the closing outer valve. There were no lights in the air-lock—or, if there were lights, they weren't working—but after a while he heard the hissing that told him that pressure was being built up.

Suddenly the inner door opened and glaring light blinded the Commodore. He could just see two dark figures standing there, with what looked like pistols in their hands. Through his helmet diaphragm he heard somebody say, "What did I tell you, Captain? A bleeding kangaroo in full armor, no less. Shall I shoot the bastard?"

"Wait!" snapped Grimes. He hoped that the note of authority would not be muffled from his voice. "Wait! I'm as human as you."

"Then prove it, mister!"

Slowly the Commodore raised his gloved hands, turning them to show that they were empty. He said, "I am going to remove my helmet—unless one of you gentlemen would care to do it for me."

"Not bloody likely. Keep your distance."

"As you please." Grimes manipulated fastenings, gave the regulation half turn and lifted. At once he noticed the smell—it was like the stink that had hung around his own wardroom for days after the attempted interrogation of the prisoner.

"All right," said one of the men. "You can come in."

Grimes shuffled into the ship. The light was out of his eyes now and he could see the two men. He did not have to ask who or what they were. Uniform regulations change far more slowly than do civilian appearance. He addressed the grizzled, unshaven man with the four tarnished gold bars on his shoulder boards, "We have already spoken with each other by radio, Captain. I am Commodore Grimes. . . ."

"Of the Rim Worlds Confederacy's Navy. But what's the idea of the fancy dress, *Commodore?*"

"The fancy dress?" Then Grimes realized that the man was referring to his spacesuit, so obviously designed for a nonhuman. What would be his reaction to what Grimes was wearing underneath it—the scanty rags and the rank marks painted on to his skin? But it was of no importance. He said, "It's a long story, Captain, and I haven't time to tell it now. What I am telling you is that you must not, repeat not, attempt a landing on Lorn until I have given you clearance."

"And who the hell do you think you are, Mister so-called Commodore? We've had troubles enough this trip. What is your authority?"

"My authority?" Grimes grinned. "In my own space and time, the commission I hold, signed by the President of the Confederacy . . ."

"What did I say?" demanded the Mate. "And I'll say it again. He's some sort of bloody pirate."

"And, in the here-and-now," continued Grimes, "my missile batteries and my laser projectors."

"If you attempt to hinder me from proceeding on my lawful occasions," said the tramp Master stubbornly, "that will be piracy."

Grimes looked at him, not without sympathy. It was obvious that this man had been pushed to the very limits of human endurance—the lined face and the red-rimmed eyes told of many, too many, hours without sleep. And he had seen at least one of his officers killed. By this time he would be regarding the enemies infesting his ship as mutineers rather than mutants, and, no longer quite rational, would be determined to bring his cargo to port come Hell or High Water.

And that he must not do.

Grimes lifted his helmet to put it back on. In spite of the metal with which he was surrounded he might be able to get through to Williams in *Corsair's* control room, to Williams and to Carter, to give the order that would call a laser beam to slice off *Sundowner's* main venturi. But the Mate guessed his intention, swung viciously with his right arm and knocked the helmet out of the Commodore's hand. He growled to his Captain, "We don't want the bastard callin' his little friends do we, sir?"

"It is essential that I keep in communication with my own ship," said Grimes stiffly.

"So you can do somethin' with all the fancy ironmongery you were tellin' us about!" The Mate viciously swatted the helmet which, having rebounded from a bulkhead, was now drifting through the air.

"Gentlemen," said Grimes reasonably, looking at the two men and at the weapons they carried, automatic pistols, no more than five millimeter calibre but deadly enough. He might disarm one but the other would fire. "Gentlemen, I have come to help you. . . ."

"More of a hindrance than a bloody help," snarled the Mate. "We've enough on our plates already without having to listen to your fairy stories about some non-existent Confederacy." He turned to the Master. "What say we start up the reaction drive an' set course for Lorn? This bloke's cobblers'll not open fire so long as he's aboard."

"Yes. Do that, Mr. Holt. And then we'll put this man in irons."

So this was it, thought Grimes dully. So this was the immutability of the Past, of which he had so often read. This was the inertia of the flow of events. He had come to where and when he could best stick a finger into the pie—but the crust was too tough, too hard. He couldn't blame the tramp Captain. He, as a good shipmaster, was displaying the utmost loyalty to his charterers. And (Grimes remembered his Rim Worlds history) those consignments of seed grain had been urgently needed on Lorn.

And, more and more, every word was an effort, every action. It was as though he were immersed in some fluid, fathoms deep. He was trying to swim against the Time Stream—and it was too much for him.

Why not just drift? After all, there would be time to do something after the landing at Port Forlorn. Or would there? Hadn't somebody told him that this ship had crashed in mountainous country?

He was aroused from his despairing lethargy by a sudden clangor of alarm bells, by a frightened, distorted voice that yammered from a bulkhead speak-

er, "Captain! Where are you, Captain? They're attacking the control room!"

More as the result of years of training than of conscious thought he snatched his drifting helmet as he
followed the Captain and his Mate when they dived
into the axial shaft, as they pulled themselves hand
over hand along the guidelines to the bows of the
ship.

XXII

"THEY'RE ATTACKING the control room!"

The words echoed through Grimes' mind. *They* must be Sonya and the Major and his men. They must have breached the ports. So far there was no diminishing of air pressure—but even such a sorry rustbucket as *Sundowner* would have her airtight doors in reasonably good working order. All the same, he deemed it prudent to pause in his negotiation of the axial shaft to put his helmet back on. Luckily the rough treatment that it had received at the hands of the Mate did not seem to have damaged it.

Ahead of him, the two *Sundowner* officers were making rapid progress. It was obvious that they were not being slowed down by emergency doors and locks. The Commodore tried to catch up with them, but he was hampered by a spacesuit.

Then, faintly through his helmet diaphragm, he heard the sounds of a struggle, a fight. There were shots—by the sharpness of the cracks fired from small calibre pistols such as the Captain and his Mate had been carrying. There were shouts and screams. And there was a dreadful, high squeaking that was familiar, too familiar. He thought that he

297

could make out words—or the repetition of one word only:

"Kill! Kill!"

He knew, then, who *They* were, and pulled himself along the guideline with the utmost speed of which he was capable. Glancing ahead, he saw that *Sundowner's* Master and his second in command were scrambling through the open hatch at the end of the shaft, the hatch that must give access, in a ship of this type, to Control. He heard more shots, more shouts and screams. He reached the hatch himself, pulled himself through, floundered wildly for long seconds until his magnetized boot soles made contact with the deck.

They ignored him at first. Perhaps it was that they took him—in his tailed suit with its snouted helmet—for one of their own kind, although, by their standards, a giant. *They* were small, no larger than a terrier dog, but there were many of them. *They* were fighting with claws and teeth and pieces of sharpened metal that *They* were using as knives. A fine mist of blood fogged the face plate of Grimes' helmet, half blinding him. But he could see at least two human bodies, obviously dead, their throats torn out, and at least a dozen of the smaller corpses.

He did not give himself time to be shocked by the horror of the scene. (That would come later.) He tried to wipe the film of blood from his visor with a gloved hand, but only smeared it. But he could see that the fight was still going on, that in the center of the control room a knot of spacemen were still standing, strill struggling. They must either have lost their pistols or exhausted their ammunition; there were no more shots.

Grimes joined the fight, his armored fists and arms flailing into the mass of furry bodies, his hands crushing them and pulling them away from the humans, throwing them from him with savage violence. At first his attack met with success—and then the mutants realized that he was another enemy. Their squeaking rose to an intolerable level, and more and more of them poured into the control room. They swarmed over the Commodore, clinging to his arms and legs, immobilizing him. *Sundowner's* officers could not help him—they, too, were fighting a losing battle for survival.

There was a scratching at Grimes' throat. One of his assailants had a knife of sorts, was trying to saw through the fabric joint. It was a tough fabric, designed for wear and tear—but not such wear and tear as this. Somehow the man contrived to get his right arm clear, managed, with an effort, to bring it up to bat away the knife wielder. He succeeded—somehow. And then there was more scratching and scraping at the joint in way of his armpit.

He was blinded, helpless, submerged in a sea of furry bodies, all too conscious of the frantic gnawings of their teeth and claws and knives. His armor, hampering his every movement even in ideal conditions, could well contribute to his death rather than saving his live. He struggled still—but it was an instinctive struggle rather than one consciously directed, no more than a slow, shrugging, a series of laborious contortions to protect his vulnerable joints from sharp teeth and blades.

Then there was a respite, and he could move once more.

He saw, dimly, that the control room was more

crowded than ever, that other figures, dressed as he was, had burst in, were fighting with deadly efficiency, with long, slashing blades and bone-crushing cudgels. It was a hand-to-hand battle in a fog—and the fog was a dreadful cloud of finely divided particles of freshly shed blood.

But even these reinforcements were not enough to turn the tide. Sooner or later—and probably sooner—the mutants would swamp the humans, armored and unarmored, by sheer weight of numbers.

"Abandon ship!" somebody was shouting. It was a woman's voice, Sonya's. "Abandon ship! To the boats!" And then the cry—fainter this time, heared through the helmet diaphragm rather than over his suit radio—was repeated. It is no light matter to give up one's vessel—but now, after this final fight, *Sundowner*'s people were willing to admit that they were beaten.

Somehow the armored Marines managed to surround the crew—what was left of them. The Captain was still alive, although only half conscious. The Mate, apart from a few scratches, was untouched. There were two engineers and an hysterical woman with Purser's braid on her torn shirt. That was all. They were hustled by *Corsair*'s men to the hatch, thrust down the axial shaft. Grimes shouted his protest as somebody pushed him after them. He realized that it was Sonya, that she was still with him. Over their heads the hatch lid slammed into its closed position.

"The Major and his men..." he managed to get out. "They can't stay there, in that hell!"

"They won't," she told him. "They'll manage. Our job is to get these people clear of the ship."

"And then?"

"Who's in charge of this bloody operation?" she asked tartly. "Who was it who told the Admiral that he was going to play by ear?"

Then they were out of the axial shaft and into a boat bay. They watched the Mate help the woman into the small, torpedo-like craft, then stand back to allow the two enginers to enter. He tried to assist the Captain to board—but his superior pushed him away weakly, saying, "No, Mister. I'll be the last man off *my* ship, if you please." He noticed Grimes and Sonya standing there. "And that applies to you, too, Mr. Commodore whoever you say you are. Into the boat with you—you and your mate."

"We'll follow you, Captain. It's hardly more than a step across to our own ship."

"Into the boat with you, damn you. I shall be ... the ... last ..."

The man was obviously on the verge of collapse. His Mate grasped his elbow. "Sir, this is no time to insist on protocol. We have to hurry. Can't you hear *Them?*"

Through his helmet Grimes, himself, hadn't heard them until now. But the noise was there, the frenzied chittering, surely louder with every passing second. "Get into that bloody boat," he told the Mate. "We'll handle the doors."

"I ... insist ..." whispered the Captain. "I shall ... be ... the last ... to leave ..."

"You know what to do," Grimes told the Mate.

"And many's the time I've wanted to do it. But not in these circumstances." His fist came up to his superior's jaw. It was little more than a tap, but enough. The Master did not fall, could not fall in these conditions of zero gravity. But he swayed there, anchored to the deck by his magnetic boot soles, out on his feet. The two engineers emerged from the lifecraft, lugged the unconscious man inside.

"Hurry!" ordered Sonya.

"Make for your ship, sir?" asked the Mate. "You'll pick us up?"

"No. Sorry—but there's no time to explain. Just get the hell out and make all speed for Lorn."

"But . . ."

"You heard what the Commodore said," snapped Sonya. "Do it. If you attempt to lay your boat alongside we open fire."

"But . . ."

Grimes had removed his helmet so that his voice would not be muffled by the diaphragm. "Get into that bloody boat!" he roared. And in a softer voice, as the Mate obeyed, "Good luck."

He replaced his helmet and, as he did so, Sonya operated the controls set into the bulkhead. A door slid shut, sealing off the boat bay from the rest of the ship. The outer door opened, revealing the black emptiness of the Rim sky. Smoothly and efficiently the catapult operated, throwing the boat out and clear. Intense violet flame blossomed at her blunt stern, and then she was away, diminishing into the distance, coming around in a great arc on to the trajectory that would take her to safety.

Grimes didn't watch her for long. He said, "We'd better get back to Control, to help the Major and his men. They're trapped in there."

"They aren't trapped. They're just waiting to see that the boat's escaped."

"But how will they get out?"

"The same way that we got into this rustbucket. We sent back to the ship for a laser pistol, burned our way in. Luckily the airtight doors were all in good working order."

"You took a risk..."

"It was a risk we had to take. And we knew that *you* were wearing a spacesuit. But it's time we weren't here."

"After you."

"My God! Are you going to be as stuffy as that Captain?"

Grimes didn't argue, but pushed her out of the boat lock. He jumped after her, somersaulting slowly in the emptiness. He used his suit reaction unit to steady himself, and found himself facing the ship that he had just left. He saw an explosion at her bows, a billowing cloud of debris that expanded slowly—broken glass, crystallizing atmosphere, a gradually separating mass of bodies, most of which ceased to struggle after a very few seconds.

But there were the larger bodies, seven of them, spacesuited—and each of them sprouted a tail of incandescence as the Marines jetted back to their own ship. The Major used his laser pistol to break out through the control room ports—but all the mutants would not be dead. There would be survivors, sealed off in their airtight compartments by the slamming of the emergency doors.

The survivors could be disposed of by *Corsair's* main armament.

XXIII

"WE WERE WAITING for you, Skipper," Williams told Grimes cheerfully as the Commodore re-entered his own control room.

"Very decent of you, Commander," Grimes said, remembering how the Mate of *Sundowner* had realized his long standing ambition and clobbered his Captain. "Very decent of you."

He looked out of the viewports. The grain carrier was still close, at least as close as she had been when he had boarded her. The use of missiles would be dangerous to the vessel employing them—and even later might touch off a mutually destructive explosion.

"You must still finish your task, man Grimes," Serressor reminded him.

"I know. I know." But there was no hurry. There was ample time to consider ways and means.

"All armament ready, sir."

"Thank you. To begin with, Commander Williams, we'll open the range..."

Then suddenly, the outline of *Sundowner* shimmered, shimmered and faded. She flickered out like a candle in a puff of wind. Grimes cursed. He should have foreseen this. The mutants had access to the Mannschenn Drive machinery—and how much, by continuous eavesdropping, had they learned? How much did they know?

"Start M.D.," he ordered. "Standard precession."

It took time—but not too long a time. Bronson was already in the Mannschenn Drive room, and Bronson had been trained to the naval way of doing things rather than the relatively leisurely procedure of the merchant service. (Himself a merchant officer, a reservist, he had always made it his boast that he could beat the navy at its own game.) There was the brief period of temporal disorientation, the uncanny feeling that time was running backwards, the giddiness, the nausea. Outside the ports the Galactic Lens assumed the appearance of a distorted Klein flask, and the Lorn sun became a pulsing spiral of multicolored light.

But there was no sign of *Sundowner*.

Grimes was speaking into the telephone. "Commander Bronson! Can you synchronize?"

"With *what?*" Then—"I'll try, sir. I'll try . . ."

Grimes could visualize the engineer watching the flickering needles of his gauges, making adjustments measured in fractions of microseconds to his controls. Subtly the keening song of the spinning, precessing gyroscopes wavered—and, as it did so, the outlines of the people and instruments in the control room lost their sharpness, while the colors of everything momentarily dulled and then became more vivid.

"There's the mucking bastard!" shouted Williams.

And there she was, close aboard them, a phantom ship adrift on a sea of impossible blackness, insubstantial, quivering on the very verge of invisibility.

"Fire at will!" ordered Grimes.

"But, sir," protested one of the officers. "If we interfere with the ship's mass while the Drive is in operation . . ."

"Fire at will!" repeated the Commodore.

"Ay, ay, sir!" acknowledged Carter happily.

But it was like shooting at a shadow. Missiles erupted from their launchers, laser beams stabbed out at the target—and nothing happened. From the bulkhead speaker of the intercom Bronson snarled, "What the hell are you playing at up there? How the hell can I hold her in synchronization?"

"Sorry, Commander," said Grimes into his microphone. "Just lock on, and hold her. Just hold her, that's all I ask."

"An' what now, Skipper?" demanded Williams. "What now?"

"We shall use the Bomb," said Grimes quietly.

"We shall use the Bomb," he said. He knew, as did all of his people, that the fusion device was their one hope of a return to their own Space and Time. But *Sundowner* must be destroyed, the Time Stream must, somehow, be diverted. Chemical explosives and destructive light beams were, in these circumstances, useless. There remained only the Sunday Punch.

The ships were close, so close that their temporal precession fields interacted. Even so, it was obvious why all the weapons so far employed had failed. Each and every discharge had meant an appreciable alteration of *Corsair's* temporal precession rate, so that each and every missile and beam had missed in Time rather than in Space. Had

Corsair been fitted with one of the latest model synchronizers her gunnery might have been more successful—but she was not. Only Bronson's skill was keeping her in visual contact with her prey.

Getting the Bomb into position was not the same as loosing off a missile. Slowly, gently, the black-painted cylinder was eased out of its bay. The merest puff from one of its compressed air jets nudged it away from *Corsair* towards the target. It fell gently through the space between the two ships, came finally to rest against *Sundowner's* scarred hull.

At an order from Grimes the thick, lead shutters slid up over the control room ports. (But the thing was close, so close, too close. Even with the radar on minimum range the glowing blob that was *Sundowner* almost filled the tank.) Carter looked at Grimes, waiting for the order. His face was pale—and it was not the only pale face in Control. But Serressor—that blasted lizard!—was filling the confined space with his irritating, high, toneless whistling.

Sonya came to sit beside him.

She said quietly, "You have to do it. We have to do it."

Even her presence could not dispel the loneliness of command. "No," he told her. "*I* have to do it."

"Locking..." came Bronson's voice from the bulkhead speaker. "Locking ... Holding ..."

"Fire," said Grimes.

XXIV

TIME HAD passed.

How long, Grimes did not know, nor would he ever know. (Perhaps, he was often to suspect later, this was the next time around, or the time after that.)

He half opened his eyes and looked at the red haired woman who was shaking him back to wakefulness—the attractive woman with the faint scar still visible between her firm breasts. What was her name? He should know. He was married to her. Or had been married to her. It was suddenly of great importance that he should remember what she was called.

Susan . . . ?

Sarah . . . ?

No . . .

Sonya . . . ?

Yes, Sonya. That was it. . . .

"John, wake up! Wake up! It's all over now. The Bomb blew us back into our own continuum, back to our own Time, even! We're in touch with Port Forlon Naval Control, and the Admiral wants to talk to you personally."

"He can wait," said Grimes, feeling the fragments of his prickly personality click back into place.

He opened his eyes properly, saw Williams sitting at his controls, saw Serressor, near by, still youthful, and with him the gangling adolescent who was Mayhew.

For a moment he envied them. They had regained their youth—but at a dreadful risk to themselves. Even so, they had been lucky.

And so, he told himself, had been the human race —not for the first time, and not for the last.

He thought, *I hope I'm not around when our luck finally does run out.*

There are a lot more
where this one came from!

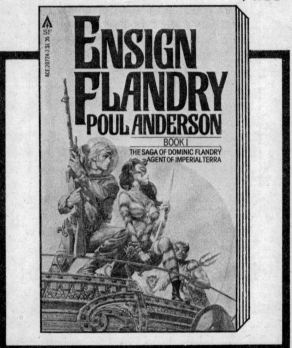

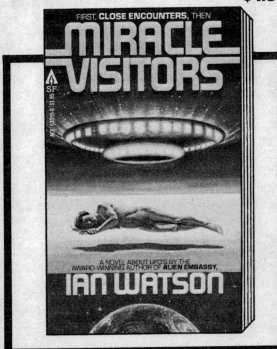